He'd lay t
that her blo
made of boring linen.

At least she'd surprised him by dodging behind the tree to change. He thought she'd make a fuss and insist he find a private room inside the fort.

Then she came out from behind the tree. Glancing over the saddle, he froze. Whoa. Ignore her, he commanded himself...but he couldn't.

Contrary to looking less feminine in pants and work shirt, she looked more. He'd always remembered her as a spoiled adolescent, but she'd finally grown into a woman. Still spoiled, but an inexperienced, *virginal* woman.

Peering at what she gripped in her hand, he gulped. Rolled into a ball, her bloomers were flaming red. Not boring linen.

"What do you want now, Roughrider?" she snarled. "What are you staring at?"

"Red becomes you."

With a click of her tongue, she threw them over his head.

* * *

The Proposition

Harlequin Historical #719—September 2004

Praise for Kate Bridges's books

The Surgeon

"Bridges re-creates a time and place to perfection and then adds an American touch with warmhearted characters and tender love."

—*Romantic Times*

The Midwife's Secret

"This is truly a story which will touch your heart and stir your soul. Don't miss this delectable read."

—*Rendezvous*

Luke's Runaway Bride

"Bridges is comfortable in her western setting, and her characters' humorous sparring makes this boisterous mix of romance and skullduggery an engrossing read."

—*Publishers Weekly*

The Doctor's Homecoming

"Dual romances, disarming characters and a lush landscape make first-time author Bridges's late-19th-century romance a delightful read."

—*Publishers Weekly*

KATE BRIDGES

THE PROPOSITION

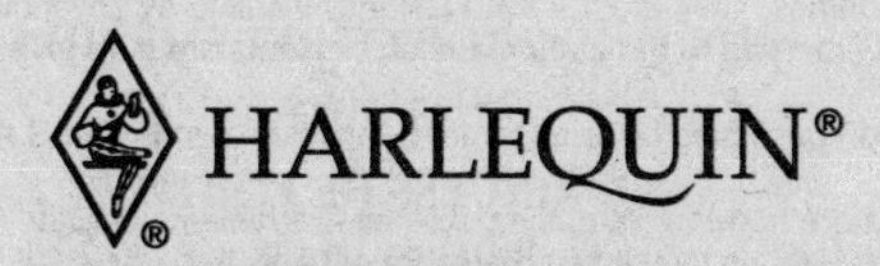

TORONTO • NEW YORK • LONDON
AMSTERDAM • PARIS • SYDNEY • HAMBURG
STOCKHOLM • ATHENS • TOKYO • MILAN • MADRID
PRAGUE • WARSAW • BUDAPEST • AUCKLAND

ISBN 0-373-29319-4

THE PROPOSITION

This edition published by arrangement with Harlequin Books S.A.

www.eHarlequin.com

Printed in U.S.A.

Available from Harlequin Historicals and KATE BRIDGES

The Doctor's Homecoming #597
Luke's Runaway Bride #626
The Midwife's Secret #644
The Surgeon #685
The Engagement #704
The Proposition #719

Other works include:

Harlequin Books

Frontier Christmas
"The Long Journey Home"

This book is dedicated with everlasting thanks and deepest respect to my agent, mentor and friend, Charles Schlessiger. Thank you, Charles, for taking a chance and believing in an unknown writer. It's a pleasure working with you.

I'd also like to thank my friend and fellow writer Janine Whalley for her generous contribution of time and advice on the matter of horses. Thanks, Janine, for patiently answering every question I had regarding stallions, broodmares, foals and training. Any mistakes I may have made in the story are my own.

Chapter One

Alberta, July 1892

Unaware of it, the man astride the horse dominated her attention. For three days running, Jessica Haven had watched Sergeant Major Travis Reid exercising the stallion on the oval track inside the fort, desperately trying to have a word with him, and for three days running the officer had ignored her. Today she'd force him to listen.

Sitting in the bleachers beside her, awash in early-morning sunlight, a small group had gathered to watch. The men concentrated on the dangerous bucking of the unbroken mustang, but Jessica knew the women focused on Travis.

"It's a pity he's leavin' his horses," said the banker.

"Sad shame what happened to his wife," whispered the commander's sister.

The officer twisted in the saddle. Leaning forward in concentration, his dark head tilted and body flexed, he melded with the sculpted lines of the horse. Dressed in the work clothes of the North-West Mounted Police—loose white shirt tucked into tight black breeches—he ran a large hand over the stallion's neck and whispered something into its mane.

His hard muscles coaxed the animal into submission.

Jessica fanned her heated face and rearranged her flowing cotton skirts around her ankles, uncomfortable that it was obvious the man stirred her. Her absence of two years hadn't changed his ability to dominate her senses.

Roughrider, his men had nicknamed him, a man skilled at riding untamed horses.

The name suited him, she thought, watching him dismount. He was rough. Travis was a master horseman, the Mounties' best. Jessica had heard he also excelled at tracking outlaws, that he'd been promoted four times in three years. He'd risen from corporal to sergeant major faster than prairie lightning.

"Sergeant Major!" she shouted, jumping out of her seat and racing into the stables behind the intimidating man and beast.

Rows and rows of horses filled the stalls. Warm gashes of sunlight filtered through plank walls; the soothing scent of fresh straw and oats drifted around her.

"The girth wasn't tight enough. I had to fix it." Swinging one long leg off the saddle, Officer Reid spoke to a stable boy. "The stallion has a tricky habit of holding his breath when you saddle him, keeping his chest expanded. Next time walk him a few paces till he exhales, Shamus, then tighten the girth again."

"Yes, sir."

"May I help you, Miss Haven?" Another Mountie, carrying a pitchfork, stepped into her path. "You're looking exceptionally fine. Welcome home. Is anyone escorting you to the pub social this eve—"

"No, thank you." Panting, Jessica dodged through the workmen. "Officer Reid!"

Travis eyed her, then turned sharply on his black leather boot, broad shoulders twisting, ready to leave.

The insult burned deep. The man still had a way of brushing her aside. "Travis! I'd like a word with you! Please!"

She dashed out and nearly stumbled over a cluster of barn cats. Four small kittens froze in her path, the smallest one, a tawny fur ball, hunched its shoulders and peered up at her.

Laughter bubbled in her throat. She lifted him, tucking his entire body into one palm. Pressing her face into the downy neck, she enjoyed the tickle on her skin and its barnyard scent. "You're so soft. A child would adore you."

Travis turned around. The rippling shadows beneath his white shirt tightened in wary response. He said nothing, simply stared down at her as she drew closer. Her bonnet, sliding off her head but tied at her throat, bobbed along her spine. Her blond hair, braided neatly at the side, brushed along her shoulders.

Don't be nervous, she told herself. *Remain cheerful and simply ask the man.*

Stroking the kitten, Jessica swallowed in a stew of emotions. Travis had the same solid jaw and firm cheeks she remembered. She looked lower. And there was something compelling about the physique of an active man, the straining and stretching of ropy muscles knotted from hard work and perseverance.

"Hello, Travis."

His lips tugged into a cool line. "Back from charm school, are you?"

Her face heated, even as she nodded in agreement. *Charm school.* It was what her father had told everyone to cover his shame, but so far from the truth it was laughable. And her own shame made her go along with the story.

Travis's deep blue eyes, almost navy in color, flickered. "The mayor's daughter has returned to Calgary. Let's all bow and bid her good welcome."

He tilted his head in mock acknowledgment, a finger of his black hair falling on his forehead.

Hiding her humiliation, she lowered the kitten to the ground, near a bowl of water where his bigger black-and-white brothers and sisters were drinking. "Make way for the little one," she coaxed. The kittens parted and she smiled softly.

She felt Travis's gaze beating down on her tilted head. She wished she could erase the past.

He'd once called her a spoiled young woman. And shamefully, it'd been true. It had begun five years ago when she'd convinced her father to outbid Travis on a feisty stallion so they could buy it and she could learn to ride. Travis hadn't had the money to compete, but he'd tried to convince her the horse wasn't suitable for an inexperienced girl because of its size and temperament. She remorsefully admitted now that the stallion had attracted her simply for its color—a speckled gray with almost purplish mane and tail. And Travis had been right. She hadn't been able to handle the horse and got such a fright she was still put off by large animals.

She *had* been rude. Self-absorbed. But in her defense, she'd also been young and inexperienced, and she'd learned a lot of things in the grueling years since.

Remain cheerful. "I heard you're leaving for Devil's Gorge tomorrow."

"How do you know? I told very few people where I'm headed for my leave."

"The commander's wife told me. They joined us for dinner a few nights ago."

He clicked his tongue in disapproval.

Unaffected, she continued. "I came to offer you a proposition. To pay you to take me along." Her mouth parted with a silent plea. He had to say yes for her world to regain its balance.

"Absolutely *not.* I'll pass on your proposition. This is a personal leave and a difficult seven-day journey. Ask at the livery stables if you want to hire a guide."

The fluttering in her stomach tightened. Desperation trembled in her voice. "I already have but they've got two men out on trail and only one left. He leers at me and I just couldn't spend an entire week… Even though I'd bring a chaperon. You know our family's butler, Mr. Merriweather."

"You've got to be kidding." Travis stalked down the middle of the stalls, ducking buckets and workmen. Horses' heads turned to watch him as he passed. "Ask at the big hotel. They hire out to travelers and tourists."

She raced behind him, barely keeping up with his long stride. She'd worn her best dress to make a favorable impression, a shimmering linen with dancing blue flowers, but now felt like a silly child tagging behind.

He glanced to his left at a groom brushing the coat of a splendid Clydesdale, then stepped into the stall. Travis took the brush and demonstrated. "Press harder. You've got to put muscle behind it. You're grooming not only the coat, but you're massaging the muscles beneath. The mare enjoys it."

"Yes, sir."

Travis's caressing hands worked over the horse. His hands were soiled and massive. Dirt streaked his palms, gilded the hairs on his knuckles, yet there was something pleasant and mesmerizing in watching him. He came from a working-class family of three rough-and-tumble brothers—with one younger sister—while Jessica came from a quiet political family of two daughters. Watching Travis's transfixed gaze, it was obvious to her how much he cared for these animals. Anyone who fell beneath his masterful touch would feel adored and needed.

"Officer Reid?" called another man. "The palomino in the corner is coughing."

Travis reared his head. "When did that start?"

"About an hour ago."

"Any other horses coughing?"

"No."

"Take him to the smaller barn and isolate him immediately. I'll take a look as soon as I'm done here. Only light exercise for the next three days."

"Yes, sir."

Travis came out of the stall and she leaped forward to appeal to him once more, but a movement on the straw floor caught her eye. The tawny kitten peered up at her. She laughed softly. "Watch out, you'll get trampled." She lifted him. "Are you following me?"

The kitten meowed and she was snared. "It's a sign we're meant to be together." Her pulse rushed with eagerness. She blurted to the stable boy passing by, "Is he for sale?"

Travis groaned.

"He's still too young to be separated from his mother," replied the youth. "Won't be ready for a coupla weeks."

She gulped at the comment. "I wouldn't want to separate him from his mother. But when he's ready, may I buy him?"

"I reckon you could have him," said the boy, taking the kitten from her. "I'll save him for you."

Jessica smiled. She hadn't felt this sense of happiness in a long while.

Travis shook his head and the gentleness in him evaporated, replaced by ice. "Still trying to buy the pretty things that attract your eye."

Travis had no right to be rude. "It's not for me—" She stopped herself.

"Goodbye, Jessica." Two hundred pounds of power and brawn pivoted away from her.

"Wait!" She chased after him. "There's no guide at the big hotel as qualified as you. And now that my father has discovered my plans, he won't let me go unless I'm escorted by a Mountie. Devil's Gorge *isn't* a light jaunt into the mountains and no one seems eager to go."

He spun around. "Then why do you?"

She had prepared for the question for days, but it still prickled her skin. "I'm trying to locate Dr.…Finch."

Travis frowned. "I know him. He's been through here before. He's helped a lot of folks."

Helped was not the right word. "I've—I've been tracing him for the last year and a half and I hear he has a base in Devil's Gorge."

"I thought he set up his practice on the West Coast, north of Vancouver."

Is that what the Mounties thought? She fumbled with her drawstring purse. "But I heard it from someone in Montreal, and another source since."

"At the charm school?"

She looked away and nodded.

"Why are *you* looking for him?"

"I'm writing an article on doctors for the *Pacific Medical Journal." On quacks and charlatans.*

He assessed her. "You're a medical journalist?"

She nodded.

"Why would you need to work?"

"I enjoy it. It's something I'm good at, and...I'm needed."

He pondered that for a moment.

"It's an interest I began in Montreal. I'm still learning, but they've published three articles already."

Dr. Finch had hurt a lot of people. She believed he'd gone by another name in Montreal—by Dr. King. When she found him, she'd expose him and Travis could jail him.

The blue in Travis's eyes deepened, as if he couldn't quite believe she was no longer solely occupied with ball gowns and fancy dinner shows. "And I imagine by speaking to him, you could write a better article, perhaps land an interview and a better paycheck."

There was always a monetary bonus to getting an interview with any subject, but she'd fight her way to Dr. Finch for no money.

"I told you," he said. "The only thing I want on my leave is to be left alone."

He stalked past her. The stall boards rose to just above his waist level, but met her at shoulder height.

"I know you're delivering your horses. You're selling your three prize broodmares to a buyer who will be meeting you there."

He stopped and faced her.

"The superintendent told me. Why are you selling them so far away? I would think there'd be plenty of buyers here."

"I *did* sell them here when the buyer was visiting, but he *lives* there. And it's as far away as possible, which is fine with me."

She didn't understand his answer. "Why?"

"That's no one's affair but my own."

"I thought breeding horses was... You seem so good at what you do. You seem to love—"

"It's no one's affair but—"

"Your own," she finished. "Listen, I'm prepared to pay you as my part of the bargain. *Lots.*"

He walked away.

"One hundred dollars," she shouted after him. "And another hundred on safe delivery!"

He turned toward her, his eyes misty. "It's always about money with you people, isn't it?"

Her throat clamped. "Not always."

Not anymore. But no one knew about her problem—or at least believed how Dr. Finch had deceived and devastated *her.*

She followed Travis as he walked around the stalls. "Mighty fine horse," she said about the beautiful bay in the corner. Its muscles glistened reddish brown.

Travis didn't respond, but she saw him grow rigid.

"I said, it's a mighty fine mare."

He cleared his throat, but his head didn't turn in the bay's direction. "She'll bring in a fine dollar."

"What kind of horse is it?"

He blinked but still didn't look at it. "Some people call them running horses, some call them quarter horses."

"On account of their speed, ma'am," said Shamus the stable boy, passing with an armful of straw. "Their muscular legs and rump make them excellent at racing the quarter mile."

Travis's gaze followed the boy. A muscle in the man's cheek quirked. "And also at maneuvering through cattle, which makes them excellent on cattle drives. This one's sold to a rancher."

She found it odd that he wouldn't look at the horse. "Ah, one of the broodmares you're selling."

That seemed to make him angrier. He scowled. "Let me make myself clear, Miss Haven. I don't care what you're up to, who your friends are or what you do with your time. Leave me alone."

She felt dizzy and wavered on her feet. She knew his response stemmed from Caroline, and Jessica was sorry that she'd caused the woman any grief. But it was unfair of Travis to blame Jessica for everything.

"I'm sorry to hear about your wife," she murmured.

He didn't respond. His mouth tightened.

"I said, I'm sorry to hear about Caroline's passing."

"Hmm." The pain that settled in his eyes was enough to stop her heart.

"Poor Caroline," she continued. "It was a terrible way to go. I—I know it happened months ago, but I heard it only last week when I arrived on the train."

"Did you now?"

She flushed at his insinuating tone.

His body stiffened. "Let's not coat things with honey. You never liked Caroline and she never liked you."

A flash of tears pricked her eyes, but she blinked them away. It was too difficult to keep begging him face-to-face. She whispered as she left, "A person can change."

Later that evening when everyone had left the stables for supper, Travis leaned against the stall and slid his arms over the boards. "Happy anniversary." The pain of despair gripped him. "Twelve months today." He cocked the hammer of his revolver and aimed it between the two eyes. "What makes you think I'm going to allow you to live while Caroline died?"

Standing in the stall, the quarter horse looked straight back at him, dipped its head into the feeding bucket and chewed.

A year ago, witnesses had told Travis that it hadn't been the broodmare's fault. The raccoon had spooked Caroline more than it had the horse as they'd jumped the fence, but Caroline had lost control. Riding sidesaddle, she'd slipped off and had fallen to her death. With Caroline's foot caught in the stirrup, the horse had immediately stopped. The mare was a sound animal that had done what it'd been trained to do, but Caroline had died from internal bleeding. Killed on impact, the fort's surgeon had told Travis, and not the horse's fault.

Travis looked into the mare's dark eyes. "Son of a bitch."

It was more a curse at himself than the beast. He could no more shoot a viable horse than he could shoot a child. The joke was that everyone thought he was a tough leader, always in control of himself and the situation. And so he harbored his grief.

And his rage. It simmered below the surface, ready to jump at the slightest trigger, as it had earlier today at the sight of *her.*

"Miss Haven says you're a mighty fine horse." Travis wiped his mouth on the cuff of his sleeve and smirked. "A mighty fine horse that killed my wife."

The horse shifted. Straw rustled.

Travis couldn't stomach looking at the mare, yet it drew his gaze at the oddest moments. He hadn't once touched its coat since the accident, fed, watered or saddled it, although God knew this wasn't the first time he'd pressed a gun to its head.

And always, always, he fell short, coward that he was.

Since he allowed the Mounties to train with his

horses, they allowed him the use of the stables and it'd been easy to ignore its care. He planned on continuing to ride for the police and training new recruits in tracking and horsemanship, but he'd sell every goddamn horse he personally owned. The fact that he'd dreamed of and acquired a ranch of his own had in effect snuffed out every blissful dream Caroline had held.

They'd only been married for three short months, but those few weeks had filled him with such a glorious anticipation for what life had to offer that he had feared it would someday shatter.

He stared at the horse. He'd already sold his land and six stallions. It'd taken him months to find the right buyer for his broodmares. He'd received other offers, but the bidders all lived in the area, which meant he'd forever be haunted by this broodmare's offspring. Taking it to Devil's Gorge in the middle of the mountains, where they traded more with folks from British Columbia than Alberta, would cure that sorry problem.

Tomorrow morning he'd be leaving without Jessica Haven. Thank Christ he wouldn't be bearing the responsibility for the safety of another woman.

Crazy fool, some had called him for keeping the horse this long. Frankly, he'd fallen into a numb pit for the past year, coldly going through his duties, never raising his voice. Only since the beginning of this week had any sentiment returned—he'd felt the rage building for days, anticipating the year's anniversary with rising gloom. A thundercloud churned within him and he wasn't sure he could control it if it spewed. He was grateful he'd be alone to handle it.

He slid his revolver back into his shoulder holster. Stepping back into darkness, he glared at the mare. He softened and whispered, "I miss you, Caroline."

He heard footsteps in the straw and spun at the intrusion.

"Roughrider," called one of his friends. "I've been told to remind you that your sister's expecting you at her pub and the commander and his wife are waiting. He needs to speak to you about something urgent first. Something about the mayor's daughter."

With a looming premonition of trouble, Travis sensed he hadn't seen the last of Miss Jessica Haven.

Chapter Two

Remorseful that she'd had to go to such lengths to get to Devil's Gorge, but nervously praying her tactic had worked, Jessica opened her wardrobe chest and removed an old shawl. She'd done the thing she knew the sergeant major would despise most. She'd used her father's status to manipulate Travis.

She walked down the hallway, peered into her younger sister's bedroom and smiled. "Are you coming, Eloise? The pub social begins at eight."

Lamplight danced around the room. Her sister's sixteen-year-old best friend, Bessy, sat perched on the iron bed. Eloise was tall and blond, Bessy round and dark. They shared a love for clothing, and laughter.

Rubbing glaze on her lips, Eloise peered up from her dresser mirror. "Our stepmother says it's not good to appear eager around men." She giggled on the velvet stool. "And the place will be filled with Mounties."

"My purpose in going isn't to impress a man. I'm going to speak with the commander to arrange tomorrow."

Eloise sighed. "Do you have to go away again so soon?"

"I won't be as long this time," Jessica said tenderly.

"Why *aren't* you trying to impress a man? Honestly, I dare say you haven't been kissed since Victor left."

Jessica's face heated. Two-and-a-half years ago, they'd done a lot more than kiss. "What's that you're putting on your lips?"

"Something *Mother* gave me." Eloise had less difficulty than Jessica in calling their stepmother of four years Mother, but it was still awkward. "It makes my lips shine. I hope it attracts a suitor."

Bessy giggled. "Can I try some?"

"Pa will be cross to see you in cosmetics," said Jessica.

"Don't be so old-fashioned. Look what I'm going to order next." Eloise tossed her a folded paper.

Jessica read the headline and silently screeched at the name. *Dr. Finch.* "An electric corset?"

"It operates on a battery, a small box, and it says that no woman should be without one."

Jessica read. "For functional irregularities. Weak back. Hysteria and loss of appetite. Kidney disorders." Angered, Jessica glanced up. "This is nonsense."

"It's not. It's signed by a real doctor. It's for getting an elegant figure and good health, and I want both of those."

Jessica took note of the Vancouver address. Vancouver. Her hopes fell. She wondered again who she'd find in Devil's Gorge. "Promise me you won't order this until I return."

Eloise rose, silk billowing around her hips. She shrugged a slender shoulder. "Well, all right."

Removing her spectacles, Bessy raised a contraption made of two blue suction balls.

"What on earth is that?" Jessica tossed the newsprint to the bed.

"An eye massager." Bessy closed her lids and pressed the rubber balls on them. Air blew the dark bangs off her forehead. "Last summer when Dr. Finch came through town, he told me if I do this three times a day for two years, it'll help restore my sight."

"Honey, it's only blowing air on your eyelids."

"It's improving the blood flow to my ocular nerve. I can feel the tingling." Bessy replaced her eyeglasses and tucked the contraption into her reticule. "You don't know what it's like to wear spectacles."

"How much did that cost your folks?"

"Only fifty dollars to restore my sight."

Jessica gasped. Most men earned a dollar a day. She knotted her hands in her skirt. The poor girl and her folks would know the truth soon enough.

"It's worth a try. What's the harm?" Bessy asked.

Jessica remembered that she'd once thought that herself. Placing an arm around each girl, she led them down the stairs and out the door. "The harm is you're being taken advantage of for your money and integrity."

While they walked, Jessica peered at her sister's trusting face and saw a reflection of herself before she'd gone to Montreal, before she'd relied on Victor Sterling, her father Franklin Haven, and Dr. Abraham Finch. Her father had promised to ship Jessica permanently back to Montreal for her own good if she confided in her sister about her own shameful flaws.

You'll ruin your chances with another man if you let your confinement be known. Father had tried to be helpful but had succeeded only in tearing a rift between himself and Jessica.

Her new stepmother, Madeline, was barely older than Jessica. The mayor's four-year-old marriage had gone through difficult times with several separations during the first three years. Jessica's stepmother had an ill sister who lived a hundred miles away, and she would often leave for months at a time to care for her. Jessica had always suspected there were other underlying problems—such as dealing with two adolescent stepdaughters and their doting father. However, since Jessica had been away, Madeline's sister had miraculously recovered and the mayor and his wife seemed happier.

Neither one was particularly fond of the fact that Jessica had a job, but she believed both were grateful that it occupied her time. Her father likely saw it as a healthy distraction to Jessica's worries, and Madeline was likely grateful it gave her more time with her husband.

Madeline was kind enough, but she and Jessica lacked a sentimental bond. Jessica's real mother was a faded memory of a woman with gold earrings and ready arms for hugging. She'd slipped to her death on a patch of ice when Jessica had been six.

Neither her stepmother, sister, nor the family butler knew the true reason for her trip to Montreal to the "charm school," otherwise known to Jessica as Miss Waverly's Home for Unwed Mothers.

It'd been agony going, but nothing compared to the agony of returning empty-handed.

They turned the corner at the pub and bumped into a crowd of uniformed officers, one of whom was standing at the back speaking with the commander and his wife, glaring at Jessica.

She could almost hear Travis Reid's growl.

Heavens, she thought, trying to shrink from his visual range. *So he's been told the news.*

She'd never seen him in his scarlet uniform. The vision took her by surprise. The deep red color brought out the thick black luster of his hair, sharpness of his black eyebrows and cutting bite to his dark blue eyes.

"Oh, my word," whispered Eloise. "A whole herd of handsome Mounties."

"Miss Haven," said Superintendent Ridgeway, the fort's commander. "Hello."

Jessica nodded warmly to his wife and the group exchanged pleasantries. Standing beside the commander was his sister—a possessive woman in her forties and widowed. She stepped toward Travis and draped an arm through his. "Are you coming inside?"

"In a minute."

"I'll save you a seat."

His gaze speared Jessica's. She was riveted by the anger infusing his dark face. He was going to Devil's Gorge anyway, so what would be so difficult in taking her along?

"We'll go inside and wait for you there," said Eloise. "Our folks are already inside," she explained to the others, pointing to the stained-glass door. The group made way for the women. "My father has arranged for a photographer from the newspaper."

That was why everyone was dressed up, and although Jessica felt like an outsider wearing her everyday skirt, she had no desire to be photographed. Quigley's Pub belonged to Travis's sister and her husband, and the town had been invited to celebrate in the birth of their first child.

Jessica was struck again by the differences in their families. Travis came from labor-class roots. His folks had settled in Canada from Dublin almost thirty years ago and owned a busy cattle ranch. The senior Reid had been an Irish copper, disenchanted and seeking his fortune in the great new world. Two of his three sons were already Mounties, following in his police footsteps. But a cloud of rumor surrounded them—that the senior Reid had taken bribes in Ireland and was chased out of the country. Jessica's father often reminded her that their lineage could be traced to English royalty, but she never mentioned it. Being the mayor's daughter entailed enough difficulties.

As she dared a glance at Travis's sweltering dark looks, she could very well imagine him with a sword to someone's throat, whispering a black threat. He'd never do it for money, but if the cause were right—

"Let me join you young ladies inside," said Annabelle Ridgeway, a round matron dressed in green ruffles. Pulling the commander's sister with her, she followed Eloise and Bessy inside. Several Mounties stood at the door, ushering them in. When one of the officers winked at the younger women, they blushed and smiled.

The commander chewed on an unlit cigar and nodded to Jessica and Travis. "It's all worked out. Travis is leaving at six in the morning, and you and your chaperon are going with him. I'll leave you to figure out the details."

"Oh," said Jessica, catching her breath as the older man entered the pub, leaving them behind. Travis didn't budge. Nor did he speak, but he was seething.

She felt like a moldy piece of cheese being inspected. "Say something, please."

"Congratulations. You got your way. You used your power and position—your *father's,* not even your own—to force your company on me. Now it's an official order from my commander. I have to escort the mayor's daughter safely to Devil's Gorge."

"This is important to me. It's not a trivial whim—"

"Neither was my journey. It was supposed to be a

personal leave. I've been arranging it for months and was looking forward to being alone. Now I have to watch over you."

Her loose wavy hair bounced on her shoulders. "You don't have to watch over me. Mr. Merriweather and I are perfectly content to—"

"I have to watch over *two* incompetent—"

"I said you don't have to watch—"

"You haven't changed a bit."

His cold words felt like a slap in the face. "Why do you dislike me so much?"

"Because I *know* you."

She stumbled back.

No, you don't, she wanted to scream. *You knew me years ago but you don't know me now.* It was something words alone couldn't prove. Only the passage of time could. But she'd done more damage by forcing his hand like this.

She pressed a shaky palm to her gurgling stomach. She wouldn't argue. But when her lips trembled, her mood darkened. "What makes you think you're so superior to me?"

"Ha," he snorted. "I think *I'm* superior? I'm not here to prove anything to you. I wanted you to leave me alone. Why do you have to butt into people's lives? You butted into Caroline's and now you're butting into mine."

"I didn't want that for Caroline—"

"I don't want to hear—"

"She made it difficult—"

"Leave her alone. She's dead."

The cold blade of truth sliced the conversation.

Jessica spun away and headed for the pub, the fabric of her long-sleeved blouse whipping through the air.

"We'll meet you in the morning at the fort's gate, at five minutes to six."

"I'm not finished speaking." His grip on her arm ripped her from her spot.

Her head snapped back, blond hair swaying against her chest. "I am." She tried to yank free but his hold was like a wooden clamp.

"You'll listen to me until I say you can go."

The man was a vain mule but she would tolerate him for the duration of her cause. She'd never *ever* trust him. Lord only knew how condescending he'd be if he knew the truth. She trembled and tried again to pull free.

He held fast and drew her closer, an inch away from his patronizing face. "I'll supply your horses."

She didn't flinch. "But we've got two perfectly—"

"I said I'll supply them. The broodmares I'm bringing are valuable, and I won't chance the interaction of horses whose temperaments I don't know."

"All right. You bring them."

"And I'll pack the supplies and food."

"But Mr. Merriweather—"

"You and Giles can each bring one small bag with a change of clothes."

"But that's not nearly—"

"One bag. Can you manage or not?"

"One bag," she repeated. "And my reticule of course, plus my small duffel with my notepad and pencils."

"I said one."

She nodded slowly. "Okay. One." She aired her frustrations in one big exhale. "Are we finished?"

"Seven days and nights," he said, holding open the door for her to enter. But he was no gentleman, she thought. "That's all I've promised. When we get there, there'll be a Mounties' outpost with three men you can count on for further help, and a small inn where you can stay while you're writing. I'll be heading back immediately, so you and your chaperon can find your own way home."

It was better than nothing. However, she stormed by him in annoyance.

Peering around the noisy crowd, she tried to find the hosts. She'd give her regards then leave. Mr. Merriweather needed to know they had to repack. Maybe the mercantile was still open for her to buy a lighter bag. Luckily, it was Monday and she'd already done her banking earlier today.

The soft sounds of a fiddler and accordion player wafted above the chatting heads, a lively melody winding through a cloud of cigar smoke. Jovial diners filled one side of the pub, feeding on cabbage and beans while on the other side, people threw darts at dartboards, raised their glasses at the walnut bartop, or clapped along to the music.

"There you are, Travis," said his sister Shawna, coming up beside them.

Jessica was surprised to find Travis still at her side. When she turned to look, she brushed against his rock-hard chest. His presence dominated her.

Shawna, long black hair tumbling over her shoulder while she held a three-month-old baby in her arms, peered tentatively at Jessica and nodded. "Miss Haven."

The baby boy, with lids closed, balled up one tiny fist and sucked on the other's loose fingers. Jessica smiled. She had that to look forward to. "Shawna, I want to offer my congratulations and wish you and your family the best."

The woman kept her distance. "Thank you."

Jessica knew she wasn't welcome even though invitations had been extended to the whole town. Her father always went to these events—for the company of his friends, yes, but Jessica knew he also went for harmless political reasons, to have his photograph taken and name written in the papers. It seemed to work, for the town had reelected him twice, and most folks genuinely liked him. Except the Reids. "I'm leaving now. I've got an early start in the morning."

Travis grumbled but Jessica ignored him. She noticed the commander's sister, the eager widow, waving to him from the opposite side of the pub and felt more ill at ease.

"You won't be joining your father, Miss Haven?" Shawna nodded at the well-tailored heavy man in the corner with the slim redheaded wife at his elbow.

"I've come only to give my regards to you. Good night."

"Good night," Shawna offered a bit too readily.

A man bumped Jessica from behind as she swung away.

"It's dark," said Travis. "You need someone to walk you home."

"I'll be fine," Jessica hollered above the crowd, squeezing past his sister.

She couldn't help but overhear the sister's whispered comments to her brother. "What's this I hear about you taking her to Devil's Gorge? You know how Caroline felt about her...how we *all* feel about her."

Travis whispered something back but Jessica was already out of earshot and heading to the exit. She burst through the doors, eager for calm, pine-scented air and the privacy to slow her beating heart.

Her walk home was only two blocks, but the streets were darker and lonelier than when they'd come. She picked up her pace. A man skidded beside her and nearly made her jump.

"Travis, you scared me."

"Just wanted to make sure the mayor's daughter got home to her mansion safely."

She bristled. People treated her politely because of who her father was, and never, it seemed, on her own merit. "My house is in view. You can leave."

"One bag," he reminded her.

"I'll manage."

"Quarter to six at the fort's gate."

"Quarter to…"

Now he wanted her there even earlier than before.

"Do you think we'll be able to stand each other for seven days?"

Her heart quivered at the question. "Yes," she answered dutifully, knowing it was best to appease him. She no longer cared what he thought of her personally. Nothing mattered except finding Dr. Finch and having him return her most precious gift.

She'd been unable to trace any adoption agencies in Montreal that had dealings with a Dr. King or Finch, but someone at the university had told her Dr. Finch was planning an agency out West. Devil's Gorge, she figured, was as good a starting point as any to search. An adoption agency for a fee, she imagined, and wondered if her baby had been sold.

She couldn't tell Travis more or he might react the same way her father had, or worse, he might jeopardize her plan.

Her father's words rang in her mind. *You weren't lucid that night, honey. Your accusations against Dr. Finch have proven to be false. Please don't say any more about them. People will think you've lost your mind, and it will ruin your future chance of marriage.*

But, she reminded herself, Travis was a police officer. He'd been sworn to uphold the law, despite what he might think of her character or reputation if her problems were revealed.

Leaving Travis behind, she ran across the dirt street to the stylish board-and-batten home with its pillars and broad white porch. She couldn't recall clearly what'd happened seventeen months ago on the night of her delivery, so she needed to locate the attending doctor—Finch or King, or whatever name he went by—and ask him.

Now, she'd go inside the house, quietly latch the door and silently prepare for the morning. But what she ached to do, standing on the rooftop of her father's unblemished mansion, was to shout up and down the streets.

She wanted to speak about the unspeakable. The disappearance of her child.

Chapter Three

To Travis's displeasure, his traveling companions arrived at Fort Calgary two minutes late. Travis slid his pocket watch back to the inside of his suede-leather vest. His spurs jangled. The weight of his guns shifted at his hips. Leaning against the pine logs of the palisade gate with the horses tethered inside, he looped one worn, black leather boot over the other and watched the unlikely couple shuffling toward him. Each dragged a square leather sack.

"Hmm," Travis muttered to himself. "Too heavy to carry."

Morning light broke through the dark clouds. The streets were quiet, although he heard the faint hooves of two horses echoing beyond the steel bridge leading to the center of town, thudding softly beyond the store facades, restaurants and the big hotel. Another workday was beginning.

Flecks of apricot highlighted Jessica's braided hair and puffy face, still rumpled from sleep. For the first time in years, he had the opportunity to take a long look at her.

Other men considered her pretty but she was rather plain, in his opinion. And a bit old, in her early twenties, to still be unmarried. He, on the other hand, was close to thirty. If you took away her fancy clothes, starched blouse and embroidered skirt, untwisted her hair from the fancy knots, you'd be left with an undistinguished blonde, face freckled from the outdoors and with a much-too-eager smile.

Money-bought prettiness.

But she wasn't wearing her usual display of gold rings and necklaces. Come to think of it, she hadn't yesterday, either. Only one thin, gold chain adorned her throat, with a cluster of ridiculous silver baubles strung through her ears. Frivolous and boring is how he'd describe her.

And it was strange, meeting a woman who wanted to work. His sister Shawna had founded the town library, and sometimes she helped at the pub, but her husband owned the pub. That was different. He sucked in a breath, wondering how on earth these two in front of him planned on riding through nearly two hundred miles of narrow mountain paths dressed like that. And their bulging bags obviously needed to be repacked. If they couldn't balance the weight, no horse should.

He stepped out and tilted the brim of his black-felt Stetson. "Morning."

"Fine one it is, sir," said Giles Merriweather. "Not too hot and not too cold. Not too many bugs, but just enough to keep life interesting. Are the horses inside?"

Travis nodded and stepped aside for the old gent to enter. He was an English butler, emigrated from Plymouth thirty years ago and he'd adopted and adored everything Western since. A wide sombrero topped long gray hair, a blue-denim shirt complete with silver rivets draped a narrow chest, and tight denim trousers flanked meaty legs. Too tight to move comfortably.

Travis was also wearing denim pants, his rugged Levi's, miner's pants that could take the abuse of a trip like this, but his were old and relaxed.

"New boots," Travis said as the man squeaked by in shiny brown leather.

Merriweather beamed, huffing as he passed. "I bought them yesterday."

Blisters by nightfall, thought Travis.

"Good morning," hollered Jessica, yanking on the leather straps of her huge bag, her impeccably pressed skirt and blouse fluttering in the soft breeze, framing her curves. And there was that eager smile, trying to win him over.

Never.

"New luggage?" he asked.

"Yes," she said, a smile dimpling her cheeks. "We bought them late last night. Luckily the mercantile was still open after I left the pub."

"I suppose you thought when I said one bag apiece, I meant the biggest crate you could find." He shook his head and her smile lost its dazzle.

She held out the straps, indicating that he should take over the pulling and yanking.

She had a few matters to learn about survival in the wild.

He brushed past her, snubbing her extended hand. "Funny, but I had a feeling I'd need to bring two spare saddlebags. You're both going to repack before we leave. Congratulations, that'll make us late. And I hate to be late."

He heard her loud intake of breath. Then she clawed her bag through the gate's opening. Six muscled horses, cast orange in the rising sun, stood tethered to the hitching posts.

"Let's not make the horses wait too long, folks," he said. "I've brought you each a derringer. Pack them in your bags."

Jessica unbuckled her bag and took the small silver gun. Fifteen minutes later, after he'd helped Merriweather repack, Travis came up behind Jessica and looked down at her open bag, resting in the grass. "Problems?"

"I—I need everything in here."

He bent down and removed two pairs of shoes. "You won't need these. The boots you're wearing are enough."

"But the high-heeled ones are in case I need something a little more formal...and the buttoned red ones...I really like them and I thought just in case—"

"No." Without mercy, Travis tossed them into the discard pile. He rummaged through her things, quickly amassing two stacks. He couldn't understand why she found it difficult to pack. "One shawl is enough. You won't need two belts. And not these tonics either." He tossed out four glass bottles.

She grabbed one. "But these are my face creams and hair soaps."

"One plain cake of soap can service your entire body." His look swept from her toes all the way up to her head. "Including your hair, if you must wash it in the next week."

Her eyes narrowed. Her smile hung like a crooked picture, he thought, weak with no genuine feeling behind it.

"Let me guess," he said. "First time in the mountains?"

She scowled. That was more like it. At least a scowl was genuine.

"Yours, too, Merriweather?"

"Ah, but I'm looking forward to the adventure, sir."

Travis scrutinized her pack. He removed a wide-brimmed cowboy hat and tossed it up to her. "Wear this to protect your head. No sense packing it. Get rid of the bonnet." Then he pulled out a speckled flannel cloth. "What's this?" It looked like an infant's nightdress.

With an embarrassed gasp, she snatched it from his fingers. "It's private."

He snatched it back. "You don't need it."

Her face reddened. She grabbed it again. "It's…a gift for someone."

He couldn't believe the frivolous things she was carting. "No gifts."

"But—"

"No gifts."

She jumped at the tone of his voice. With her brown hat in one hand, she scrunched the flannel cloth with the other but didn't move to put it in the discard pile.

"What's in this compartment?" he asked.

She flew to her knees, pushing him out of the way, surprising him with her strength. "That's my personal business." She blushed considerably.

He moved to unbuckle the pocket but she snapped it from his hands. "*Personal* business," she shouted.

The pocket was square and thick, as if it carried paper. "All right, all right. You get the idea now. If that's your writing journal, remember, you only need to write in one. And just *one* pencil."

Ten torturous minutes later, he was strapping Merriweather's saddlebag to one of the broodmares. The butler stood twenty feet away, laughing with one of the guards.

"One more thing," said Travis to Jessica. "You better change before we leave."

When he turned around, he towered over her. She eyed him carefully, then looked down at her clothes, smoothing her blouse with a graceful hand. Two long braids of hair, flung over jutting breasts, sparkled in several shades of gold. A natural rouge sprang to her lips, deepening the outline of her mouth. "Why?"

"Church clothes aren't for riding. Too much starch."

"I'll be fine."

"I saw a pair of cotton pants in your pile."

"My sister threw those in." Her earrings dangled at the side of her head, catching a beam of sunlight. "I-I'm not taking them."

He rearranged his Stetson. "They're the only sensible thing you're bringing. You won't be comfortable in anything else while riding astride."

"Astride? I'll be riding sidesaddle."

"No sidesaddle."

Her lips puckered. "But—"

"No sidesaddle!"

They glared at each other. He didn't have time for this. Sidesaddle was how Caroline had fallen to her death.

"Must you always shriek?" She hurled her hands to wide hips and anger found her tongue. "Have you ever thought of having your head examined?"

He leaned toward her, tightening every muscle, but she didn't back off. "Just once when I agreed to taking you on this trip."

"Do you have to be so domineering?"

"*Yes.* I'm the sergeant major, remember?"

"*Roughrider.* Grand. Just grand," she whispered. Digging into her discard pile, she yanked out the ivory pants. "Wait here while I slip behind that tree. God sakes," she muttered, stalking away, hemline flinging through the air. "If the man follows me, he's liable to accuse me of wearing too many underthings and *must* I bring these stockings? And am I aware of the weight of my lacy bloomers?"

Lacy bloomers. For a moment, he fumbled at the saddle.

With exasperation, he shook his head. He'd lay ten bucks that they were made of boring linen.

At least she'd surprised him by dodging behind the tree to change. He thought she'd make a fuss and insist he find a private room inside the fort.

She came out from behind the tree while he was tightening the lines on another broodmare.

Glancing over the saddle, he froze. Whoa.

Ignore her, he commanded himself. He forced his gaze down to the saddle, but it crept back to her. The brim of his hat shadowed his eyes.

She bent over her pack and began stuffing the discarded items into her original bag, which they'd leave behind with the guard. Travis had already arranged to have them sent back to her home. Contrary to looking less feminine in pants and work shirt, she looked more. Gone was the flowing fabric that concealed her body. Ivory pants clung to well-shaped thighs. Rounded hips swelled to form an hourglass figure. Fabric clung to her smooth behind, and when she walked, the black belt cinched at her waist accentuated her bounce. A simple white blouse, oversize, folded into her waistline. The shadow of her corset hinted at what lay beneath, while the top two buttons of her collar remained open, revealing light and gold shadows illuminating a slender throat.

He'd always remembered her as a spoiled adolescent, but she'd finally grown into a woman. Still spoiled, but an inexperienced, *virginal* woman.

Frivolous and boring is how he'd describe her, he reminded himself.

Peering at what she gripped in her hand, he gulped. Rolled into a ball, her bloomers were flaming red. Not boring linen.

"What do you want now, Roughrider?" she snarled. "What are you staring at?"

"Red becomes you."

With a click of her tongue, she threw them over his head.

Jessica noticed things about him that a conservative woman should not. The way he yanked at his gloves when he was mad—which was almost all the time; the way he instinctively reached for his guns at an unexpected sound; how rough his knuckles were as he tugged the reins; and how forlorn and desolate he looked when he thought no one was watching.

Travis was the type of man that all good mothers in Calgary warned their daughters against. Temperamental, moody, and thought the world spun around him.

The man was trouble. Still, Jessica needed him and the thought was daunting.

For now, she considered herself fortunate that he took the lead on the trail, which allowed her and Mr. Merriweather the opportunity to fall behind, single file, and gain their bearings.

"We'll be following the Glacier River most of the way," Travis shouted two hours later from fifty feet ahead, speaking above the thundering of the water. Turning his huge body around in the saddle to talk, he ducked beneath pine boughs and aspen leaves. The wind lifted the needles, filling her nostrils with cool forest scents.

"Lead the way, sir," Mr. Merriweather shouted back. "The foothills are a sight to behold."

Jessica nodded, trying to unwind her stiffened shoulders and mask her apprehension of riding so high off the ground. It scared her to be responsible for the broodmare she was leading, with a rope tied around its neck and ponied to her mount. Travis had steered away from taking any stallions on the trip, he'd explained, for stallions too close together often fought. Travis rode a gelding but she and Mr. Merriweather each rode mares. *They* led compact quarter horses—or running horses or whatever name they went by—to be sold when they reached Devil's Gorge, but Travis led a massive Clydesdale broodmare. Whenever the Clydesdale snorted, the other animals waited for its lead. She was the dominant one.

"The horses are shod only on their front feet," Travis hollered. "That's where they take most of the weight and strain. In case any of them kick in such close proximity, their back hooves were left unshod for minimal damage."

Jessica didn't like the sound of that. If the information was supposed to comfort her, it only served to glue her gaze to the back of Mr. Merriweather's broodmare. It was the striking bay she'd noticed in the stables yesterday. Whenever the broodmare adjusted its footing on the rocky path, Jessica jerked back, thinking the horse was about to kick.

"Relax," Travis told her around noon, leading them into a small clearing.

"Right," she said, trying not to look too grateful to Travis for finally stopping so she could rest.

He swung off his horse, surveyed the area, declared it was time for lunch, then walked the horses two at a time to the river's edge to drink before she and Mr. Merriweather had even removed their gloves.

Travis returned to the shady knoll. "You're a pretty good rider, Merriweather."

"I spent a lot of time in foxhunts with my father." The older man clutched at his back, then limped away toward the river, leading two horses. "I'll water these two."

Grass swished beneath Travis's big boots as he approached her. He didn't look directly at Jessica, but took the reins of her horse. Still, she felt the sting of embarrassment at his soft words. She watched the tiny creases at his eyes move while he spoke. They gave him distinction, a weathered, attractive look of matured experience.

"Don't fight her so much. She doesn't like when you sit rigid. If you spread your arms to your sides, you can lean in tighter and she'll adjust to your weight. Pat her neck once in a while. Maintain the contact. She's going to be your friend for seven days."

Then his gaze was direct and she felt her head swim.

Squinting up at him in the patch of sunlight, Jessica nodded and slid her cowboy hat to her back. Her temples were drenched with perspiration, and her legs felt like rubber trying to hold her upright.

"Let your body flow with the rhythm of the mare."

Jessica lowered her lashes. "I'll try."

"We'll rest here for two hours. Soon as the heat of the day subsides, we'll head out again."

He took care of the horses first, removing saddles and hitching the animals to a lush grassy spot where they could graze. Then he tended to her and her butler. Jessica felt awkward, more of an observer than assistant, knowing she was making Travis work harder on account of her and Mr. Merriweather's presence.

Finally, as Travis was preparing the horses to leave, she jumped up from her spot by the boulders where they'd eaten their smoked beef and coffee, and met him on the other side of his beautiful bay. The horse he'd avoided looking at yesterday.

"What's her name?" she asked.

Jessica's voice startled him. He'd been deep in concentration, sliding on his work gloves. He stared at the mare for a length of time before tackling its gear. The other horses were ready; he'd left this one for last.

"They've got names, don't they?" Jessica repeated.

"My broodmares do. But the Mountie workhorses, the ones we're riding, don't. There's too many to name." He yanked on his large left glove, opening and closing his fingers. He seemed so slow with this horse compared to how he'd been with the others. And his face was flushed. "The one you're leading, the roan," he said, nodding behind her shoulder, "is called Seagrass. My Clydesdale goes by Coal Dust."

"Ah, because of her black color. And this one?"

She noticed a drop of sweat rolling down his forehead. "...Independence."

"Independence." Jessica stood in awe at the size of her. "May I help you with her?"

His expression changed. His white sleeves rustled in the wind, outlining the muscles beneath. "She's got a burr in her mane. If you put on your gloves, you could comb through it with your fingers and then I wouldn't have to.... Much obliged."

"I...I don't mean to sit idle." She tugged on her brown-leather gloves. "It's just that I'm unsure how to help."

He nodded and heaved a saddle blanket on top of Independence.

She grabbed the other side. They worked tranquilly together. She was making headway with him, Jessica thought, and wondered if and when she should tell him some of her allegations against Dr. Finch.

"What happened to the perfume you always used to wear?"

Her responding smile came gently.

His mouth tugged upward in kind.

That wasn't so hard, she thought, was it? He looked much better in a smile than a scowl.

"I didn't think the horses would appreciate it."

"That showed good judgment."

"Go ahead and say it. It's the only good judgment I've used today."

He inclined his dark head. The brim of his hat concealed his eyes. "Not the only. Your choice of shoes was good. Unlike your friend over there." He motioned to Mr. Merriweather, who was massaging his sock feet. "Will he be all right?"

"Sure."

"What about his back?"

"He's…he's not used to riding. It uses a lot of muscles you forget you have."

"I've seen him pull out those binoculars a few times. What's he looking at?"

With his mouth open in amazement, the butler had his collapsible binoculars aimed above the fir trees.

"A rusty-colored hawk," she answered. "See it circling? It's got a wingspan of four-and-a-half feet. The largest hawk in North America, they tell me."

"They?"

She turned back to Travis. "He's the president of the Birdwatchers Society."

Travis grumbled. "I suppose that's harmless enough. But it better not get in the way of anything I'm doing."

Spoken like the controlling man he was.

Jessica reached out and timidly patted Independence's shoulder. The mare stirred and took a step backward.

"Easy," Travis said to her. "She senses your fear."

"Sorry. I'm trying to maintain contact." Summoning her courage, she plunged forward and grabbed the horse's mane where she saw the cluster of burs.

The horse startled at the jab.

"Whoa," Travis warned her.

Jessica gulped. "Just this one last burr." When she yanked on the hairs, the horse lifted its hind leg.

"Be careful," said Travis, looking somewhat overwhelmed. He gripped the bridle and the mare settled.

"But she seems so mild mannered."

He peered down at her, eyebrows drawn together, facial muscles tensed. "You still need to be careful."

His mood shifted to one of stormy anger. What on earth had she done to cause it?

"You need to be gentle on *her*." His eyes sparked with a stab of emotion. Whatever was bothering him, it seemed to suddenly deepen. "She's in foal. The mare's...pregnant?"

"How far along?" she whispered.

The mare didn't look pregnant. With a shiny coat, she had just enough fat on her so her ribs were slightly visible.

His voice rumbled as he turned away, she swore to hide his face. "About two months."

"How do you know when it's not visible on the mare?"

"A good breeder keeps track of dates when his mares are bred. And I also did a thorough manual examination."

He nodded, lowering his eyes to the saddle.

Her hand fell to rest on the horse's neck. With a moan of empathy, Jessica recalled her own months of confinement in the Montreal house, stepping out for fresh air to trim the backyard hedges, watching her figure grow while in a torrent of mixed emotions. Then feeling the first tiny kick in excited anticipation with no one to share it with, only to have lost it all.

Chapter Four

"The last time you were in Calgary, you were rumored to be engaged to that Englishman. Victor Sterling, was that his name?"

The personal nature of Travis's question and the sudden vibrancy to his voice unnerved Jessica.

Standing in an ocean of green prairie grass and dwarfed by her horse, she tried to untangle the leather straps from her saddle. As they made camp, last remnants of fading light silhouetted the mountain peaks and gushing river waters behind Travis. The sky was twilight blue, on the verge of turning black.

In the distance, Mr. Merriweather limped between the trees. He hummed a cowboy tune while collecting firewood.

She dug her boots into parched soil. "That was his name."

The moon, a glowing yellow ball, skimmed the straight lines of Travis's shoulders. The quality of lighting was changing on their journey. The general lighting of the vast prairies had washed everything equally but in the rugged foothills, the enclosures cast shadows across his body and face, highlighting his unique stance and the outline of his lips.

He tied a rope between two evergreens, forming a hitching line for the horses.

Irritated by her gloves' bulkiness, she removed them, turning her back on Travis and hopefully his curiosity.

"What happened to your engagement?"

"It was never really official," she said with begrudging frankness. "He had to… Victor had to return to England."

"But I thought—"

"Victor never made it."

"What do you mean?"

Resentful of the questions and the raw emotions they evoked, she pulled her arms tighter to her chest. Last year when Jessica wrote to his parents to enquire about his whereabouts, thinking that maybe Victor, the natural father of her child, might help her look for their baby, she'd been informed of the horrible news.

She avoided Travis's cold stare. "Victor's ship never reached London. It went down in the tail end of a hurricane." Her despair intensified. "Victor drowned."

His large hands stopped working on the rope.

Slowly, he turned to face her. His stern attitude dissolved. "I'm sorry."

Quietness consumed them.

She nodded, looking down at her pack, wishing he'd leave. Then she heard him walk away, leading two mares in the direction of the river. Dry leaves and pine needles crackled beneath the horses' hooves, while Travis's spurs echoed between the foliage.

She untied the metal pots from her saddlebags. It bothered her that he apparently assumed it was Victor's death that'd stopped their marriage. But their relationship had been nothing like Travis and Caroline's; Travis had cared deeply for *his* wife.

Victor had been a youthful English professor at Oxford. He'd come to Canada to discuss the possibility of setting up an affiliated university, possibly choosing Toronto, Vancouver or Calgary. As mayor, Jessica's father was eager for Victor to choose *their* town, for it would bring financial and social gains to the community. Her father had introduced them. Jessica, an insatiable reader, had shared with Victor her adoration for the romantic poems of William Wordsworth, the travelogues of Mark Twain and the adventures of Chaucer's *The Canterbury Tales.*

She'd fallen in love for the first time. He'd never actually proposed, but he'd fed her imagination, telling her how much she'd adore Oxford when she saw it and the joy he'd find in showing her London. She thought it meant he loved her, that he was assuring her of their future. In hopes of showing the depth of her feelings, she'd succumbed to his advances. They'd made love three times, but Victor had turned ashen when Jessica had informed him she was late in her cycle.

He was a man who'd simply been in love with poetry and words. A far cry from Travis's practical nature.

Later, she'd discovered from Victor's valet that he'd been engaged all along to another woman in England, a richer one with three London homes who was paying his traveling bills. At the news of Victor's death, Jessica felt a deep sorrow for her child for the loss of his father, but not for herself.

Are you a close friend? Victor's father had written in his letter. Jessica had never answered.

And *her* father had never received his university.

She flinched as she untied a small shovel. Her anger

returned—at the way she'd been treated by Victor, and then her father. She understood the scandalous way she'd behaved and how the town would look down on her if the truth was known, but to blazes with her shame, *and her father's.*

Jessica was furious at her own vulnerabilities and shortcomings, but it was pointless to look back. She'd look ahead to the promise of a future with her child. She was saving every penny she earned, for if and when she found her son, she'd make her own way. A seventeen-month-old child needed her.

If she let herself dwell for a moment on the harm that may have come to him, or the uncertainty of her claim against Dr. Finch, she wouldn't have the strength to carry forward. So she pushed the pain out of her mind.

"Here, let me help you with those." Mr. Merriweather removed her saddlebags.

One was filled with her clothing, the other with food supplies Travis had packed. As the elderly man lifted the weight to his side, his face strained beneath his sombrero.

"My dear old friend, you're in discomfort. Is there something you're not telling me?"

"It's nothing to worry about. As soon as we've unpacked and I've started dinner, I'm going to slip out that bottle of medicinal tonic, sit back and relax."

"You need medicine?"

"A simple brew bought from Dr. Finch three years ago. I bought three bottles and there's still an ounce or so left."

She brushed the hair from her eyes, upset that even her dear old butler had a cure from the charlatan. "What's the tonic for?"

Mr. Merriweather removed his sombrero and combated flies. "General pains. *Gentlemen's* problems," he said with an embarrassed laugh.

Uncomfortable with the topic, she collected the small utensils and carried them to the flat part of the site. "Sorry, I didn't mean to pry."

Walking back and forth between the horses and the campsite, she unloaded what she could. Ill at ease, she crossed her arms against her white blouse and looked around, waiting for Travis to return with the second set of horses. She wondered what she was supposed to do to help.

Mr. Merriweather struggled on his feet to put dinner together while Travis tied the horses to the hitching rope. Jessica settled onto a log by the burning fire. It warmed her face while they ate sausages and biscuits.

"It's not what I normally prepare for dinner," Mr. Merriweather apologized. "This is Sunday, and on Sunday evenings we usually have roast fish and baked potatoes, my special recipe from Plymouth. The ones the pilgrims brought to America, you know."

"This is delicious anyway," remarked Jessica. "And seeing how you cooked and Travis took care of setting up camp, I'll wash the dishes."

Mr. Merriweather floundered for something in the pack beside him, a shadowy figure in blue denim. "My word," he gasped in the semidarkness, face glued to the side of an ancient maple tree.

Travis looked up from his plate and stopped chewing.

Jessica craned her neck in alarm. "What is it?"

"A family of hummingbirds. They're nesting inside the trunk of that tree."

She found his wide-eyed expression humorous. "We've gone from seeing the largest hawk to the tiniest bird."

The old gent peered through his binoculars. "I've never in my born days seen anything so magnificent. Look how they spin their wings together."

"Marvelous," said Travis, jumping to his feet. Jessica detected sarcasm. "The blue plumes sparkle in the moonlight and the beaks, various shades of yellow and orange, capture the shimmering glow of the stars."

"Oh, you understand," whispered Mr. Merriweather in glee.

"Don't move," murmured Travis, coming closer with the butt end of his log. He hammered it into the bare ground three feet away from Mr. Merriweather. "Prairie rattler. The only poisonous snake in Alberta. Average length, three and a half feet."

Mr. Merriweather jumped up and shrieked as the mottled serpent slid to safety in the grass. With a yelp of her own, Jessica flew to her feet.

"He's gone," said Travis, peering into the brush.

"But we didn't hear him rattle," said Jessica.

"They don't unless they feel threatened. He wasn't about to bite."

The butler clutched at his chest. "My poor beating heart."

Jessica smiled through her trembling. "Are you all right?"

The old man nodded. "Is this what we're to expect for the rest of the trip?"

"No." Travis's face was illuminated by the golden fire. He stood a head above the both of them. "They're prairie rattlers, most likely after your hummingbirds. There aren't any in the mountains. It's too cold. But there are just enough here to keep life interesting. Same like the bugs, remember?"

Mr. Merriweather slapped a mosquito on his neck. "Quite right, quite right." He shook his head and sat back on his log. "Jolly good, I've witnessed a live rattler."

"And you didn't need binoculars to see it." Travis cleared the tin plates.

Jessica eyed her log but no longer felt like sitting down. She shooed away the flying insects.

"Are you still going down to the river to wash these plates?" Travis asked her.

She wished she hadn't volunteered.

He grabbed a tin bucket. He was a commanding force of bulky shadows and straining muscles. Permeating the pine-scented air, his laughter was the first she'd heard in two days. "If your chaperon approves, I'll go with you."

Damn, the woman was distracting.

Wondering why he allowed her to bother him, Travis led them to a clear spot by the river. He scoured the area for more rattlers, found none, then slid their tin cups onto a granite boulder.

She'd been distracting him all day—her ineptness at handling the horses, her eagerness to help with chores as if the offer would erase that she'd gone above his head to order him here and even how she spent her time mostly with her butler, taking little regard of *him.*

Travis, on the other hand, couldn't turn a corner without being alerted to her presence. When she stood beside him grooming Independence, he found the air stifling. When she asked a question, his normally quiet composure chafed in self-defense, and if, God forbid, their eyes met accidentally, his pulse began a rhythmic tap. His reactions annoyed him.

And made him miss his wife more.

Grumbling, he lifted his Stetson and allowed the cool breeze to curl beneath his pressed hair. It felt good. Jessica kneeled on the boulder.

In the stables this morning, the other men had been eager to replace him when they'd heard he was leaving for seven days with the mayor's daughter.

"I'll deliver your broodmares," the farrier had said, winking while making a final check of the horseshoes. "A man could always use pretty female company."

She was pretty and she was female, but Travis could pass on her company. Standing back in the brightness of the moon, he watched her.

Although he fought it, a glimpse of the smooth side of her cheek played with his thoughts. Jessica lowered herself to the rushing river. Her braids dipped below her shoulders. Beneath her fresh, white blouse and trousers, her youthful body contrasted against the century-old, twisted trees behind her. Glowing skin in its prime versus rough, mossy bark. Yet both images brought a strange comfort to him. Did all women use lotions on their face as Caroline had, mint powders on their teeth and vinegar to rinse their hair?

It was a silly thought, he acknowledged, so he turned away to concentrate on his task. He dipped the bucket into the moving mass of water.

Victor's death had surprised him. He had no idea she'd had such turmoil in her life. Maybe it was one of the reasons she'd left for finishing school—to get her mind off Victor.

He cleared his throat. "Is Dr. Finch expecting you?"

The question seemed to rattle her. Fumbling, she laid one clean tin plate upon a boulder, the clanging echoing over the river. Dipping a dirty plate into the water, she scrubbed a sliver of soap against it.

"No," she said softly.

"Then how do you know he'll have the time to be interviewed?"

Her lips drew together. "He'll listen to my request."

"You may not find him. He's needed in several towns and travels quite a bit, from what I hear. Doctors are hard to come by in this part of the country."

"I suppose that's why people are so ready to trust him. Because they need to. They want to."

"Why don't you like him?"

She started at the observation. The fabric of her blouse billowed, accentuating jutting breasts, narrow waist and full hips.

He turned away, his gaze settling on the flowing river and trees lining the distance. "It's obvious you don't. Every time his name is mentioned, you stiffen like a fishing rod that's snagged an unwanted catch."

Even in the golden light, he saw defiance in her eyes.

"He charges a lot of money for his cures," she countered.

"There's no law against a man turning a profit."

"Some of his cures don't work."

He watched her long fingers sweep the inside of a cup. "Some of them do. I imagine when you're dealing with the health of a patient, unfortunately, there's no answer for everyone." He scrutinized her. "Why did you want to pay me so much to get you to Devil's Gorge? Two hundred dollars, if I recall."

The lines of her shoulders hardened. "The money's still open, if you like."

He scoffed. "That's not why I brought it up. Why is it so important that you speak to Dr. Finch?"

"I need him for my article, to give it authenticity."

There was something more to her position; Travis sensed it.

"Why do you like him so much?" she asked.

He anchored one boot between two rocks and rebalanced his weight. "He helps a lot of folks. He helped me get a conviction in the trial against Pete Warrick."

"What trial?"

"The huge one that just finished." He noticed her pause. "I forgot—you were out of town."

Her gold necklace shimmered around her slender throat. "Was it a medical case?"

"No."

"Then how did he help you?"

"He was the sole eyewitness in a string of unsolved robberies that happened across southern Alberta and B.C. over the course of the past two years. He placed Pete at the scene of a store crime one hundred miles due south of here, the only person ever captured."

He watched her digest the information.

She frowned as if something didn't make sense. Then she rose, her expression fiery, her body challenging. "There are two other doctors in town. Are they friendly toward Dr. Finch?"

He studied her critically. "Why wouldn't they be?"

She shrugged, but seemed flustered by his scrutiny. "Journalists are supposed to ask questions."

Maybe, but she seemed to have a bigger stake in this. His gaze again fell to her creamy throat. "The fort's surgeon, John Calloway, joined us for dinner once after the trial and seemed to like Dr. Finch just fine. And Dr. Virginia Bullock says she and Dr. Finch shared the same physiology professor in medical college."

"What?" Jessica's plate clattered to the pile, the bang surprising them both. A flock of geese fluttered fifty feet away then tore off into the sky. Quickly recovering, Jessica scooped the plate and continued washing. "How's that possible?"

He stepped back from her to catch a breath. "Dr.

Bullock attended the university in Toronto, but she told me her professor emigrated from Glasgow twelve years earlier. That's where Dr. Finch went to school. During the trial, they compared notes about their quirky professor. He used to write lists and lists of anatomical glands, organs and bones. He made his students reorganize them according to their placement in the body, starting from the head and working down."

She rubbed the back of her neck, looking very disturbed.

"Glasgow," Travis repeated. "That's where Dr. Finch earned his medical degree. He's Scottish."

She slumped down on a protruding boulder.

"You *have* done some digging about his background for this interview, haven't you?"

"The University of Glasgow," she whispered, incredulous.

"What's this interview about, exactly? What's the topic?"

The breeze whirled around her hair. "There's a man," she said. "A man I've been tracking in Montreal. His name is Dr. King. My topic is about charlatans and their influence in modern society. How their practices have sparked the current laws for licensing of legitimate doctors. Up until recently, almost anyone could call themselves a doctor."

"And you think Dr. Finch knows something about Dr. King?"

"I thought… But his attendance at the University of Glasgow places him in a different…" She flushed. "You're a policeman. Do you know anything about medical con artists and charlatans?"

He shook his head. "Not medical. We've had our share of passing carnival men who've duped folks out of money. We've had store owners and bankers who've been apprehended with their fingers in the till. But no run-ins with dubious quacks."

The animation in her face distracted him again.

He shoved a hand into a pocket. "I've heard about charlatans, though, in the big cities out East—in both Canada and the States. I've heard that in Philadelphia they have these medical museums. Innocent folks go in thinking they're going to see something unusual, but many are cornered and led to believe they're dangerously ill themselves. They're taken to a backroom and sold expensive treatments."

"There was a museum like that in Montreal. The police disbanded it."

"And Dr. King knew something about it?"

"I'm convinced he was involved, although he was never caught."

"Well, if Dr. Finch can help you locate this charlatan, I'm sure he will. Because of him, I won a major trial. Pete Warrick's doing seven years' hard labor."

Devastation fell across her face. "A doctor's word is sacred, isn't it? I mean, no one goes against the word of a doctor."

"Not without powerful proof. Do you have any against Dr. King?"

Her lashes swept downward. "No…"

"That's a big accusation with no proof. You could be brought in front of a judge yourself for slandering the doctor's reputation."

She scoffed. "That's the same thing my father told me."

"You should listen to your father."

The wind kicked up around them. She sprang to her feet, collecting the plates and cups. "The puzzle pieces are spread in front of me," she said firmly. "All I have to do is join them."

"It seems to me that you have an opinion on everything."

"I'm close." With a burst of militancy, she blew the hair from her face. "I can feel it."

They were standing close, and he could feel it. Close enough that he could smell the soap on her hands.

Their proximity made him uncomfortable. He stepped away to lift the empty bucket. When the wind curled and shifted, he smelled vestiges of smoke. Wary, looking down the flowing river, he straightened and sniffed again.

"What is it?" she asked.

"A campfire."

She peered through the darkness. "I don't see it."

"It's a smudge fire. They're using moss to keep it burning low."

"Why would they do that?"

His muscles tensed. "They're hiding it on purpose. There's two or three of them behind us."

"Who?"

"I don't know. Earlier today along with the hawk you and Merriweather were watching, there were vultures flying in the sky. They were circling something a mile or two farther down the trail. They eat scrap food and anything a traveler might leave behind."

"What does that mean?"

He grabbed her by the elbow, pulling her arm so hard against his chest he stole her breath. "Is there any reason *you* can think of why someone might be following us?"

She hesitated, and that worried him.

"No," she whispered.

"Are you sure?"

She yanked from his powerful grip, spun around

and dodged him. "Wh-what on earth would they want from me?"

He ran a hand across his dry mouth and cursed aloud. If she didn't know anything about them, then there was only one logical explanation, one that had loomed in his fears since he'd begun planning this critical journey.

"Then someone's after my horses."

Chapter Five

With a growing sense of frustration, standing behind a cover of bushes while preparing for bed, Jessica stretched her right arm behind her back as far as it would go and grabbed for the last hook and eye on her corset. She shuffled in the dirt. Perspiration broke out on her forehead. With a moan and a final tug, she managed to unhook it. The red corset flung off her body and ricocheted between a poplar tree and white spruce. A cool breeze whispered over her naked breasts.

"You damn miserable piece of cotton, I should—"

"Is everything all right?" Travis called in the darkness.

Shocked by the proximity of his voice, she scooped her corset and clutched it to her body. "Stay out there!"

"I'm not coming after you. I'm merely wondering what the fuss is about."

"I'm fine. A little difficulty with my clothing. Go on now. Run along."

There was a pause. "Yes, ma'am," he said in mocking tones. She relaxed as his footsteps grew distant. He called to Mr. Merriweather about stacking fire logs.

She was still touchy from the thought someone might be following them. Every noise spooked her.

Looking down at her corset, as much as she could see of it in the dark, she rubbed her fingers along the intricate column of hooks. At home, she and her sister always helped each other secure their stays, but Jessica was alone on this trip. The corset clasped at the back, which was half the problem.

Tomorrow, she'd have to devise something different to wear beneath her clothes. Her chemise, perhaps, and an undershirt on top of that to support her as she rode.

Beyond the bushes, Mr. Merriweather called to Travis above the spitting fire. "For a man who thinks someone's following us, you don't seem to be very worried."

She heard a rustling of branches, then Travis's low voice. "There's no sense getting your long johns twisted in a knot. Overreacting doesn't solve anything."

Jessica slid her night shift over her head and listened to their conversation.

"You're not worried at all?" continued the butler.

"I'm concerned, but they won't come near us for at least three more days."

"How can you be so bloody well sure?"

"Because that's what I'd do if I were them. I wouldn't make a move now because we're too close to the police fort. Dozens of policemen who don't take kindly to horse theft. It'll take us three days to cross the border of Alberta into British Columbia. It's deserted in the interior. That's when I'd make my move."

The butler gasped. "Why don't you arrest them tonight?"

"I can't arrest anyone unless a crime's been committed." He paused. "Tomorrow evening we'll be passing through the village of Strongness. I know some men there who've worked for me before. Good men. I'll get their help with this."

"Good show! But for tonight, shouldn't we be sleeping in a ring, facing outward, head to toe in our bedrolls with our guns drawn?"

Travis laughed. "Where'd you read that? An adventure novel?"

"Well, as a matter of fact, Cherokee Joe—"

"Cherokee Joe?"

"He's a brilliant Indian I read about in a jolly good Western series, written by an Englishman from Hong Kong. My word, Cherokee Joe could smell a trap a mile away. And he could wring a coyote's neck with his bare fists."

Jessica recalled the story and smiled to herself as she folded her daytime clothes to stuff them in her pack.

"First of all," said Travis, "there aren't any Indians in the West named Joe. And Cherokee Indians have never lived in this territory."

"But this man was special. His wife was a European princess who happened to meet him on one of the king's trips—"

"That's crazy." Travis whistled. "Why would he marry a princess? What in the world might they have in common?"

"Their mutual love for an injured buffalo, of course—"

"I've met several Indians. None of them would want to marry a European princess. They're smart."

"But I haven't gotten to the part about the Mountie."

"Let me guess. It's a lovers' tug-of-war between Cherokee Joe and the Mountie for the princess."

"No, no," said Jessica, stepping out backward from behind the bushes, dragging her saddlebag to the large pine tree. She propped it beside the others. "The princess shoots the Mountie because he's trying to wrongfully imprison Cherokee Joe."

She tried to join in the light conversation, hoping to divert attention from what she was wearing, but failed miserably when she turned around and saw Travis.

Crouched by the fire, he was unrolling blankets. Mr. Merriweather was nowhere in sight. She peered around for him then spotted the movements of his arms behind a far tree as he wiggled out of his clothes.

Travis had removed his hat, vest and shirt. His powerful set of shoulders gleamed bronze in a white sleeveless undershirt. It struck her that she'd be sleeping within yards of him tonight.

He hesitated at the sight of her, looked her up and down, clenched his jaw then turned back to his bedroll.

They were both embarrassed. Although she'd tried to cover her white nightdress with her shawl, the shawl only reached to her waist. The bottom half of her gown, and her high woolen stockings, were visible. It was definitely improper to be seen in her nightclothes by a stranger. The last time she'd been with a man... The consequences of her tryst with Victor burned in her mind.

Desperately wishing she could sink into the darkness of the night, she tugged the shawl tighter. She'd removed her braids and the wind nipped at her disheveled hair. What else could she do but pretend everything was normal?

Travis finished with one bedroll. He untied the leather ties for another, stood up and shook it out.

"So I gather you read the book, too?"

She nodded. "Mr. Merriweather loaned it to me and my sister years ago. The story is very dramatic."

"The Mountie sounds like an incompetent fool."

"He was a bit on the slow side."

"Written by an Englishman from the colony of Hong Kong."

"Um-hmm. I'm sure Mr. Merriweather wouldn't mind loaning it to you. You might learn from Cherokee Joe's tracking methods."

"Thanks but I'll pass."

He had a way of making her feel inadequate, as if she always said the wrong thing, did the wrong thing.

She walked closer. "May I claim one of the bedrolls?"

"Any one you like. I'll keep the fire burning so we'll be warm all night."

He rose to his feet. The campfire spit and popped beside them. Even though the air was hot, she shivered when she looked at him.

Flames of fire reflected off his profile—across the darkened jaw, the straight nose, the rigid cheekbones.

A confusing mix of feelings raced through her. *They would sleep together tonight.*

She recalled that for a brief time as an adolescent, she and Caroline had competed for his affections. Caroline had always won every silly rivalry they'd ever set. But Jessica had dreamed of how his kiss might feel. A *real* kiss, not like the two he *had* given her—once when he brushed her cheek at a wedding, and once at a Christmas social. Now as his full lips parted and his gaze glossed over her mouth, she wondered still.

She should have thought before she spoke, but her anger at herself for wondering about his kiss made her want to distance herself. "Why didn't you think about horse thieves before we left? Surely it's something you should have considered on a journey with your prize mares."

His face darkened. "I was keeping my plans quiet. Just a few of my men and the commander knew the exact day I was leaving and where I was heading. Thanks to you and your stunt of going above my head, the whole town discovered it overnight."

She stepped back at his rebuke. "I didn't realize."

Menacing, he stepped forward, bridging the distance she wanted to widen. "If I lose any of my horses, I'm holding you responsible."

She'd messed up his plans again. As if she were that same spoiled woman he accused her of being.

The corner of his mouth twisted. "You and your father finagled a prize stallion out from underneath me years ago. This time, maybe you'll have to reimburse me for my trouble, and these ones will cost you a lot more."

"Travis, I didn't realize—"

"Ready for bed, all?" Mr. Merriweather hobbled out from the tree, wearing a long cotton night shift similar to hers.

Travis shook his head at the friendly man. "Forget the rattlers, forget the horse thieves. I'll tell you one thing I *am* worried about. Your feet. Seems to me you can barely walk."

"My feet will be fine."

"How many blisters do you have?"

"Just two. One on the bottom of each foot."

Travis stalked to his pack and withdrew a roll of cloth. "Tomorrow morning, wrap your feet with this gauze before you shove them back into your boots."

His eyes narrowed on the two of them standing by the fire. He peered down at her legs, apparently for the first time. His bare, muscled arms tightened. His gaze roved her lower half. "Is that what you're wearing to bed? Both of you—only nightshirts?"

"What's wrong with them?" she asked.

"You're not sleeping in a castle. You're sleeping in the middle of the wilderness!"

Jessica was too startled by his booming voice to respond. He always seemed to be teetering on the edge of anger, and she always seemed to be pushing him over.

"If we have to jump up in a hurry, Merriweather, because we're getting mauled by bears, how are you going to protect us naked beneath a nightshirt? And you, Miss Charm School, what about you? If you have to jump onto a horse, are you willing to ride in that *thin little thing?* For God's sake," he said, stomping to the third bedroll and flinging it into the air, "think of how Cherokee Joe would dress!"

"In his clothes!" shouted Mr. Merriweather. "By George, his clothes. That's why you're still in your pants and undershirt. That's what you're sleeping in, aren't you?"

"Put some pants on, woman," Travis grumbled with fury, brushing past her so only she could hear. She withered at his next words. "With your back to the fire, I can see through your whole damn gown."

From beneath her covers, Jessica watched Travis stir the fire then check the horses. Apparently, he couldn't sleep, either. She stilled with nervous expectation. She wanted him to return to his bedroll and fall asleep so she could get something from her pack, something she'd forgotten and didn't want him to see. If he caught her, they'd certainly clash again.

She squirmed on the hard ground, trying to forget about the flat rock lodged beneath her back. Six feet to her left, Mr. Merriweather snored. Draped near her feet, Travis's bedroll lay empty. He'd tried going to sleep alongside the both of them an hour ago, but had risen only moments earlier.

Her gaze traveled the fifty feet of moonlit space and rested on Travis's hands. He patted the horses one at a time. His handling stopped short of Independence and Jessica was riveted again by the discomfort in his manner. What was it that he didn't like about that horse?

Her eyes stung from weariness. The long day had tired her, not so much the physical exertion, but the mental strain of being on her guard with Travis. And discovering Dr. Finch had gone to medical college in Glasgow. She'd thought he was lying about his education. This was the first time she'd heard of Dr. Virginia Bullock having the same professor.

Jessica considered the problem, adamant she was still somehow correct. Could it be Dr. Finch's discussion with Dr. Virginia Bullock had been framed in front of Travis in such a way that he only *appeared* to have had the same physiology professor? Why?

Hearing the jingle of spurs approaching the campfire, she closed her eyes quickly and pretended sleep. The heat of the fire warmed her lids and touched her lips.

After waiting two minutes for the sound of rustling blankets, she heard none.

Go to bed, she wanted to scream.

Slowing opening one eye, she found him seated on a log, long legs spanned in front of him, hands propped on solid knees, a stick in his hand as he turned red-hot coals.

She had to admit, he was pleasant on the eyes. Blue-denim pants hugged a flat waistline, molded lower to firm thighs then bunched slightly at the knees before falling above pointed black boots. The muscles of his bronzed arms tensed with his movements, then relaxed, then tensed again. A knot formed in her stomach as she watched him being *him.*

The strain in his face had lifted. The wrinkles between his eyebrows that appeared whenever he looked at her had faded. His mouth, parted slightly, slackened in the red light. Deep black hair framed his temples, and the rough shadow of a beard reminded her again how much he looked like a dangerous pirate.

He was rude and arrogant and had treated her badly since the minute she'd approached him for help.

But she couldn't deny how good he was at what he did. He was a master in leading the horses through the foothills, an expert in supplying food and drink and shelter. While she watched the serenity in his face, she was mesmerized by the pleasure he seemed to derive from being the boss and taking charge of everyone and everything.

A horse neighed. Travis turned his head in that direction, as a concerned parent might, then instinctively rose, armed with his Colt revolver. He made his way to investigate. He scoured the ground then seemed satisfied that all was well. Perhaps he'd thought it was a rattler. Because he remained with the horses, she figured it was her chance to jump up to her pack.

Sliding out from her covers, she tugged her boots over her stocking feet. She bunched her nightgown in one hand above the ivory pants she'd decided to sleep in—tomorrow she'd try sleeping in her blouse, too, but for tonight she was already changed—then heaved to her feet. Her pack was still resting beneath the pine tree, ten feet away. She'd be back before he realized she was gone.

Kneeling, she undid the bulging side pouch, rifling through her journal, her pencils, her money, her papers, until her fingers touched soft flannel. With a gentle smile, she pulled it out, held it to her face and inhaled the calming scent of clean fabric. Perhaps it was superstitious of her, but she'd never be able to fall asleep if she left her infant's nightgown alone in the cold. She would tuck it beneath her pillow.

She worked with speed to retie her side pocket.

There were three things in her pack she had no intention of telling Travis about. *Three secrets.* He'd already seen this one when he'd helped her pack at the fort, and had tried to make her toss it out.

Pivoting with the soft flannel concealed beneath her own nightgown, she remembered what he'd yelled this morning when he'd seen it. *"No gifts!"*

She didn't have many gifts she could offer her son when she found him, but a simple nightshirt from his mother surely wouldn't intrude on Travis's time or space.

When she wheeled around, Travis was standing in front of her.

She riveted in alarm. "Why'd you scare me like that?"

"What are you doing?"

Breathless, she was hit by a cold pang of loneliness. Loneliness that she was in dark, unfamiliar territory, that she was a mother without her child, that she had to constantly defend herself to this man.

"I'm a little cold. I got another piece of clothing."

He crossed his bulging arms over his chest and continued to block her path. When he looked lower to the flannel cloth she was clutching, her grip tightened.

She knew as they neared Devil's Gorge and Dr. Finch, she'd have to tell Travis something more. *Something about her missing child.*

So far he hadn't given her one reason why she should trust him. If she divulged her secrets, he might tell her the accusations against Dr. Finch were preposterous, that her secrets nullified any agreement he had with the commander to escort her. Travis was so harsh toward her he might say he didn't care about her problems and demand she and her butler return to Calgary. Tomorrow evening they'd be passing through a village—maybe he'd order them to stay behind there.

She couldn't divulge anything until it was safe to do so, until they were beyond the point of no return.

But glaring at the uncompromising cut of his profile, she realized she was tackling more than she could handle.

"Are you warmer now?"

"Yes, I am."

Darkness wove an unwanted air of sensuality between them. Only a nightgown separated her skin from his. But this time, there was no fire behind her and she knew he couldn't see her naked figure through the sheer cloth. He took a deep breath, though, and she felt as if the oxygen around her was being sucked away.

The scent of ferns mingled with the scent of his skin. Above them, moonlight rippled through a canopy of branches. Circular swirls of light softened the steel-hard cut of his jaw and sharp black brows. She caught the deep glimmer in his eyes as they searched her face. Cool, clean air filtered up her gown and over her bare flesh. Tiny hairs bristled on her skin; her breasts felt heavy. That lonely ache throbbed inside of her.

She remembered the last wedding reception they had attended, each with their families, years ago before the rivalry with Caroline had begun. And before the mayor and Caroline's father had declared war on each other. Travis's kiss on her cheek had been soft and smooth because he'd just shaved; his kiss now would be rough.

Roughrider.

She had an urge, a need, to be touched. Her body flushed with heat, her heart pounded as she imagined his hands sliding along her skin.

But he'd been nothing but rude and miserable to her since this started.

"Good night." She stepped around him and left him staring after her, a solitary figure in the dark.

Chapter Six

The second day passed in misery. Travis knew he urgently needed to do something to shake her out of his mind. He'd spent a restless night watching the stars, analyzing sounds in the cool wind for indications of trouble, but mostly trying not to breathe the same air as the provocative woman sleeping three feet away perpendicular to him.

In the morning they arose with the rising sun. The more he ignored Jessica, the more he craved to look at her. She tumbled out of bed, her cheeks creased with the lines of her bedding, cheerfully hauling water from the river to boil coffee, asking Merriweather how he felt, timidly making her way to the horses to say hello.

Hello to the horses!

Later astride his horse, while he led them through rolling hills and thicker trees, Travis assured himself his craving had nothing to do with disloyalty to Caroline. Caroline may have understood it, for she'd always raised her eyebrows at the frequency of his desire. *He* was taken by surprise by his physical sensations whenever Jessica brushed by. His skin bristled, he inhaled deeply, his pulse stopped for a beat and he avoided eye contact. He kicked himself every time it happened.

He'd seen that need in animals, a physical alertness of the male to the female species. But for cripe's sake, he wasn't an animal and should be thinking more with his brain than his urges. One year had passed since he'd even *noticed* another woman. Was his body making up for lost time?

Behind him on the trail, Merriweather hollered in a weary voice. "Shall we stop here for our midday rest?"

Adjusting his hat, Travis slowed his gelding and peered through a ring of firs to a clearing beyond the river's curve. He knew he'd been pushing the other two hard. It seemed the more irritable Travis got, the harder he worked them. This was taking its toll on the butler.

"It looks fine. We'll stop for two hours."

"Can you see anyone behind us on the trail today? Anyone following?"

"No sign of them," said Travis. "I'll take a closer look while we're resting."

They dismounted. Where the sunlight penetrated the forest, wildflowers grew in abandon—lady's slipper, Indian paintbrush, and a variety of heathers.

Merriweather limped through the trees to the river, five hundred feet to the west. While Travis untied his saddle, he watched the old man then shook his head in sympathy and concern. Jessica was also watching. When Travis turned his head to locate her, their eyes met above the saddle. He looked away but she *walked* away.

With ease, he slid the saddle off the first horse, then the second, then the third. He didn't expect any help from Jessica or her butler; he was grateful if they would only keep out of his way. As he slid the saddle from the last horse, he heard Independence whinny. Turning toward the sound, he noticed Jessica had led her to a tree twenty yards away.

His heart plunged. He dropped his saddle and ran. "No! Stop!"

Jessica lunged out of his path. He slammed past her to the reins and yanked Independence from the shrubs. "Never, *ever, ever,* let her eat that plant. It's yew and it can kill her. A mouthful can stop her heart!" His own heart bounded in leaps.

Her hand flew to her brown hat. "She didn't touch it. She'd didn't take one bite!"

He was standing next to her again, the last place he wanted to be. He felt the movement of her breathing and the maddening rush of his own. He said nothing but shook his head in disapproval.

Brown eyes smoldered in his direction. She tossed her hands onto her angled hips. "You think I don't know anything, but it's because you don't tell me anything. Mr. Merriweather gets your precious sympathy, but all I ever get is your blasted temper."

He gritted his teeth. "Because you're nothing but trouble."

"And you're nothing but a thorn in my behind. I want you out."

He glared at her, wishing he could say a magic word to make her disappear. Her braids were never able to contain all of her hair. Escaped strands of gold framed her heated face. Her white blouse had pulled out from one side of her waist. The creamy pants that had been crisp and clean yesterday morning were looser and stained with dull splotches of coffee and grass. The freckles on her nose had deepened in color.

She glanced at Independence, who was grazing grass by his boots. "Many people mistakenly treat me like I'm upper class. You treat me like I'm lower." Her lips stiffened; her tone was harsh. "I don't think we're so different. You were raised to believe if you worked hard, you could make a difference. Well, I was told the same."

Momentarily rebuffed, he tossed his Stetson to the grass and ran a hand through his hair. "All right, you want to know some things? This is yew." He pointed to the line of shrubs. "They've got straight, green leaves, which almost look like coniferous needles. Keep the horses away from that." He emphasized his point by gouging the air with his finger. "They can all graze in the clearing at the tall grass where I left them. But the shorter, fresh grasses, there—" he pointed past her shoulder "—have more nutrients. We'll let Independence graze there for the sake of her foal."

She squinted in the sunlight. "A kind word from the king."

She'd roused his anger, then tried to leave.

"Go ahead, run away again."

"I'm not running." She turned briskly at his other side. He felt the breeze of her movements, smelled the scent of her skin.

"Yes, you are. Just like last night when I caught you at your saddlebag. You can't face a confrontation."

"I can face anything. It's you who's not straightforward. You sit waiting until I make a mistake then you tear my head off." She ducked past him, body bouncing.

His jaw pulsed. He spun her back by the shoulders. "Would you like to be straightforward?"

His emotions whirled so he released her and she stepped back.

"Tell me what's in your pack," he demanded.

The pulsing at her throat began. Her expression reddened but she didn't respond.

"Don't pretend you don't know what I'm asking." Wild birds called above them. "In the upper right pocket, the one that's bulging and tied extra tight with leather thongs. What've you got in there?"

Her eyes narrowed. "Nothing of your concern."

He lunged for his fallen hat. "It damn well is. Everything on this journey is. And I'm going to find out for myself." With a slap of his hat across his firm thigh, he stalked toward her bags. *There was nothing she could say or do to stop him.*

"I would expect my father to rifle through my things," she called over his shoulders, "but not you."

Except that.

He stopped in the grass, settled his palms on his waist and exhaled. To be compared to her father…

He whirled around. The sun's heat bit through the fabric on his shoulders. "You're going to tell me then. What's the connection between Dr. King and Dr. Finch?"

She paled instantly, as if he'd struck the right chord.

Three more strides and he was towering at her side. "I've been thinking about what you told me, and I want to know the connection. *Now!*"

Defiance flooded through her. "You want to know, you brute? Here!" She raced to her pack, to the secret compartment he'd been staring at, and untied the strings with a fury. She shielded the open pocket with her body so he wasn't able to see its contents. "This wasn't exactly how I wanted to tell you, but here!"

She thrust a piece of folded paper onto his chest.

He staggered with the impact. Taking the paper between long fingers, he unfolded the flyer and read the headline. "A Discussion of New Medical Inventions, 7 p.m. at University Hall, May 22, 1891." It was more than a year ago. He stared at the black-and-white lithograph of a man with dark hair, mustache and beard. "So?"

"It's a lecture I attended in Montreal. The room was packed with medical personnel. Doctors, nurses, pharmacists, journalists. I even interviewed a banker who was thinking of investing money for his clients in some of the new inventions."

"And?"

"And..." She lowered her gaze to the paper, her mouth forming that firm, stubborn line he was beginning to recognize. "...that's Dr. King."

He frowned, well aware of her provocative body as she leaned over his shoulder to point across the page.

He scratched his bristly jaw. "Am I supposed to know what you're talking about?"

"Look closer. His hair is solid black. If you colored his hair white at the temples, shaved off his mustache and beard, don't you think he'd look a lot like Dr. Finch?"

Stunned, he looked up from the paper to her vibrant face.

He *knew* Dr. Finch. The man was a fine, respectable man who'd cooperated fully at the trial. For God's sake, the man was a *doctor.*

She showed no remorse, while amazement siphoned his circulation. "Hold on a minute. What you're suggesting—"

"I'm not suggesting anything. I'm *telling* you. Dr. King and Dr. Finch are the same man."

His mouth dropped open as he looked at her with ill regard. His listened in disbelief as she kept going. She *believed* this convoluted story.

"I didn't realize while I was taking notes why Dr.

King's voice sounded familiar. He had to speak loud in the lecture hall in order to be heard, at times nearly shouting. I've never heard Dr. Finch shout. He speaks softly. But two nights afterward, the voices were still echoing inside my head. I realized…the voices were the same."

"You hear voices inside your head." Then he whispered, "You're mistaken."

She balked. "You're afraid."

"What?"

She was pushing hard. Every muscle in his body tensed in response.

"You're afraid because if I'm right, then you're wrong." She ripped the paper from his fingers. "If Dr. Finch is a con man, then your police trial involving him as your solitary eyewitness against Pete Warrick… Well, you may have put an innocent man in prison."

Christ, she had a way of grinding her point home.

"With Dr. Finch's help, you might have sentenced the wrong man to seven years' hard labor." Her voice choked. "You owe Mr. Warrick the dignity to investigate my allegations."

He disengaged himself and stepped away, tucking both hands into his pockets. "Maybe you should be writing fiction."

She looked down at her boots. Then with a stifled sob, she took her paper and ran past him, past Independence and into the field. The wind blew her hair. Her hat fell off but she kept running, visibly shaken.

Why was she so upset?

With blood rushing through his veins, he chased after her. "Stop!"

"Stay away from me!" Her feet flew over the shafts of tall, green grass.

He could hear his pounding breath in the wind, feel the stretch of muscles in his legs, sense the thrumming of excitement and danger in his limbs.

He dived for her legs. They fell to the soft, grassy slope. He yanked without mercy on her shoulder, spinning her to face him until she was sprawled beneath him, pinned beneath his ribs. He lay on top. Propriety be damned.

His breath raced in triple time, loud and raspy. "You're mistaken. Admit you don't have evidence."

Her chest moved up and down beneath his as she fought for air. It was then he noticed the pliant nature of her body. It wasn't encased in a firm corset but in softer cloth. He liked the smooth feel of her warm flesh beneath his.

"You're an insensitive man. You like order in your life, but you can't have it while I'm here. I won't give it to you. I'm right about Dr. Finch, *and…you're… wrong!*"

He pinned her arms to her sides and, in a moment of red-hot fury, slammed his mouth down hard on hers.

The shock of contact subdued her. It rippled through him.

Her mouth was hot, wet and soft.

He moaned in pleasure, unable to stop himself from demanding more.

Her last words were smothered by his mouth. And then she responded.

Urgent. Rough. Delicious.

His hold slackened on her wrists. Her fingers reached up and seared a path down his neck and back, then burned across his waist. When she pressed her body up against his, he felt himself grow hard. He was shocked by the hungry desperation in their kiss.

And she was a virgin?

He was practically attacking her, but he couldn't stop.

When she moaned and tilted her body to the right, he followed her lead and rolled over so that she was on top. He could envision their position naked, her swollen breasts swaying above him.

His hands explored her flesh, traveling down her waist as he kissed her neck, her earlobe, her temple. With a solid yank, he tore her blouse out from her pants.

Then with a quick thrust of her knee that almost hit him square in the groin, it ended. Luckily, he'd dodged before she hit her target, but it was enough to stop him cold.

He slumped to his back in the weeds, enveloped by the heat of the ground, gazing up at the blue sky. What the hell had he attempted?

She rose above him in the grass, a proud form peering down at him, full lips rounded over white teeth, dusty rose in her cheeks, loose tendrils of hair flying across her face.

Panting uncontrollably, she threatened, "If you try that again, I'll shoot you."

It took Jessica more than an hour to recover from his kiss. Then she took her time preparing lunch.

Shielding her eyes from the campfire smoke, she stood above the hanging frying pan and tossed in the apple slices. The sugary scent of bubbling raisins and fried apples filtered through the air, likely down to the river where Mr. Merriweather and Travis were catching fish.

How dare he put a hand on her while she'd openly beseeched him for help. What had possessed him to tackle her to the ground and...and press his mouth against hers?

A masculine display of power?

With her thoughts still turbulent, she wiped her lips from his sting. If he didn't believe her about Dr. Finch's masquerade, then Travis wouldn't believe that the doctor had taken her child. She'd hoped by opening up to Travis he'd be on her side, but it now placed her in a more vulnerable position. He was taking Dr. Finch's side.

The fact remained she needed Travis to get her safely to Devil's Gorge, and if he thought about it, if he were at all intelligent, maybe he'd see he needed *her* to help uncover Dr. Finch's true identity. Even if only to prove her theory wrong so that Travis could know his police witness was untainted.

She stirred the apples. And now two of the three secrets in her saddlebag were out—her infant's nightgown and the flyer about Dr. King's lecture. Travis hadn't shown respect for either one, so she didn't dare reveal the third. He would hold it against her—

"Merriweather caught another trout!" Travis interrupted her thoughts, calling up from the slopes of the riverbank.

At the deep boom of his voice, she ran the back of her hand over her hair. "Wonderful," she said weakly.

"We'll add it to the other two and that should be enough for lunch." Travis bent down beside her, a wall of looming muscle. He'd already gutted the fish. He rinsed them in the pail of water with the others, then proceeded to skewer them onto a stick above the fire. The scales glistened in the sunlight, catching tiny rainbows of color.

Stealing a glance at Travis's face, lost in concentration, Jessica tingled at the thought of his burning kiss. She studied the outline of his lips and remembered how seductive they'd been. He'd coaxed her to wrap her arms around his neck. But she'd only been pretending to enjoy it in order to fool him into turning over so she could knee him and escape. However, she was shocked at how easily the ruse had come to her, and the urgent nature of her response. He'd been rough and direct and animalistic compared to Victor's soothing manner.

Without warning, Travis's dark lashes twitched. His probing gaze flew up to meet hers.

She felt herself blush at being caught watching him. Wheeling to her pan, she stirred and nearly burned her hand from the heat. "Our dessert's ready." Briskly, she took the cooking towel, wrapped it around her hand, then removed the pan from the fire. She set it down on a flattened rock.

"It smells good." Travis slid the stick full of fish into place over the fire.

"It's a recipe I learned from one of my friends in Montreal."

She watched him shift his weight, his large black boots scuffing the dirt, his muscles primed for work. She peered through the tangle of greenery toward the riverbank. "Will Mr. Merriweather be joining us soon?"

"He says he'd like to eat by the river. I'll bring him the first plateful as soon as it's ready."

"That's all right, I'll do it."

"There's no need for you to run around."

She stopped herself from arguing further about silly things. They watched the fish cook. Their discomfort with each other stretched. Reaching for a supply bag, she pulled out three plates. Not knowing where else to look, she peered at Independence, grazing in the short green grass where they'd tied her.

"Does your buyer know she's pregnant?"

"It's in our contract. He wanted her to be bred before I delivered her."

"She must need a lot more feed because of her condition."

"Actually, no. The most common mistake people make is overfeeding a pregnant mare."

"She's a fine horse." Jessica studied the reddish-brown muscles as the horse turned. "Why do you always leave her till the end, after all your other horses have been looked after?"

Travis adjusted the stick, then stood up. If she were to stand on tiptoe, she might be able to reach his face.

For a moment, she wasn't sure he'd answer, that he'd keep his thoughts to himself as he usually did. Then his blue eyes deepened. "Caroline was riding Independence when she fell."

"*That's* the horse I heard about?"

He nodded.

"No wonder you can't..."

He shrugged a massive shoulder.

"The mare is wild, then. She's unpredictable. Mr. Merriweather and I should stay away from her."

"She's gentle," he said slowly. "Caroline was spooked by a small animal, which caused her to slip and fall."

How awful. She watched the corded muscles of his throat as he tried to bury the pain.

It certainly explained some things about his anger. Whenever he was around that horse, he was a volcano waiting to erupt.

Gripped by sympathy, she realized they'd both been through a lot since their adolescence, since those frivolous years she'd spent vying with Caroline for his attention. Poor Caroline.

Weaving around him, Jessica found their clean cups and aligned them on a log beside the plates. She would talk about something safe. "There are many things I don't know about horses. They're a mystery to me."

The age lines about his mouth and eyes softened. "Jessica, about what happened earlier between us with that kiss—"

"My father was always too busy with work and people to teach me much about horses." Reaching for the coffeepot, she spun away to avoid him.

His voice rumbled from somewhere above her head. "It won't happen again, and you don't have to be concerned about your safety if—"

"I mean, we had those two fine show horses that pulled our buggy, but I wasn't allowed to go near them as a child for fear of pestering them." She slid her braid off her cheek.

As she clutched the coffeepot handle, he came up from behind and placed a callused hand on top of hers. She quaked beneath his touch. "I know you hear me." His breath was warm at her throat. "But I won't talk about it anymore."

He released her and she fought for equilibrium.

Neither spoke while they searched for clean cutlery. She scuffed the toe of her boot in the grass.

He stood motionless, drawing an invisible pattern on a fork with his thumb. "What would you like to know about horses that your father didn't teach you?"

She wiped her hands on a towel. "You'll think my questions are silly, they're so simple."

His glance slid to her blouse. "Try me."

"How high is Independence? I mean, I know you measure from the ground to the top of her withers, but the size of my hands and your hands are so different, whose hands do you use?"

He smiled and it disarmed her. "She's sixteen hands.

We don't use either of our hands to measure. A hand is considered to be four inches."

She studied his lean, tanned face. "Oh."

Beside them, the frying fish crackled. Travis bent at the waist, extended a powerful arm and rotated the stick.

"Why do we mount horses from the left? One time, my father took me riding and as I approached the horse from the right, he yelled at me to go around to the other side. I never could understand why and he couldn't give me the reason."

The wind changed direction and Travis squinted in a puff of smoke. She pulled away, fighting the sting in her eyes, while his arm came up to touch her back protectively. Escaping his gesture, she dodged around the fire.

"No wonder you have a fear of horses. Your father doesn't sound like the most patient teacher."

"He's all right. Used to dealing with adults, I suppose, and not inquisitive children."

"Most people are right-handed. Horses are trained to be mounted from the left for the ease of the rider. It dates back to the time when men wore swords and it was easier to mount. If you mounted from the right, you'd make the horse very nervous. It can be done, though. I once knew a left-handed old man who'd trained his horse to be mounted from the other side. He owned the horse straight from birth. When the old man died, no one else could ride him. They wound up setting it free to roam wild."

Travis's demeanor changed when he talked about the animals, from serious to animated.

Taking the towel, she lifted the lid from another pot. "The rice looks almost done." She stirred. "Have you ever had to destroy a horse because of a broken leg?"

"I have, and it wasn't easy." He lifted a fork and poked the side of one fish. The scales flaked nicely.

"I never could understand why we have to shoot them when they break a leg."

"I tried to save one once when I was fourteen. The horse had a bad fall jumping a ditch, but I was determined I could heal the fracture." He shook his head, entranced by the thought. "It was soon obvious I couldn't and my father had to shoot it. In the end, I realized it was the most humane thing we could do. Bad leg fractures never heal on a horse because of the weight of the animal and the need to keep the bones immobilized while healing, which is impossible."

"Is that why you're interested in training horses? Because of the one you tried to save when you were fourteen?"

He nodded, smiled easily, and her body felt warm and heavy in response.

"And that's why you're trying to save this one, why you haven't destroyed Independence after Caroline's accident. You can't because you like the mare too much."

The smile faded, replaced by a probing query. "You're reading too much into it. I'm selling my horses, remember?"

"Why?"

"It's time to move on in my life. Horses are expensive and they take up too much time when I could be doing other things."

After witnessing him talk about the animals, she wasn't sure she believed his reasoning.

"What about you?" He peered through the smoke, studying her with intensity. "When did you take up writing?"

"I used to write stories when I was young. Nothing very good. Then in my senior year, I kept a journal and wrote about events that happened in Calgary. I discovered I was better at writing about real events than made-up stories."

He removed the fish from the fire and slid them onto a clean plate, his movements swift and sure. "You surprised me when you said you write for the *Pacific Medical Journal.*"

"How so?" She scooped rice onto her plate and Mr. Merriweather's, acutely conscious of Travis's watchful eye.

"I never thought I could have a serious conversation with the mayor's spoiled daughter."

His confession brought a flash of sadness to her, that he thought of her in those terms. "Well, I've written all sorts of *serious* articles. New techniques in suturing, medical vacancies at various hospitals, how to use creolin as an antiseptic."

"And you got started in Montreal at the finishing school." He spooned rice to his plate with strong, long-fingered hands.

She nodded, uncomfortable with the topic. Turning her attention to the fish, she took a whole one for Mr. Merriweather and half for herself. "I made some friends who didn't have a lot of money for doctor's care. I got involved in helping to raise money for them, and educating girls in basic health and hygiene. I started attending lectures at the local university, always bringing a pencil with me. Before long I guess my natural desire to write took its course."

The rich outline of his shoulders strained against his shirt fabric. When he leaned over his plate, the top of his dark head brushed hers. It sent a nervous tingle up her spine.

"It seems odd that the mayor's daughter would have the opportunity to mingle with people who needed basic care."

And there it was, what he really thought of her.

She could reveal a little of her past, couldn't she? She could test him and watch the reaction in his eyes. But the fear, the constant fear she lived with about disclosing her illegitimate pregnancy censored her speech. The truth *would* ruin her reputation and her family's.

But she couldn't help herself. "There was this home I used to visit, called Miss Waverly's Home for Unwed Mothers."

"You mean the rich girls from the charm school visiting the poor girls from the Home to dole out charity?"

Her sympathy toward him evaporated. "What have you got against rich girls?"

"Money seems to buy everything in this world."

She felt her face tense. "It didn't buy your love for Caroline."

His expression churned with emotion. "What do you mean by that?"

"Nothing except that money doesn't buy everything. Caroline came from a poor family, yet you chose her anyway. Money didn't buy your love. I was giving you an example and hoping you might extend the courtesy to me."

"Money drove a wedge between your family and hers," he countered. "It destroyed them."

"That had nothing to do with me."

She lifted two plates in her hand, ready to deliver one to Mr. Merriweather. She moved forward but Travis blocked her path.

"What would be the motivation for Dr. Finch to assume the identity of Dr. King?"

They were back to that. At least, she thought, Travis was weighing what she'd told him earlier.

But it was the question she couldn't answer, the one

that nagged at her at night. Why would Dr. Finch have taken her baby? "Money, as you say. It affects a lot of people adversely."

"He makes a fistful already as a traveling doctor. He eases pain and cures sickness. He doesn't need more money. I can't see it in him."

"Then power."

"That's intangible. It would never hold in court."

"How about insanity?"

"I met the man. You know he's not insane."

"We'll see." She balanced the plates in her hands and kept walking, leaving Travis behind. Maybe Dr. Finch had taken her baby because he was a sick, twisted man who hurt children. A sob clung to her throat. Her misery at that thought was so acute it squeezed her heart.

Insistent, Travis leaped beside her. "What's *your* stake in all of this?"

She gave a choked, desperate laugh. Revealing that to him wasn't a risk she was willing to take.

"I don't like him. Now step aside. I'm going to take my meal with Mr. Merriweather."

Chapter Seven

So he'd kissed her, Travis thought after dinner several hours later. So what.

So frivolous and boring she wasn't.

At sundown Travis turned in his saddle to speak to his companions, his guns shifting around his hips. "The mercantile's around the first bend!"

They galloped out of the narrow path into a clearing that marked the village outskirts. A cool wind kicked up, blowing through his vest, refreshing his energy. "The best inn is on the other edge of town. We'll stop there first, get our rooms, then come back to the mercantile for food supplies. I also aim to buy a bigger pair of boots for our friend here, Cherokee Joe."

Merriweather grumbled. A wagon groaned by in one direction while a young couple on horseback tilted their hats hello in the other. Travis craned his heavy body to make sure Jessica was following closely. He watched her sigh, which lifted her breasts beneath her buttoned blouse, and accentuated the pull on several upper buttons.

A man could sure get lonesome looking at her.

And carried away by his imagination.

Their serious conversations of the past two days were a lot different than the trite observations they used to make on social occasions. She was smart and it surprised him.

He wondered if he'd been too harsh, judging Jessica by her behavior when she'd only been a teen. Hell, while growing up, he'd done and said plenty of idiotic things himself.

But Jessica had an opinion about Dr. King that Travis couldn't shake, and didn't understand.

Travis nodded to pedestrians on the boardwalk and waved to a familiar barkeep who was making his way to the saloon.

"Good evenin'," shouted the barkeep in a laughing voice. "Did you bring your rowdy brothers, Travis?"

"Not this time."

"That's too bad. The men in the saloon will be disappointed. I haven't had a cigar that good since the winter of '83."

The flare of street lamps bounced off the windows of several stores, although the sky wasn't completely dark yet. Strongness, with a head count of five hundred, was a natural resting stop at the base of the Rocky Mountains. It hadn't changed much in two years, nor in the ten since he'd first stopped here with his father and two brothers.

Hearing voices above him on the saloon balcony, he peered up and saw a woman dressed in scant clothing arguing with a man in a faded suit, no doubt one of her tawdry customers. Out of politeness, Travis's instinct was to divert Jessica's attention.

He let his horse slow so that he rode beside her. "Have you ever been in Strongness before?"

"You know I haven't." Distracted by the sounds of a

piano and loud voices, she glanced past his shoulder to the direction of the saloon.

"I used to come through here with my brothers. Selling cattle to the interior towns."

She frowned at his talkative nature, but they passed the saloon and he relaxed.

When they reached the inn, the innkeeper's wife was just entering the front door with an apron full of brown eggs. Heavyset with a rounded back, she pulled at her single braid of long, black hair. A shock of white lined its center part. She spotted them. "Travis! How wonderful to see you! Are you staying the night?"

"Only one, Miss Penelope."

"If I wasn't full of eggs right now I'd squeeze you with a big hug! Did you bring your handsome brothers?"

"Not this time."

"That's too bad. Esmerelda will be disappointed. She hasn't laughed so hard since that travelin' show passed through here during the summer of the large potatoes."

"We'll need three rooms, all beside each other if possible, for me and my friends here. This is the mayor of Calgary's daughter, Jessica Haven, and her butler, Giles Merriweather."

"Pleased to meet you. Here, let me put these down in the kitchen and I'll be right out to help you with your bags."

"My goodness," she said three minutes later as the group dismounted at the corner. "The mayor's daughter. I don't have any fancy rooms like they have in Calgary."

"I don't need anything fancy, ma'am. Your home looks beautiful, especially after a woman's been on the trail for two days."

Miss Penelope took a gander at Jessica's attire, raised

her eyebrows and looked to Travis with a secret in her eyes. Travis felt his neck grow hot.

"Esmerelda will be so disappointed you're traveling with your lady friend," the large woman whispered in passing.

"She's not my lady friend," Travis tried to assert.

Miss Penelope winked.

Despite his sore body, Merriweather insisted that the older woman not lay a hand on any of the bags, that he would carry them in himself.

"Imagine having a butler of your own," said Miss Penelope with wonder, wiping her boxy hands on her apron as she watched Merriweather. "Sheer luxury, I say." She saw her husband and daughter coming down the boardwalk carrying jars of prunes. "Dearest! Come here and say hello to our guests. Have you ever thought of hiring me a butler?"

"I thought I was your man," replied her tiny, chuckling husband Zeb.

Esmerelda laid down her jars. She had the same thick black hair as her mother, minus the white stripe. "Hello, Travis," she cooed.

"Hello, Esmerelda," Travis echoed.

"Are you alone, or did you bring your charming brothers?"

"I'm alone."

She looked crushed. "What are Mitchell and Donovan up to these days?"

"Well, Mitchell's spending a few months at the Officer's Academy in Toronto—"

"Your younger brother's a commissioned officer!" Esmerelda clapped her hands.

"And your older brother?" asked her mother.

"Donovan's been on the road…for a few years." It

was a sore point Travis didn't care to talk about. After his huge clash with their father, Donovan had left town. No one knew his whereabouts.

"Come in, come in," said Miss Penelope, shooing them up the stairs to the second floor of the sprawling inn.

"We'll take this opportunity, Miss Penelope, to have our riding clothes washed." Travis took the room nearest the hallway stairs, at the point of trouble if any should occur. He placed Jessica in the room next to his, and the butler in the far one. In the ten minutes it took for the men to settle their bags and come out with their soiled laundry, Jessica had also changed into fresh clothing. She stepped into the hall dressed in a peach-colored blouse and brown skirt, swinging a brown shawl around her shoulders and drawstring purse from her wrist. She'd brushed the braids out of her glossy hair.

"What is it?" Her hand flew up to her cheek. "Do I have dirt on my face?"

"No. No." *The peach color brings out the peachy tones of your skin.* Travis swore under his breath. He was starting to sound like Merriweather when the old man described his pretty birds.

After they freshened up, Travis insisted they board their horses at the livery stables. "Are Claude and Bill McGraw still working at the stables?" he asked the innkeeper.

"Yup," said Zeb. "Good men, those two."

"We'll take our horses there for the night. But first, I've brought you a little present, Miss Penelope."

Jessica coughed and shot him a deep scowl. Travis remembered he hadn't allowed Jessica to take any gifts on the trip. He'd made her leave behind a child's nightgown. This was different, though. Gifts to the innkeeper assured their safety. He gave Jessica a conspiratorial wink, but it didn't seem to appease her.

The heavy woman removed the mason jar from the velvet pouch. She smiled, revealing one gray tooth. "You remembered."

"What is it?" asked Jessica. "A jar of marmalade?"

"To some, it might appear that way. But this is amazin' face lotion the superintendent's wife makes from orange peel and brown sugar and a bunch of other stuff. It does wonders for my and Esmerelda's complexion. Considerably better than that expensive lotion we bought from Dr. Finch."

Travis and Jessica eyed each other. "When was Dr. Finch through here?" she asked.

"Let's see now. Two months ago, I believe. Could have been three. Or was that last year?"

Travis shrugged at Jessica's glare. The innkeeper and his entire family had always been lousy with dates and times.

"It was during a storm. Snow or rain, I can't recall. But I served him fish, I remember. With a dash of oregano and a pinch of dill."

The two groups parted at the side door. Travis led Jessica and Merriweather and their six horses around the back alley to the stables.

"Claude McGraw!" Travis bellowed upon entering the double doors.

Claude popped up from the corner stall, a headful of orange hair and well-toned muscles. "Well, sound the trumpets and raise my shorts as flags—" He stopped himself from his usual bout of swearing when he caught sight of Jessica. "Howdy, Travis. Did you bring your crazy brothers?"

"Not this time."

Claude slapped his thigh. "That's too bad. Bill will be disappointed. Honest to God, I've never seen a faster threesome of brothers, climbing up these columns and swinging from the rafters with six pints of ale—"

"Claude," Travis interrupted.

"But you won the bet, fair and square. You were always the most serious of the three, trying to outdo and outrace everyone. It's a wonder to me how you managed to hang on by one arm with that young woman strapped to your—"

"Claude! This is business!"

"Well, why didn't you say so? Let me get my brother."

They turned serious. When his burly brother joined them, Travis introduced them to Jessica and Merriweather.

"I heard you got shot a while back," said Bill.

"Minor leg wound," declared Travis.

Jessica shot forward, concerned. "Where?"

"Hunting accident in my thigh."

"Does it bother you?"

"Only when I get tired."

"Don't worry about him, ma'am," said Claude. "He's as strong as an ox."

Travis disregarded her pinched expression and explained their problems of being followed. Jessica stood beside him, nervously tapping her foot, while Merriweather went around with Bill to help settle the horses in their new stalls.

"I can see why someone might want to get their hands on your horses." Bill whistled. "The broodmares are beauties."

"The last one, there, is in foal."

"We'll take good care of 'em. Now, you say you want us to follow you to Devil's Gorge. To stay between your camp and theirs. Do you want us to take any of your horses?"

"No, I'll take care of them. I just want you to cover us as we ride."

"Not a problem, not a problem."

"You'll be well-paid."

"I imagine so," said Claude, "what with your new position as sergeant major." He squinted at Jessica, who stepped closer to a bale of straw. "You sure there's only two of them, Travis?"

"I only saw two. But they're well-armed."

"You saw them?" Jessica crossed her arms, her slender fingers cupping an elbow, oval face tilted toward him.

Travis nodded, standing tall and straight in blue shirt and black suede vest.

She swayed against the straw bale. When her face darkened, he wondered why she was getting mad again. "When?" she asked curtly. "When did you see them?"

"I doubled back today while you were frying apples. I stopped about three hundred yards from their camp. There's two of them. One's skinny, the other one's muscular. Both in their thirties. I don't know them."

Her mouth compressed. "I thought you were fishing with Mr. Merriweather."

"Nope. Merriweather did all the fishing."

"You left us out in the open where we could be attacked while you doubled back to get a look at them?"

He leaned over the stall boards, reminding himself to be patient with her. Sometimes she reacted illogically. "I knew you'd be safe." He glanced at Merriweather, who was catching up with their conversation. The older man nodded in agreement as he led Independence into an empty stall. "You see, your good butler understands."

"You couldn't have known who'd be safe!" She patted the broodmare, her quick hands conveying her irritation. "What if you'd been hurt? We wouldn't have had a clue what happened to you. Why didn't you tell us?"

"Merriweather knew."

"Why didn't you tell *me?*"

"You don't need to be bothered with these details," he scoffed. Looking toward the other men, he stepped to his mount and removed its saddle. "You're a woman and it would only worry you. It's the men who do the protecting."

At the sight of battle in her brown eyes, he realized the other men were staring from behind the horses, amused.

"We can continue our discussion outside on the way to the mercantile." Travis tipped his hat to the two brothers and grabbed her by the wrist. She fought but he held firm and pulled her toward the doors. "Claude, I'll pay you extra if your men will guard my horses tonight. We'll meet you here in the morning at five."

Travis led them down the darkened alleyway behind the storefronts. When he finally released her wrist, she stepped back, rubbing the joint and glaring at him.

"I can't go on," Merriweather interrupted as he collapsed on a stoop. He was still fully clothed in blue denim—his second set of Western gear since the first was being washed by Miss Penelope. Exhaustion fluttered through his normally peppy voice.

"Don't worry about your feet," said Travis with some concern. "They'll feel better after they slip into a new pair of boots." In a friendly turn, Travis clapped the man on his back. "I'll buy you a bigger size and something with a square toe, not pointed."

The butler stretched his legs and groaned. "Don't waste your money. The problem's not my boots."

"Then what is it?"

"It's my backside."

Jessica squatted to his side. She patted the old man's arm with a tenderness Travis wished she'd shower on him. "A sore spine from riding in the saddle? My back is sore, too."

"Try lower," came the weary reply. "Try hemorrhoids."

Travis clenched his teeth and sucked in a breath, sympathizing with the man's discomfort.

"Oh, my dear Mr. Merriweather." Jessica's shawl dropped from around her shoulders. Rocking back on her legs, she was at a loss for words.

"It's all right when I'm standing." The butler raised his boot to dig his square heel in the dirt. "It's only when I ride that it hurts. I can't imagine," he added with a humorous lilt, "Cherokee Joe having this problem."

"Yes, well, hmm," said Jessica.

Travis looked at the butler and the old man began to chuckle. It was sort of funny. Travis felt a rising rumble of humor. Their deep laughter echoed through the winding dirt path and off the pine buildings. Travis hadn't realized how tense he'd been for days. Weeks and months.

And to add to his warm laughter, he realized he'd finally be rid of these two. If her chaperon couldn't go on, then neither could she!

Jessica wasn't laughing. He could see she was thinking.

An endless feeling of freedom soared through Travis. Sometimes, when the stars aligned in his favor, the world was a wonderful place. "You made an honest attempt on this trip. Both of you, really. You should be proud of your efforts. As much as I complained...I haven't laughed this hard for quite a while. You made that possible and I thank you."

He tipped his hat and spread his arms wide, gesturing in the alley. "Take your time getting back. Rest at the inn for two or three days, and I'll hire the men to escort you back to Calgary. Drop your horses at the fort when you reach it." He bounced toward the mercantile, big boots scraping the dirt, spurs tapping loudly to his laughter. "I've still got supplies to buy, so you two take care, now, y'hear."

"Don't you dare walk away." Jessica's cold voice chilled the hairs on the back of his neck.

Leery, afraid of impending doom that might shatter his newfound glory, Travis swung around to face her. He shrank at the determination he saw blazing in her dark eyes.

"If you've finished with your aggravating little speech, chew this for a spell. With or without Mr. Merriweather, I'm still going with you."

It was chaos in the alleyway of Strongness. For five grueling minutes, Jessica listened as both men shouted at her nonstop. Mr. Merriweather sat perched on his stoop, bent halfway over with large hands propped on thick legs, bellowing streams of words, while Travis pointed his fingers and flailed his long arms for emphasis.

She could barely understand Travis for the speed of his words. He snarled, "And if you think I'm going to waste any more of my precious time—"

Mr. Merriweather belted out, "Your father will have my hide—"

"—don't know a thing about riding. It's like I have to hold your hand every step of the blasted way—"

"—thought I'd seen it all in Plymouth but the women here think they have every right—"

"You two are giving me an earache." She raised her

arms in truce. When the men stopped yelling, she rubbed her hands together in the chilled air. "Why don't you men argue your terrific points to each other while I go into the mercantile to start on the supplies?"

She scooted away, smiling.

Mr. Merriweather shouted, "Come back here, young lady!"

Jessica froze on the pathway.

She hated when he yelled at her. The last time he'd done it was ten years ago when she'd taken three of the honeycombs he'd intended to use for baking apple pies and dispersed them among her school friends.

"Your father's ordered me to be your chaperon. I intend to fulfill my duty, so you'll need to return with me. Thank you very much."

Her stomach clenched with apprehension as she turned around. She really didn't want to argue with her dear old friend. "I'll tell my father it was entirely my decision and that you did everything you could to fulfill your duties. It's my responsibility to see my own way, and I won't...take direction from anyone else on this. I'm fully grown, Mr. Merriweather, and not the little girl you used to supervise. Surely you know I have a head on my shoulders and won't do anything to compromise that."

She peered at Travis's disapproving stare. "You know this man's an officer," she added weakly.

Although it hadn't stopped the snake from stealing a kiss earlier today. Travis must have been thinking the same thing because he averted his face and kicked at the dirt.

The butler rose. "But people will think—"

"I don't care. The trip's too important for me to turn back."

"It's only an interview. Dr. Finch will likely travel

back to Calgary within the year. This isn't urgent business. It can wait until then."

Mr. Merriweather obviously didn't know the full story. "I—I don't want to wait. What I do to earn my living is vital." And the need to find her child was beyond question.

"What about your reputation? Isn't that vital?"

Jessica cowered beneath the man's honesty. He hadn't known about her pregnancy, and would be shocked to learn of it now.

"I've seen that look in your eye before." The old gent sighed. Mr. Merriweather was such a good friend. She was sorry to leave him behind.

"It means stay out of your way," the butler added. He trudged closer. "I can't win on this, can I?"

She shook her head.

Mr. Merriweather kissed her cheek. "We'll talk about it more in the morning. I'll try and rest and maybe... maybe if I take an extra dose of that tonic.... Well, I'll see you back at the hotel."

"Thank you," she whispered, which left her standing alone with Travis. His face was a brooding mask again, and she was learning she needed to back away when he looked at her like that. "We have a deal," she insisted calmly, slowly backing out of the alleyway in the opposite direction the butler was going. "You agreed to take me to Devil's Gorge, and I'm holding you to it."

Travis lunged after her, brushing his rough shoulder against her smooth one. "My orders were to escort you *and* Merriweather to Devil's Gorge. Half the deal has just walked away."

She felt her skin flush at the nearness of him. "But the other half is standing right here. You know as well as I, the commander's meaning was that *I* get to Devil's Gorge."

"The trail up until this point has been easy, but you can barely keep up. What lies ahead is brutal. You can't take it."

"I can take anything you throw at me and more. So, it's off to the mercantile we go." She peered through the dark alley. "Which store is it? I can't tell from the back."

She walked away but he grabbed for her. He missed her but caught her shawl, which ripped from her shoulders. She gasped, scooped to the dirt to retrieve it, then struggled to run.

This time when he lunged, he anchored two firm hands on her waist and spun her one hundred and eighty degrees around to face him. His strength was so mighty he lifted her legs off the ground and planted her a foot closer.

"Why aren't you worried about your reputation? Doesn't it mean anything to you?"

His hold was rigid and encompassing. The night's chill on her skin contrasted with the heat emanating from his hot hands on her waist. If he squeezed, he could crush her ribs.

"Everyone's worried about my pristine honor." If they only knew. She struggled unsuccessfully. "Why don't you admit you don't give a hen's feather about my reputation? You want to be rid of me for your own convenience!"

She hadn't meant to shout. It only aggravated the bull more. "No one talks to me like this," he said.

"Remove your hands!" She twisted but he laughed with a coldness that sent a tremble up her back. "What are you going to do? Hold on until you squeeze obedience from me?"

His black hair gleamed in the light of the distant street lamp. "You're going to be in deep trouble if you continue to insist you're going with me. Take it back or I'll—"

"You'll what?"

"I'll show you what I can do to your reputation!"

"You wouldn't dare. I'll kill you. I'm not worried!"

He fended off a slap. *"Dammit, maybe you should be."*

He yanked her, slammed her body against his and lowered his head. His kiss was rough and urgent. Too shocked to move, she waited, listened in the darkness for an opportunity, hoped he'd unhand her so that she might flee.

His right hand slipped down and traced the small of her back, making her well aware that they were sandwiched together. Now, she told herself. Try now.

But then just as quickly, he had her from behind, cinched his arm through hers until they were tighter pressed. His hand came up for the buttons at her throat. She struggled to catch his thieving fingers. Her gasp did nothing to stop his kiss from developing further, becoming firmer, more possessive.

Who did he think he was!

He was mad, and she was madder to allow this. To wonder where it might lead if she slackened her grip and responded to his wild kiss.

How could she deny her attraction? At times he could be so caring and protective, so sympathetic while he struggled to feed and water his mares.

That's when Travis moaned, loosened his hold, trailed his fingers lightly over the tip of her breast and that's when her wave of anger turned. His moan seemed to hold the weight of the world, as if he was struggling to forget about Caroline, to forget about the mare, to clamp his wounded heart and run as far from his wounds as possible.

Her nipple tightened beneath the cloth where he stroked her. She connected with his pain, understood his anger at the loss of his wife. When his lips surged over hers, he pressed her mouth open with his tongue, and she was shocked to find herself responding.

His hardened body molded against her. Her hands slid up his sleeves, over tight forearms and firm biceps. She rose on tiptoe to allow her arms to go farther, past wide shoulders to his throat. She twirled the soft, damp hair at the back of his neck with her fingertips, feeling his shivering response beneath her touch.

She felt warm, even as she trembled. An urgency rushed out to greet him, to kiss him back tenfold.

Then he snatched her by her arms and tore her body off his. "You see?" His voice was deep and rusty. "You see what I can do?"

He dumped her to her feet on the hard, unforgiving ground.

Chapter Eight

Catching her breath, Jessica wondered what had compelled her to linger those few lustful seconds in Travis's foreboding arms. Wrenching himself free, he stalked ahead of her in the alleyway while she took the time to calm her pounding heart.

She pressed a hand to her hot face and assured herself what she felt was anger and pity toward Travis, for anything more would be disgraceful.

Gulping, she walked into the mercantile, slid her drawstring purse onto the counter, tugged her fingers through her knotted hair and nodded hello to the store owner. A stooped man with thin spectacles, he stood behind the till grinding coffee beans. She hoped he hadn't been peering out his back door minutes ago, witnessing that offensive kiss. Victor's kisses had never started out as insults hurled in the dark, nor as wrestling matches.

"Howdy, Mr. Brown." Travis entered behind her, every hair and fiber in its place as if he'd just come from a meeting with the pastor. She wanted to kick him.

In the bright lantern lights, three other customers

walked up and down the aisles. The scent of newly ground coffee wafted through the warm corners. The storeowner gazed up at Travis and smiled in recognition. Travis appeared to be well-liked wherever he went and for some reason that ruffled her.

Did everyone in the blasted town know him and his brothers?

"Before you ask," she squawked at the store owner, unable to control her temper, "the answer is no. Travis didn't bring his rowdy, handsome, charming, crazy brothers!"

The owner scratched his chin. "Sir, you've got brothers?"

"Two. And a sister." Travis adjusted his vest. When he looked at her, his jaw tightened.

He could complain all he wanted, she thought. Despite his cruel kiss, she would still be going with him in the morning and there was nothing he could do to stop her.

"Do tell," said Mr. Brown.

"Well, my younger brother—"

"We're here to buy provisions." Jessica slapped the counter, hoping to dispel the stories before they began again.

"Yes, ma'am, I can see that," said the store owner, speaking slowly, as if he were addressing a youngster. "Plain as day, what with Corporal Reid carryin' that bag of beans to the counter and reachin' for his billfold."

The two men smiled at their silly joke.

Travis strode away to the glass counter that contained smoked meats. "We'll add a roll of smoked turkey. And actually, it's Sergeant Major now."

"Land sakes." The owner adjusted his spectacles. "Whaddya know. Do tell."

"Well, the last promotion came as a surprise, but the first—"

"I'll take this sack of cornmeal," she interrupted, huffing as she hoisted it to the counter. She'd heard enough of Travis's stories.

"You like that stuff?" Travis asked.

She nodded, slightly calmed by his question. She believed if she loaded up on supplies and if he allowed her to buy them, it was an indication she *was* going with him tomorrow.

Travis sighed, and in that one long exhalation, she sensed an acceptance of the inevitable. He was stuck with her.

With a fresh bounce to her step, she pulled her arms behind her back, dangling the beaded purse from her fingertips. It swung against her backside while she scrutinized shelves.

The store overflowed with cooking utensils, cleaning supplies, rope and nails and pulleys for the outdoors, meat and canned foods, even pharmaceuticals. It was a huge place, she supposed, because the village was an in-and-out traveling point for the mountains. The town sat like a sprocket on the map with several trails leading into the Rockies—some for coal miners, some for the cattle trade, some for tourists and mountaineers, others for access to British Columbia.

She stopped dead-cold when she reached the counter of medical aids, unable to believe her eyes.

She recognized Dr. Finch's trademark—a small crown imprinted with black ink onto his products.

"What is it?" Travis stepped beside her.

"Dr. Finch has been here."

The store owner joined them. "I reckon everyone in this part of the country knows Dr. Finch. I'm his official representative for the nearest fifty miles. Did you need something here, ma'am?"

"No, I..." She picked up a baby's teething ring, made of rubber. It had a colorful wooden rattle on its other end and as she tilted it, the beads inside clacked softly. Her heart ached beneath her breast. She'd never bought a rattle for her own newborn.

"Mr. Brown," called another customer. "Could I get a pound of these coffee beans, please?"

"Excuse me a minute, folks." The owner hollered as he left, "Do you want me to grind them?"

"This is the man you're accusing." Travis cupped a sturdy hand over the rattle and tenderly stroked the painted streaks of midnight blue, turning it over beneath the warm light. "He sells a thing of beauty."

Entranced by the gentle way he held it, Jessica tried to bury the sorrow springing from her throat. "Looks can be deceiving."

Each assessed the other.

"How about some of these other devices? They look useful. There's a hearing horn that my father could use. He's going deaf in one ear."

She rang her hand along the glass, tapping above the smooth wooden horn that was similar in size to a trumpet. "I can't argue with this device. It's helpful. I'm not so sure about the others. For instance, these wooden boxes stacked beside your arm."

Travis lifted one of the painted white boxes, rotating it and stopping to study the wires along the back. "I've never seen one."

"They're shock boxes. They operate on a battery. When you're feeling ill, you hold it over the area that's weak, press a button and it gives you a small jolt. It's supposed to cure you of almost anything, but the people I spoke with in Montreal say they're useless."

Bending lower, his holsters sagging against his

thighs, Travis pointed to the lower shelf. "There are tonics here that do a lot of good. Take for instance the herbal lotion there in that green glass. It looks similar to what Merriweather was drinking."

"Herbs mixed with opiates and alcohol. I don't know if they do much more than relax the body."

Travis studied more items. "There's something for the first criminal I ever arrested," he said with a laugh. "He could use that nose straightener."

The product was made of rubber and similar to a clothes pin.

Tapping her fingers along the glass, Jessica dragged her shawl by the other arm. "Quackery. The practice of unproven or ineffective medicine in order to make money or to maintain a position of power. Don't we have laws against that?"

He studied her more seriously this time, weighing her question carefully. "You can't prove something's ineffective until it's been used for years. And then you have to prove that the doctor selling it to you had harmful intentions."

"So we're back to where we started."

"If no one gets hurt by these products, and Dr. Finch is honestly trying to help, what's the harm?"

"What's the harm? Do you know how often I've heard that? Some people do get hurt."

The store owner slid behind the counter. "Do you need some Queen's Herb, Travis?"

"Queen's Herb?"

"Tobacco," Jessica answered. "It's the cure-all for whatever ails you. Gastric problems, nervous problems, throat discomfort. Have a stomachache? Smoke a pipe. Cough stopping you from milking the cows? Try chewing tobacco."

But some folks did swear by its potency, and she couldn't discount its power. In her observations, tobacco *did* calm nerves. She wondered if half these products worked as placebos in folks' minds rather than true medicines for their bodies. People believed what they wanted to believe.

Travis flagged his hand at the store owner. "No need for Queen's Herb, I feel fine. If you could tally up what we owe, we'll be on our way."

With packages in hand, Jessica headed for the door. Travis pushed it open for her with a long extended arm. The sign on the door made her stop. Travis let the door close as she read.

"Good Lord," she whispered. *"Foster home in Riverpoint Junction now accepting children for adoption. Funded by Canada's new Children's Aid Society."* She ripped it off the storefront. "Travis, where is this?"

"Riverpoint Junction is thirty miles south of Devil's Gorge."

Thoughts whirled inside of her—of hope, of possibility. "I'd like to go."

"Thanks for telling me," he said, trying to clamp the conversation. "I'm sure you'll make it there someday." He opened the door again.

She ignored his request to leave. "Is there a foster home in Devil's Gorge?"

"No."

"How long ago were you there?"

"Two years."

His answer wasn't good enough to convince her. There had to be more. "Mr. Brown," she said, racing to the back of the store. "Is there a foster home in Devil's Gorge?"

"No, ma'am, not that I know of."

Her breathing began to race. "How long ago were you there?"

"Just last month."

"This foster home, here in this town." She pointed to the paper, her pulse beating in her throat. "How long has it been open?"

"I reckon a little while."

"Who tacked the flyer to your door?"

"I did."

"Who gave it to you?"

The old man peered around her shawl to Travis, as if wondering why all the questions. "The couple who run the foster home gave it to me when they were passin' through two months ago, on the way to her sister's wedding."

"What do they have to do with Dr. Finch?"

He shrugged. "Nothing that I know of."

"But there's an imprint in the paper, a little crown in the bottom corner printed in black ink like on the rest of Dr. Finch's products."

"I don't know anything about that."

"May I keep this paper?"

"Sure. I've got another few behind the counter."

A sudden wave of fear burned in her cheeks. "Are they—are they nice people? Good people?"

"Why, heavens, yes. Love kids, those two. With their own kids, I reckon they've got near a dozen in their home."

She nodded and slowly headed out the door with Travis for the second time.

"What was that all about?" he grumbled. They strode briskly along the boardwalk.

How much should she tell him? "This Children's Aid Society is a new organization formed by the government. To help children. I've heard of them but never seen a foster home. I'd—I'd like to write an article about them for the journal. Please, could we go?"

He stopped under a street lamp, his face hidden in shadow beneath the brim of his Stetson, his shoulders a yard wide. She prayed for his trusting nature to surface.

"It's half a day's ride off our trail, and half a day's ride back. My personal leave doesn't extend that long. I'm only going to say this once, Jessica, and I want you to listen carefully. *No.*"

"Dr. Finch, how can we ever repay you?"

Standing above the examination table in his office in Devil's Gorge, Abraham Finch swelled with pride. Gripping medical scissors and a surgical needle, he raised his shoulder and rolled it along his large jaw, collecting the perspiration he felt dripping from his white-haired temple. "There's no need, Mr. Beckham. Your wife's recovery is payment enough."

Abraham tucked a sheet beneath the old woman's pale face as she awoke from her drug-induced sleep.

Surgery hadn't been an option he'd planned, but the man had insisted Abraham relieve his wife's pain. She'd broken her arm three months earlier and the splint Abraham applied hadn't helped. Loose bone fragments inside were grating on muscles and nerves, causing swelling and acute pain. Abraham had told Beckham what he told all his patients—that he was a general practitioner, not a full surgeon—*yet*—and he wasn't able to perform the necessary operation to scrape out the fragments. However, Beckham persisted and was willing to pay any price.

Leaving for Vancouver within days, Abraham had been unable to resist the extra money and compliment. Damn right he had the talent to be a surgeon. Damn right it was about time he tried.

"There now, you see," said Abraham, drawing a soothing hand over her bare arm. He gazed at the stitching. He'd had only two nights of practice with a needle and flap of leather, but he'd done a decent job. Yes sir, mighty clean repair. The trick had been to suture the internal layers one at a time, all the way up from the bone.

"When should I bring her back to remove the stitches?"

"Right. Ah, let me think."

"When I had my leg stitched up from that train accident back East, they took them out a week later."

"Yes, of course. Bring her back one week from tomorrow." Abraham wouldn't be here, but his medical assistant would take good care of the couple. How hard could it be to yank out a line of thread? Abraham would read his journals tonight to study the technique of suture removal and show his assistant what was required. Young Hopkins never refused an order, washed his hands before and after every duty and hadn't a clue his employer had never graduated from medical college.

Beckham stared through the open door to the medical diploma hanging on the office wall. "I read that as we came in. Glasgow University. My uncle's from Glasgow. Don't suppose you know him? Edwin Beckham?"

"No sir. But then, Glasgow is large."

Washing his hands, Abraham wondered how difficult other surgeries might be. There was the neighbor who wanted her hip straightened, the clerk at the bank who needed his jaw repaired and the occasional broken limb Abraham was certain he could mend if given the chance.

If they saw him now, the professors in Glasgow would be sorry they'd failed him from those miserable courses. What did examinations prove? That one could memorize paragraphs and body parts? Anything he needed to know, he could refer to a book.

The professors had been condescending and had never appreciated how difficult it'd been to rise from his background. His folks had been street performers, Gypsies who didn't mind the occasional lift of a bystander's wallet. Hadn't those goddamn professors realized how difficult it'd been for Abraham to fit in to society?

His parents had always told him he'd be naturally gifted in medicine. He was quick to think of solutions, skilled with his hands and, quite honestly, liked helping folks with their problems. Nothing brought him greater satisfaction than hearing praise for his abilities to cut disease from flesh and eradicate pain. Being paid dearly sweetened his success.

Here, people gave him the respect he'd earned. A forged piece of paper held a lot of weight. Folks felt more comfortable seeing it on his wall, with these troublesome days of licensing.

As Abraham helped the groggy woman sit up, a younger man, well-dressed and groomed, appeared at the door. "There's a letter here for you, sir, from those folks at the foster home. I took the liberty of opening it."

"What do they need, Hopkins?"

"They say four of their children are going to be adopted within the week."

"That's wonderful! Which four?"

"The youngest."

A sense of relief washed over Abraham. His dilemma of the last seventeen months would soon be over. He'd attempted something that simply hadn't worked, but…if the mayor's daughter had known what he'd done for her, she would thank him. And if not her, then certainly the prestigious mayor himself.

Chapter Nine

Jessica felt panic rise within her chest. Time was running out.

Sitting on her horse the next morning engulfed in a forest, she rode thirty minutes out of Strongness accompanied by Travis and the two McGraw brothers. Last night, Travis had agreed she could ride with them, but only to Devil's Gorge. She figured she had to tell him about her missing child before they reached the fork leading to Riverpoint Junction tomorrow evening. The truth was the only way she might convince him to ride to the foster home. The home had to contain some clues. She feared for the children. All of them.

Jessica filled her lungs with oxygen-rich air laden with the earthy scents of moss, green leaves and river silt. More than three months after she'd given birth and was told her child had died, she'd gone to the lecture hall to listen to Dr. King. Later, when she'd pieced together that he was the same Dr. Finch who'd delivered her child, she'd felt a rising elation that maybe somehow, her baby boy was living.

Two vast emotions battled inside of her—an outcry

of horror that a doctor she and other women trusted had done this to her and her child, and exhilarating hope that Dr. Finch was a con man. It meant her baby might be breathing.

May heaven strike her down, she prayed he *was* a liar.

She jostled in her saddle. She rode behind Travis but ahead of the brothers, who would part ways and fall behind at midmorning. Travis had said there was no sense hiding that they had hired guards.

They'd left Mr. Merriweather behind and the horse he'd been riding. Travis had taken Independence and tied it to his other prize mare, so he was now leading two to her one. Riding single file on the trail, the distance and the wind kept them from speaking.

This morning when she'd knocked on the butler's door to say goodbye, Mr. Merriweather could do little more than groan. His double dose of tonic had hammered him to his bed, but he'd managed to assure her he'd be fine on his own, and for her to remember her manners and the proper code of behavior she'd learned in charm school.

Charm school. What she'd learned there was that she was on her own in making life's decisions. And that people, self-absorbed young women like herself, can and do change.

Beside the trail gushing, on their left the Glacier River was getting narrower, deeper and faster. The changes in the river seemed to sum up her relationship with Travis. In their discussions, she was balancing on a *narrower* ribbon of disclosure, wondering how much to tell him and how much to hold back. In spite of her sense of impropriety, they shared *deeper* conversations and *deeper* physical arousal. And just like the river, Travis was pushing them *faster.*

She understood more about the river than she did about the man. The water originated in the mountains at a glacial point, its dangerous curves and depths plotted on the map she'd borrowed from Travis last night. While the river raged toward the flatter plains, its path grew wider and slower, but Travis's rage might flare unexpectedly at any moment.

"You'll stop here to rest!" He shouted above the wind three hours later as the sun rose higher over the mountains. He ordered the men, "Stay with Jessica while I turn back!"

She floundered, sliding off her saddle. "Where are you going?" More alarmed to be separated from Travis than she cared to admit, Jessica watched him untie his prize mares from his mount to take the gelding solo.

He galloped past her on the trail, back from where they'd come. "To check up on our friends, the ones who are following us. Talk to them if they're there!"

"Are you crazy?"

"I'll be back in three hours!"

"You don't know what those two men might do to you! They might slash your throat and take your horse right there!"

But he was already flying a hundred yards past her, his black Stetson slicing the wind, unbuttoned suede vest exposing the strength in his torso, imposing hands slapping the horse's rear. "They don't want this horse! I'll see you in three hours!"

Galloping through an acre of trees, Travis heard the horses before he saw the riders. He chomped down on his jaw but he was breathless with rage. No thieves were going to steal his broodmares.

There wasn't much he'd salvaged from the last year.

He'd given the money from the sale of his ranch to Caroline's folks. They had one son but she'd been their only daughter. They'd been devastated by her death. At Travis's insistence, they accepted his offer, sold their small cabin and moved to the southern border to be closer to their remaining son and his family.

Money from the sale of Travis's stallions went to caring for the mares. He didn't need much cash living in the officer's barracks where food and lodging were provided.

But dammit, he needed some.

He turned his head at the sounds resonating through the pine trees. A crisscross of light slanted through the tall trunks. A horse neighed. A blur of dark clothing in the distance riveted his gaze.

Travis slid his hands over his guns. Primed and ready.

He barreled his horse straight toward them.

One of the riders pulled back on his rearing horse. "Whoa, mister, where you goin'?"

Travis coaxed his gelding to a stop, feeling its muscles tighten beneath his calves. He glanced from the scrawny blonde to the bigger man speaking, who had long, black hair tied in a tail behind his back.

"Howdy." Travis nodded, conscious of the weight of the guns on his hips, *liking* the weight of his guns. "Mighty fine day for a ride. Where are you two headed?"

By the flash in their eyes and at each other, the men seemed to instantly recognize who he was. His presence caught the slimmer man off guard because his cheeks grew red and he had problems controlling his horse.

The leader glared back, gloved hands steady on his reins, his unshaven face rippling with sweat. "Up a ways."

They appeared to be drifters and their horses were average, Travis noted. Their coats could use a good grooming for they had grass in their manes and tails. Neither of the men went for the guns strapped to their sides, but the scrawny one let his hands drift downward.

"Where you headed?" the leader asked in turn.

"Devil's Gorge. Is that your destination? I noticed you behind us for two straight days."

Both men were taken aback at his blunt appraisal. Travis didn't try to hurry their reply, nor did he plan on speaking again until they did.

It took several seconds.

"Yeah, Devil's Gorge."

"My name's Travis Reid. Sergeant Major with the police. Are you having any trouble?"

The leader calmly slid his hands to the saddle horn. "No, sir, no trouble."

"I thought you might like to join me and my company."

They balked. "What?"

"We're headed in the same direction. It's a lonely trail. Sometimes discouraged miners looking for an easy target pass back and forth through here. I thought you might like police protection."

"We don't need none."

"I didn't catch your names." He glared with dead precision at the weaker of the two. "Mister?"

The slimmer man looked to his partner. "Jeb…Jeb Lake."

Travis believed him. The man hadn't had a chance to coordinate any lies with his partner, and he didn't seem smart enough to make the decision himself.

"Pleased to meet you." He shot an equally intimidating glance at the leader.

This one wasn't as easy to crack. He blinked and answered after a beat. "Andrew Garwood."

Travis leaned into the warm wind. "Well, Jeb and Andrew, what's your business in Devil's Gorge?"

"Why so many questions?" asked the leader.

"Just being friendly."

"We're thinking of doing some mining. Panning for gold, maybe."

"There's no gold rush in Devil's Gorge."

"Not yet," said the leader with a forced grin.

The other one laughed nervously.

"I suppose you'll be buying your mining equipment when you get there." Travis noticed they had none strapped to their horses.

"That's right."

The weaker man shifted in his saddle and spoke quickly. "There's no law, is there, Officer, about traveling alone on this trail?"

Travis didn't move but he noticed from the corner of his eye that the leader scowled at his partner, indicating he soften his tone.

"No, there's no law. I was merely putting forth an invitation. You sure you're going to pass?"

"We're sure," said the leader.

"Well, holler or shoot if you need help. Me and my men are well-armed for protection." With a click of his tongue, Travis tore off through the trees as quick as he'd come.

Galloping in a steady rhythm through the winding forest and along the riverbed, Travis spotted the McGraw brothers from behind, each with a broodmare tied to their mounts. Travis rose to his feet in the stirrups. The muscles in his thighs pulled while he strained to catch sight of Jessica.

She was there. He sighed in relief, and for the first

time in hours, noticed the tension in his body that had resulted from his taxing ride. Stopping to rest and water his horse every hour, he hadn't had time for lunch and his water canteen needed refilling.

Jessica turned at the sound of his horse. "Where have you been? The last time I checked it was nearly four hours!"

The brothers reined in their horses.

Travis slid off his mount. He panted to catch his breath, but a laugh escaped him. He walked toward the river, eager to slap water on his heated forehead. The others followed.

"What took you so long?" Jessica asked. "Answer me."

His breathing sounded loud, even above the rush of water. "I think you missed me."

Her brown eyes blazed. Turning abruptly to the water's edge, she propped her hands on the belt of her narrow waist. Her legs, encased in newly washed pants, were outlined in the sunshine. Her gaze followed a line of geese skimming the blue water. She repeated, "What took you so long?"

"They were farther back than I thought."

Bill turned his head. "Did you talk to 'em?"

"Yeah. I let them know we're watching." Travis recounted his conversation.

"You rode right into their path?" asked Jessica.

"Nothing like a stampeding bull to get someone's attention, wouldn't you say?"

Jessica picked up a flat stone, aimed and released. It skipped five times across the water. How'd she do that? "You could have been shot."

"They're not interested in me. If they want anything, they want the broodmares."

The brothers took it in stride. "Should we fall behind now?"

"Yeah," Travis replied. "They're about two hours back. Try to stay half an hour behind us. If anything goes wrong, fire a shot. I'll hear it."

They took a thirty-minute break to rest his horse. Travis ate a stick of jerky then set off with Jessica and all three broodmares. The McGraw brothers were to wait another thirty minutes, then plow ahead.

Travis and Jessica were finally alone. He tried not to dwell on it, or to wonder why that made him nervous.

He called back to her, "It feels strange to be riding at this slower pace after galloping for hours."

"You need to slow down."

"It's not in me."

"Then try to remember the fable of the tortoise and the hare."

Slow and steady wins the race. Was that the moral? He grinned softly to himself.

The trail grew steeper as the horses climbed. Mountains closed in around them. He stared above the treetops in the foreground to the snowy peaks in the distance. Deep crevices marred their slopes. There was a ledge halfway up on one ragged mountain, with a golden eagle soaring above it. A circle of straw dangling off the ledge told him she'd nested there. He wondered how many men over the centuries had stared at that very spot, and how many eagles had been born.

He wondered what his purpose was in life, and whether he'd ever find peace again without Caroline. Then he realized with surprise, he felt tranquil at this very moment.

The solitude of the earth and sky, the steady beat of the horses' hooves, the awareness that Jessica was following, counting on his skills, on him, melted his arguments with the world.

He wondered what she was thinking and why she was so stubborn about going to Devil's Gorge.

They rode until four o'clock, then took an hour's break. Each went about their chores in a serious mood. He was surprised how quickly Jessica was catching on to what needed doing. Without asking, she took a couple of horses at a time to the river to let them drink, visually checked each one for signs of injury and discomfort, retightened sagging lines if the packs had shifted during travel, then saw to her own needs of thirst, hunger and stretching her legs from cramps.

Due to Merriweather's absence, the casual nature of their ride had vanished. In its place was something denser, more intense, each of them guarding against intrusion, against overfamiliarity with the other.

Dusk was falling when he spoke again. "We'll camp here, Jessica, in the shelter of these cedars." He'd told the McGraw brothers to ride until dusk as well, and then break for camp.

The pleasant scent reminded Travis of the cedars reaching outside his bedroom window on the ranch where he'd grown up. He'd shared the tight but comfortable room with his brothers before his folks could afford to build the bigger house. At the time, his sister hadn't been born.

Travis and Jessica unpacked the horses and led them to the river. "Travis, could you come here? Take a look at this."

"What is it?"

The sound of water crashing over rocks lulled him in the twilight. He tossed his hat to the ground and ran a hand through deep, damp hair.

On the grassy bank Jessica stood beside Independence, a contrast of femininity against muscled speed.

She'd taken a shine to the mare ever since Travis had told her the mare was pregnant. Women seemed to enjoy talk of babies and offspring, no matter what the breed—human or animal. Caroline had been the same.

Come to think of it, so had he.

He sighed in sorrow for a past he'd never regain.

"Watch this." Jessica held the reins and walked Independence in a loose circle.

He wasn't sure what he was supposed to observe. Maybe Jessica was demonstrating the progress she'd made in getting the horse to cooperate with her commands.

"Turn this way," she said gently. The mare followed her, as did Travis's inquisitive gaze.

The breeze caught Jessica's blouse and pasted it to her back. It ruffled the cloth on her elbow as she led the horse. With arms raised like that, her figure became more pronounced. It seemed, from Miss Penelope's washing, that Jessica's cotton pants had shrunk. The fabric clung to her legs like virgin leather. Her boots, on gently sloped heels, thrust her upper body forward. His gaze lingered on the stretch of her softly rounded bosom. Still wearing no corset.

Glancing upward, he noticed a freckled cheek curving in concentration, sharp brown eyebrows flexed, straight nose held with pride. She looked more youthful today; her skin glowed. He hadn't realized how pale she'd been when she'd approached him three days ago at the fort.

Jessica led the horse in the other direction in another circle. "Are you watching?"

"Uh-huh."

A red streak of fading sunlight bounced off the river and illuminated her face.

"The mare feels comfortable with your lead," he said.

"But did you notice it?"

"Notice what?"

"Her gait is off."

Alarmed, he sprang forward. "*It is?* Walk her again."

This time, his undivided attention fell to Independence.

When he saw the slight limp, he whistled through his teeth and raced to the mare. "How could I have missed this?"

"It's hard for you to watch the horse behind you. She moves in front of me, so I watch her all day."

Feeling horribly guilty, he lifted the mare's hind leg and examined one hoof, then the other. There were no breaks in the lines of the hooves, no sand cracks or inflammation. Jessica followed him to the front. When he examined a front shoe, he spotted a pebble caught beneath it. He tried to extract it with his fingers, but it was wedged in tight. The mare stirred and tried to walk.

"Steady," he coaxed. He patted her shoulder but released the leg so she wouldn't panic. She settled. "How long has her gait been off?"

"Not long, at least I don't think so. I thought I noticed something half an hour ago, then I thought it was my imagination."

"Easy," he said to the mare, lifting the foreleg again. He turned the hoof to get a better look, then snatched at the pebble. This time he retrieved it. "Good girl. It's out. Good girl." He stroked the glossy hide. "I should have noticed it. I'm sorry, I should have seen it."

"Travis," Jessica said quietly beside him. "Will she be all right?"

Inches away from Jessica's face, Travis turned to her direction. "No harm done." He kept stroking.

"She sure is calm when you touch her."

He exhaled softly. It was the first time in twelve

months he'd touched her without gloves, and he'd only just realized it. He remembered the smooth, soft feel of her. She felt like warm, beating velvet and he couldn't pull away.

Jessica slid her hand close to his on the withers. "Is this where she likes to be patted?"

"Yeah, and down here."

Jessica followed his lead. A smile touched her lips. The cut of the moon glowed over the three of them. It was twilight again, the magical time when day turned into night.

Magical, too, because he was stroking Independence. The mare didn't deserve his wrath.

"Look," whispered Jessica, placing a tender hand on his forearm. She leaned in, her body exuding heat.

He turned to the water where she was looking. A white stork was fishing in the distance, standing in the water on stilted legs, plunging its head beneath the surface.

Jessica laughed softly and he filled with contentment.

When he spotted a huge moose drinking a hundred feet farther down the river, silhouetted in the moonlight, he nudged Jessica. "Look at that."

The animal was standing in the river, looking upstream. The bull had a massive brown coat and brown antlers.

"Whoa," Jessica whispered. "He's huge."

"As big as a horse." Fifteen hundred pounds of flesh.

"Will he hurt us? Charge us?"

"He'll leave us alone."

They stood, bodies touching, mesmerized by the animals. When the stork rustled, the moose froze, looked around, spotted them, then turned and galloped up the other side of the riverbank.

"I can't believe—"

"Too bad he spooked—"

They shared a moment of whispered laughter. Their bodies brushed.

When he turned toward Jessica, he watched her face glisten in the moon's glow. A trail of blond hair fluttered across her eyes. The horse stilled beneath their touch. Travis reached out and brushed the hair off her cheek, holding his palm over her ear to steady the tendrils in the quiet breeze.

Jessica didn't move.

"I've never really taken the time to try to know you," he said softly. "You and Caroline—"

"We fought at every opportunity over petty things," Jessica admitted. "Like silly schoolgirls."

She peered down at Independence and he dropped his hand. "You took your cues from your fathers, I suppose."

"The uncompromising mayor and his strict bylaws."

"Caroline told me your father drove hers to ruin with his laws. Every time her old man started up the brewery, yours would shut it down."

"I was told her father took advantage of immigrants. He paid them next to nothing."

"They were grateful for the work, it was explained to me. Caroline's father couldn't compete with the prices of ale from the larger breweries moving in from the East. Caroline told me once the workers learned the language, they moved on to better jobs. No harm done, even as far as the Mounties saw."

"The superintendent turned a blind eye but my father couldn't. You know how he is. He goes by the book and he follows the bylaws. He always conforms to society's rules," she added with cool observation. "Anyway, the immigrants should have been paid the same as the other workers."

It had happened before Travis's time, so he hadn't thought about it much. But now he wondered if maybe the mayor had been right to protect the folks who were too scared, or unable to speak for themselves. "Caroline's family went from being one of the wealthiest to one of the poorest. Caroline...really hated you."

Jessica turned to watch the flowing water and he watched her.

"I never held you accountable for your father's actions or arguments, Jessica. But I never rose to your defense when they talked about you. Not once," he confessed with shame.

Jessica ran her arms up her sleeves. "When we were in school, I should have let her comments slide off my back, but every time she called me the mayor's spoiled daughter, I—I lashed back with an insult of my own."

His cheek pulsed. "I didn't know that. You were both young. Fourteen, fifteen. It was a period before I knew her. When I did know her, she never called you names."

"I should have been more caring. When we sat across from each other in the schoolroom, I didn't realize her family was losing all their money.... She had fresh pencils whenever she needed them, a new slate. She wore pretty dresses, just like mine. Only later did I realize how many years she wore those dresses, how many years her mother lowered the hem and added lace to the cuffs to extend the sleeves. Now Caroline's gone and I'll never be able to apologize."

An apology to Caroline. He never thought he'd hear those words from Jessica. "When you came to see me in the stables three days ago," he murmured, "I called you...I'm sorry I called you the mayor's spoiled daughter."

"At one time I was that person. *I was.*" Jessica ran her shirtsleeve over her eyes, turned and walked through the woods.

He wondered what, in life, had changed her.

Her voice shook through the floating leaves. "I'll start the campfire."

They had much to do before settling down to sleep, but Travis stood and watched her dip through the trees. He wanted to hold and comfort her, but stood rooted. She was different from his late wife. Caroline had been tough and independent, probably *because* of her financial hardships, but if he were honest, he'd admit Caroline had never seemed like she really *needed* him to thrive.

Jessica's vulnerability reached out to him in every conversation, in every quiet moment. Jessica seemed to always need protection, and he always wanted to give it to her.

Chapter Ten

Jessica awoke earlier than she had the previous three mornings. It was still dark. Her eyes flew open, then tried to adjust to the darkness. The sun would soon be coming up over the horizon but she felt sick with nervousness. At the end of today, they'd need to make their decision at the fork in the road—Riverpoint Junction or straight to Devil's Gorge.

The horses stirred. She saw a flash of movement. Lifting herself to an elbow, she searched for Travis in the bedroll by her feet but he wasn't there.

She scoured the campsite. No sign of him. Maybe he'd gone for water for their morning coffee. They hadn't spoken much last night, each attending to their duties and alone with their thoughts. She'd been apprehensive about sharing her space alone with Travis without Mr. Merriweather's watchful eye, so she'd tucked herself in early and tried not to speak too much.

Rising, she stuck her feet into her boots then adjusted her clothing, wrinkled from the night's sleep. The chilly air filtered through her blouse. She tucked it into her pants, wrapped her shawl about her shoulders, and made her way to the horses.

She patted Independence. "Where's your master?"

The horse whinnied.

She heard a neighing far off into the distance. And then another horse. The sounds weren't coming from the river, but from the other direction. Was Travis there?

Independence whinnied again, as if in response to the other horses. Jessica remembered Travis telling her that horses were social animals and called to one another. She smiled. "Do you know those creatures? Are they friends of yours?"

A stream of sunlight hit the campsite. The sky above twinkled blue and appeared cloudless. So far on their journey, they'd been blessed by clear weather. The thought of rain, soggy clothes and damp supplies made her shudder.

Jessica followed the sound of the horses, careful to walk as silently as she could in case of trouble. But Travis wouldn't leave her unattended if he thought there was danger nearby. He'd probably gone for a walk to investigate the sounds himself. She strode through the still air, listening to the lap of the wind against the pines and the squealing of morning chipmunks.

When she came to an opening in the woods, she stood breathless in amazement. The ground dropped below her into a valley as wide as she could see. The sun was rising where a meadow of green grass met with an oblong lake. The scenery rolled for miles in both directions, with a branch of the Glacier River winding through it. And there in front of her was a herd of wild horses with Travis in its midst.

She sat in the wild grass of the hillside and watched. He was attempting to capture one of the horses. She wondered how he'd do that. He carried no equipment.

The horses stilled around him, allowing him to draw close. Travis had a powerful connection with wild horses. Even his men had recognized it with his nickname.

On the stretch of meadow grass, a mustang, a mare, stood in the open straining its mouth at Travis. It flicked its ears and tossed its head at the man three feet away.

Unaware of Jessica, Travis fixed a stare on the horse and stood perfectly still, unaffected by the animal's twitching. When it flicked its tail, Travis reached out slowly and touched its mane. The horse reared and shrieked out. Its whinny instilled ice into Jessica's spine, but Travis remained steadfast. He waited a few moments to see what the mare would do, then Travis crouched low to the ground, plucking a shaft of grass and popping it into his mouth, as if he didn't care what the mare did.

Patience. He had so much patience with horses but so little with her. Although what he'd said to her last night about not holding her accountable for her father's actions meant more than she'd been able to convey.

She feared for Travis's safety, crouched in front of a jittery herd of horses, but couldn't turn away. The mare had a spirit about it that drew her eyes to its beautiful neck, the exquisitely proportioned body, the look of fire in its eyes.

The other horses grew placid. They bent their heads to graze, allowing sparrows to land on them and peck insects from their backs.

Travis took the opportunity to rise from the grass. Slowly, he closed the distance between himself and the mare. The beast allowed him to approach. Travis reached out a second time and ran his fingers along its mane. The mare shuddered and tossed its head. Jessica heard Travis's cooing voice but couldn't make out the words.

He stood like that for a long time, it seemed, talking and patting and perhaps telling it stories about where he came from.

The mare responded, tilting its head toward him. That was the opening he sought. In one gliding swoop, Travis jumped up and hoisted himself to the mare's back.

Jessica heard a gasp escape from her lips.

He was up. The horse reared but Travis clung to its mane and neck. It galloped headlong into the wind, its mane flowing over Travis's arms, its tail billowing in the sunrise.

"Roughrider," Jessica whispered. A man accustomed to breaking in wild horses. He had a gift.

He didn't ride for long. He led the horse to the sparkling lake, or maybe the horse led him. With an affectionate pat, Travis slid off and quickly backed away. With his hands in his denim pockets, he stared for a while longer, then looked up the hill.

She could tell Travis noticed her then, because he stiffened.

Caught watching, Jessica ran a hand along her cheek and straightened her posture. Uprooted from her privacy, she jumped to her feet and waited the minutes while he walked to meet her.

"I wondered where you went," she said, apologetic for the intrusion.

"I couldn't sleep. I heard the horses."

"They're magnificent."

He nodded.

"Why did you let it go?" she asked gently. "Many men would rope the mustang and sell her."

"I'm already selling the ones I have. I don't need anymore. I'm done with horses."

"But they're not done with you."

He turned and walked past her, heading to the camp. "You're talking riddles."

"Then why did you ride that mare?" She persisted, still marveling at the image.

"Because...she spoke to me."

"I believe she did. And you rode her simply for the love of being able to."

His rugged face creased with lines of unexpected tenderness, quickly replaced with the harsher lines she knew too well.

He peered down the slope at the herd of fifty horses. The wild mare looked up. When an eagle screeched above them, the mare spooked and ran. About four dozen horses thundered behind her, a rolling stampede of beautiful colors. Brown, rust, bay, roan, speckled.

"I don't love horses." Travis rubbed his jaw and murmured. "They're not people."

Jessica asked too many questions and made too many observations, thought Travis twelve hours later as they chose a campsite for the night.

He liked it best when there was space between them, when they were riding three horses apart and left to their own solitude, as they had been all day.

"How far is the fork to Riverpoint Junction?" Jessica asked as she scraped cooked ham from a tin into the frying pan.

He tossed his Stetson to the top of the bedrolls he'd just placed on the ground and sighed. He suspected he knew what question was coming next. "It's just beyond that curve." He motioned to the roaring river.

"If we get up very early, is it possible for us to swing by—"

"No." He wondered if she'd ever stop pestering him

and why it was so important. Removing the small ax he'd brought for chopping wood, he strode into the middle of the high ground and began splicing. "You can go anywhere you want when we reach Devil's Gorge. I'm not interested."

He didn't look up again until the fire was blazing. Jessica removed the ham and dumped three-quarters of it on his plate. "That valley with the horses, how far up does it go?"

"The river is another tributary from the glacier, so it goes all the way to Devil's Gorge."

"Why don't we travel along it, then? It seems like a gentler, easier ride."

They ate their food. "It would take us twice as long. Cutting through the mountains is faster."

"Is there an actual glacier at the end of this river?"

"Of course. Haven't you heard of it?"

"I thought maybe it was a rumor. It seems so unbelievable. What does a glacier look like?"

"Well, let's see. It's icy and cold."

She smiled, Travis noticed, despite his refusal to take her to Riverpoint Junction. "Tell me something I might not know."

"It's so big it looks like another mountain squeezed between the Rockies. The color takes you by surprise. When you get up close, it looks like a block of ice, but from a distance it's turquoise. Sort of a bluish-green mixed together."

"Why is that?"

"They say its color comes from the river silt mixed in with it."

"The same color as the lakes."

He nodded and set down his empty plate. She seemed to be getting friendlier, as if she might be priming him to ask again about Riverpoint Junction. He didn't have the time to take a journalist on a trip to get an interview—getting her work completed with no regard to how the timing might affect his.

"That herd of wild horses travels up and down the valley. I've seen them before, two years ago when I passed through with Mitch."

"The horses all look the same with their spots and colors. It's hard to believe you can recognize them."

"When you study them awhile, you notice their differences."

After supper, Jessica didn't quickly disappear into her bedroll as she had last night. After grooming the horses together, they stayed up and watched the fire.

"I'd like to wash up by the river," she said.

"Wait and I'll heat up a pot of water for you. A woman shouldn't have to bathe in cold water when she can bathe in warm."

Jessica raised her eyebrows.

"Something my mother used to say to my father all the time."

She smiled and he felt that silent bond of understanding weaving between them again.

Suddenly growing solemn, she sank onto a log and folded her hands beneath her legs. "Travis, there's something I need to tell you, and then you might understand why I need to go to Riverpoint Junction. I apologize for not telling you sooner, but I couldn't…not before we passed the point of no return."

"That sounds gloomy." He lifted the cauldron of water onto red coals. He adjusted the coals beneath it with a stick so the cauldron rested straight.

"You know that I spent two years in Montreal."

"Right."

She removed her hands from under her and rubbed them nervously down the front of her pants. "You know I became a medical journalist because of what I saw there."

Leaning over the fire, he let it heat his skin. The flames colored Jessica's face red. "Because of the poor women you visited at Miss Waverly's Home for Unwed Mothers. I remember."

She stood up and walked to the other side of the fire until she was standing facing him. Her hands dipped into her pockets. "Well…I didn't actually visit Miss Waverly's Home. I mean, I did…but not as a visitor. As a guest."

He tried to understand. He poked the fire. "As a guest. You were helping out…writing medical articles."

She gulped hard. *"As a guest,"* she repeated with deliberate meaning. "Victor Sterling was the father of my baby."

Travis slowly turned toward Jessica, struck silent by her admission. Most women would have turned their heads to look the other way after a confession like that, but her gaze held firm. Her nostrils flared, her jaw tightened, and the force of anger simmered beneath the surface.

What was he supposed to think? She'd shocked him so hard he groped for words. She was a mother. With Victor Sterling. God, the man who'd drowned on his return to England. Jessica was alone to deal with this.

"You had a baby in Montreal?"

"Yes, a baby boy."

"Why did you go to Montreal to give birth?"

"My father sent me there. To save embarrassment."

"Yours or his?"

She frowned at him, then laughed softly.

But a little tremor of fear caught inside his throat at the hollow sound of her laughter. "Jessica, where's your baby?"

She opened her mouth to speak, but nothing came out. She opened it again, whimpered, then shook her head.

He waited patiently, as still as the leaves in the moonlit sky.

She pressed her hands to her face. She almost didn't need to say the words because he sensed with dread what was coming. "They told me my son died."

He closed his eyes. His heart thudded. Pulling her to his chest, he wrapped his arms around her shoulders and stroked her head gently as she mustered strength to speak. All he wanted to do was protect Jessica.

"Tell me what happened," he coaxed.

She lifted her face. "Would you believe you're the only person who's asked me that?"

"But your father surely must have asked."

"When he came to retrieve me from Montreal after my delivery, Miss Waverly told him what happened. He was sympathetic at the loss of my child…his grandson…but he asked very few questions of me. When I asked for permission to stay longer in Montreal, on my own to help the other women, he agreed and was gone the next day. Later, we communicated by letter until my recent return to Calgary."

"Tell me what happened in Montreal," he repeated.

"First—" she withdrew from his embrace "—first, I have to tell you that I don't think my baby died."

"But you were told—"

"The doctor who delivered him was Dr. Finch."

Travis walked to the fire to watch the water heat for her bathing. Crossing his arms, he tried not to show his skepticism. He cast aside his emotions—everything he felt for Jessica—and concentrated on being a policeman. These were serious allegations and he'd keep her talking until she answered every question. Disengaging himself from his own reactions was difficult, but always effective. "How did Dr. Finch get from Alberta to Montreal?"

"He started his practice in Montreal when he arrived from Scotland. He travels to this part of the country, too, he says, because we need him badly. He knows my father. Dr. Finch was the person who…who recommended Miss Waverly's. He told my father he'd take good care of me there when the time came."

"That's the personal stake you have in finding Dr. Finch."

She nodded, crossed to the other side of the fire, bent her head and studied her hands.

"What happened to your baby?"

"I don't know." She rubbed her face. "I don't know but Dr. Finch does. I was heavily sedated and some of my recollections don't make sense."

"What about the woman, Miss Waverly?"

"She's not a charlatan. If you could have seen how that elderly woman tended to us—she's a kind, frail old woman. She was an unwed mother herself and thrown out of her home forty years ago, she told us. Her daughter helps out, the one who was born illegitimate. She's married now with legitimate children. It's Dr. Finch who medicated me. I signed papers and don't recall what they said. There was another woman giving birth that night, and Miss Waverly tended to her while Dr. Finch remained with me. But I heard and felt a baby boy in my arms, Travis."

"What do you think Dr. Finch did with your baby?"

"I heard rumors he was planning to start an adoption

agency. He'd connect wealthy people with strong, healthy newborns for a fee."

"He sold your son?"

"It's possible, but I'm not sure."

"And you think he also goes by the name Dr. King."

"I'm sure it was him in the lecture hall."

Travis watched the tiny bubbles rise to the top of the water cauldron. The fire blazed. He rearranged the pot. "Did you tell your father?"

"Yes, I wrote to him. He was having marital problems the whole time this was happening but he hired a private investigator in Montreal who secretly worked with me, unbeknownst to Miss Waverly. The records show I gave birth to a girl. Miss Waverly says she saw the deceased infant wrapped in a blanket, briefly, but wasn't positive of its gender."

"So the allegations of a live baby being stolen…"

"Were proven false."

Smoke circled the air. They fanned their faces. "What about the other woman who gave birth that night? Could the babies have been switched?"

"I…I thought of that. She left Miss Waverly's shortly after she gave birth to move to a flat of her own. The investigator followed her for a while and later I visited on a friendly call. She gave birth to a little boy with hair as red as her own. He's not my child."

"Have any other babies disappeared from the home, or just yours?"

"Only mine."

"Why would Dr. Finch do it? If he was charging a fee for adoption, why wouldn't he take other babies?"

"Maybe he's crazy for power. I don't know!"

The water cauldron boiled steadily, the sound of bubbling water stretching the air between them. Sliding on his work gloves, Travis lifted the cauldron and set it on a cool log. The metal sizzled when it hit wood.

"It's a far-fetched story, Jessica."

"Dr. Finch *is* Dr. King."

"No one else knows, do they?"

She shook her head, rising to bring the other pot with cool water closer so they could mix the two.

"Not your stepmother, not your sister…not even Merriweather."

"None of them. My father may seem like a cold man to you, but I know he loves me and is doing what he thinks best. He was willing to tell his wife about my new baby, no matter if it caused more problems in their marriage. He planned to bring the baby back to Calgary so that we would live as a family beneath his roof. But when the baby passed away…he told me to keep my history quiet. That it would ruin my chance of marriage to another man and therefore any chance of future children. I'd like to have more children, Travis…someday maybe… And how could I speak out against a doctor?"

"If it's the truth, you can speak out against anyone."

"Would you help me, Travis? Please?"

"How?"

"The foster home in Riverpoint Junction has something to do with Dr. Finch. I fear for those children. Please take me there."

He considered it as he fed the flames with another log. Wood crackled, sparks flew. He restrained himself from lashing out verbally against Dr. Finch, and from prejudging Jessica. He remembered that he was a sergeant major. "If what you say is true, then the theft of a child is official Mountie business. And Dr. Finch's dirty character would throw havoc onto the conviction of Paul Warrick. *I'm* involved in this story. If what you say proves false…then it's an allegation against the good name of the doctor."

She sank to a log, crossed her arms and stared into the fire.

"As heartless as it seems, Jessica, I'd like to prove you're wrong. There's got to be another explanation, one that doesn't involve such turmoil for so many people."

He planted his big hand beneath her chin, turning her toward him, feeling her flinch at his next words.

"But you're damn right we're going to Riverpoint Junction."

Chapter Eleven

It was starting again. The pounding in his temples threatening to erupt as a headache, the ire churning his blood, the outrage at life's circumstance. Travis felt as if a dam was about to burst within him. He needed to be alone, had wanted to be alone since the beginning of this journey.

The night was quiet. It was one or two o'clock, he guessed. Beetles chirped in the trees. A loon called, then an owl. He tossed from side to back but the ground dug into him. No position was comfortable.

He gazed at the sprinkling of stars in the velvet sky. Shortly after his conversation with Jessica, he'd set her up for bathing then had left her at the campsite while he'd taken a long walk along the river. When he'd come back, she'd already gone to bed. He'd stayed up by the fire, but no matter how hard he thought, nothing was clear.

She'd turned his head upside down with her confessions. How could he feel so sorrowful for a woman he hoped was lying? This was not the Jessica he thought he knew. Hell, he didn't know anything about the woman sleeping three feet away.

Her story evoked pity and compassion. The humiliation of being sent away, and then the pain of discovering her baby had died…or had gone missing…

It also evoked anger at being dealt such a harsh blow. And she wasn't the virgin he'd assumed she was.

He blinked and snapped the blankets off his body. It was cold so he yanked on his leather jacket and stomped down to the river. The quarter moon was just enough to light his darkened path.

Standing at the river for a few moments, he swore. It made him feel good. He swore again, louder.

"No matter how many times you curse, it won't change a thing," Jessica said behind him. "I've done my share of screaming."

He spun around to see her standing on the rocky shore, a wool blanket wrapped around her body, her loose hair tumbling about her shoulders.

She looked down at his boots. "What's wrong with your leg? I saw you limping."

"It's nothing. When I get tired, the old wound flares up. It'll be gone by morning." He spun back to the raging river, feeling its power thundering through the ground beneath his pointed boots. "I'd prefer if you left so I can curse all I want."

To his surprise, he felt the rustle of her blanket against his shoulder till she was standing next to him watching the black water. "Go ahead and curse. I'm not leaving though. When you get in these surly moods, you think I don't notice but you close down and your mind escapes to somewhere else. Talk to me instead. Nothing you say or feel can scare me."

"Oh, no?" he asked bluntly. "Well, I'm mad as hell because Caroline had to die. I'm mad because you lost your kid. I'm mad because Independence is healthy and thriving."

"Don't sell your horses, Travis. You love your horses."

"Don't start that again."

"You're selling them to punish yourself over Caroline's death."

He kicked at the mud and swore. He hoped it would intimidate her so she'd leave, but she remained.

"You can't curse me away. And I know you can't bring Caroline back by punishing yourself."

She was treading into dangerous territory, into things about himself he didn't want to examine. He snapped back with unintended cruelty—anything to chase her from here. "You're very calm while doling out this good advice. If I recall correctly, you're in quite a quandary yourself."

She flung the blanket over her shoulder. "Do you think you're the only one who's entitled to be angry? Well, I'm angry, too! I'm angry at a system that believes *him* over *me!*"

"And I'm goddamn angry that I can't get you out of my system! Every time I look into your face, I imagine what it'd be like to kiss you!"

Standing before him, she suddenly spun away. "Goodbye!"

He yanked her back by her belt, sending her reeling toward him. "You said you could take anything I have to say. Then listen to this." He hauled her unceremoniously across the dirt. "I'm angry with myself for assuming you were a virgin and knew nothing about the world. And I hate myself for being jealous of Victor!"

"Shut…up!"

"I hate that when I look down at your throat, I want to rip that blanket off and the blouse beneath it. I hate that I wonder how you strap down your breasts for the ride each morning without a corset and I especially hate…that I wish *I* could have shared your bath tonight!"

She kicked toward his legs and missed. He jumped out of her range but held her at arm's length as he might a wild cougar.

"You maniac," she yelled. "I hate that I've had an affection for you since I was sixteen. I hate that when you slide your legs into your bedroll each night, I wonder how they'd feel sliding on top of mine. And I especially hate…that you're the only person I can count on to get me to Devil's Gorge!"

He panted for air, struck by her natural beauty, her untamed hair, her flaming skin.

"Goddamn you!" she wailed. She kicked hard and hit his shin. "Let me go!"

He winced with the kick. His hand slipped from her belt and she ran. But she couldn't outrun him. She had nowhere to go. He chased her up the riverbank to the campfire.

"If you think you can run, you're mistaken." They circled the fire like prizefighters in a ring. He finally caught her by the shoulders and kissed her.

"Did Victor do this?" He growled into her mouth, clawing at her buttons.

"Shut your mouth!"

"Or this?" He clasped a large hand over her breast. "Did you like it, Jesse?"

"Stop that filthy talk!" She backed up, attempting to smack him, but he caught her hand and covered her mouth with his. He was lost in a second. Her mouth was tender and soft and everything he remembered, while his tore into hers as if seeking answers for feelings he couldn't comprehend.

He whispered her name and grasped the edge of her

blanket which dragged from her elbow. When he tore it off, she gasped.

He kept urging, pressing against her, feeling as if something was just beyond his reach. Her body tensed and released. She ran her hand up to his leather lapel and gripped. In one smooth motion, he parted from her and slid his jacket down his arms. It hit the ground. Her lips were swollen, eyes ablaze, but she didn't run.

Her face tilted up toward him, lit with shadows of possibility.

His blood stirred. "Jessica. I want you. And maybe, just maybe, you want me." He curled a sure finger down the line of her cheek. "Don't you?"

"Yes," she breathed.

In the next instant, he caught her bottom lip with his mouth and sucked roughly. Jessica responded with a quivering of her body. The desperation had been building in her as much as it had in him, and the thought burned to his soul. She was what had kept him awake on these lonely nights, what he hungered for and fantasized about.

He reached to unbutton her blouse. Her fingers clasped eagerly over his, helping frantically as they raced to undress. She wore a loose shift beneath her blouse. He slid it over her head, exposing ivory breasts and large nipples. She didn't shield herself from the light and he marveled at the soft curves of her body. His rough hand gripped her waist, then curled up to capture a breast. She moaned. He unbuckled her belt while she unbuckled his. Their pants fell to the ground.

They didn't speak; they didn't have to. Each knew what they were promising and neither wished to examine but only accept what was offered tonight.

He removed her pantaloons and stockings, she slid

off his shorts. They were both bare. He reveled in her beauty, taking his time to gaze down to her slender feet.

He lowered her to his blankets, moving them closer to the fire to keep her warm. Her skin glowed in the orange light. Nestling naked on top of her, he slipped a hand beneath her bottom so that her crotch met his.

"I want this to last...so you remember it...remember me." He gave her a dozen kisses—upon her lips, her lids, her ear, her neck, her breast.

She stroked the scars on his right thigh, and moaned with concern.

"Don't worry," he whispered. "It's all right."

"Does it hurt?"

"No."

His erection slapped against her waist as he kissed her fully on the mouth, savoring the pleasure of her responsive lips. He then slid down to one breast and licked its tip.

She rolled toward him in approval, and he smiled that she was urging him to continue. Her nipple rose in greeting as he swirled his tongue and mouthed the rosy circle.

Inhaling loudly, he moved to her other breast and sucked. And then he moved lower.

He kissed her belly, around her waist, around and down to the point of her hip. She placed her palms at each side of his head and he moaned with the feeling of being held. But she couldn't hold his head for long because he slipped lower, between her legs.

With muscled arms, he pushed her knees up so her rear rested on the middle of the blankets. Gently, he spread her legs. Her scent was pleasant—bayberry soap and river water. He parted her with soft fingertips and then with the whisper of his tongue.

If she was unprepared for him to kneel between her

thighs, she lost her inhibition. No protest left her lips. Her body relaxed. When he slid his fingers along the bud, he gazed at her face. She closed her eyes and arched back slightly.

She rolled her hips. He teased her more and more, a dozen times till he believed she was hovering on the edge of light and dark.

He murmured, "Beg me for my tongue."

She smiled with eyes closed. "Give me your tongue, Travis. Bury it inside of me."

He licked her as she moaned in shameless pleasure. He craved her more than he thought possible, and had imagined doing this to her from the minute she'd stepped out from behind the tree at the fort wearing tight, ivory pants.

She pressed her knees together around his head, arched her back and shuddered in a wave of fulfillment. Her body trembled, her breathing stopped. When her rapture ceased, she clutched his shoulders.

Satisfied that he could please his lover, he ran the back of his hand over his mouth and untangled his limbs from hers. Sliding up beside her on the blankets, cradling her in his arms, he delighted in the thought of the many hours ahead of them tonight. He'd make love to her in any and every position.

Smiling, she gazed into his eyes and draped her hand across his arm as he lay on his side. He lifted the blankets and tucked them around her back to ensure she was warm.

Reaching lower, she touched his waist, grazed his thigh, then stroked his erection.

"Ahh." He closed his eyes and drifted on a cloud of ecstasy. He placed his hand over hers to keep them there.

She laughed gently, sagging into a blissful state of relaxation, closing her eyes and moving her hand up and down. On the edge of a dream, he floated there, extending the timeless moments as long as possible.

When her hand slowed, her fingers fluttering on his shaft, he was almost bursting with need.

He opened his eyes and smiled into her glowing face. Her lids were closed, her expression serene as silk.

"Jessica?" he murmured. He kissed her warm, smooth cheek.

Her mouth parted, every muscle in her body uncoiled and relaxed.

"Jessica, are you asleep?"

"Jessica?" She heard Travis's voice in her sleep, but he seemed so far away, she couldn't answer. She was swimming in a warm lake, the sun was shining, and on the shore stood Travis with a baby in his arms…no, he was leading Independence along the shoreline.

Travis shook her by a shoulder. "Sleepyhead."

She opened her eyes and blinked several times in the morning light. She was wrapped in blankets, lying by a fading fire, but Travis was fully dressed. His hat shadowed his face in the dawn sunrise while he peered down at her. His torso was silhouetted by a blue sky.

It was morning?

It was morning!

She bolted upright, surprised to find herself naked. Scrambling to cover herself with the blankets, she noticed their things were packed, their horses waiting. Everything was packed except her bedroll. A plate of biscuits and dried fruit lay on a stone by the fire.

"I couldn't wait any longer," said Travis, looking

away as she self-consciously tugged the blanket over a nipple. "The sun is up and we best be on our way."

He gave a nervous cough. Dark bristles glistened along his jaw. "I folded your pants and blouse in at the bottom of your roll. Your socks and underclothes are there, too."

The awkwardness between them intensified. She moved toward her clothes, trying not to shift the blanket off her bare skin. "My Lord, how could I have slept through your packing?"

He placed a hand on the brim of his hat and grinned. "Something made you tired."

"And I fell asleep right when—" The realization of what they'd done together swept over her. She felt the blood rush to her face. "I'm sorry."

Something flickered in his eyes. Regret? He turned his head to look at the stirring horses. "No need to apologize. Hurry up, though. I've left you some food. While you get dressed, I'll put out the fire."

Mortified that they were on such unequal footing—she naked and he fully dressed—she listened to the dirt from his shovel hit the blistery logs. She'd been physically satisfied but he'd been left on the verge. And she'd fallen asleep with her hand on *his*... Bristling with embarrassment, she tugged up one sock then another.

Even though she hadn't intended on falling asleep, she felt selfish.

But she'd been so tired, and now she felt refreshed.

On went her bloomers. She'd make it up to him. Thinking of how she might accomplish that, she blushed. Last night had been a night like no other. Their tempers had gotten the best of them and then the ripple of the river...and the scent of grass.

Making sure he wasn't watching, she raised her arms

and put on her chemise, then her tighter undershirt. It seemed silly to hide herself like this when he'd seen all of her last night, but covering up came naturally to her and getting naked didn't.

Neither of them had planned it. It had been a strange extreme in their relationship. She'd never been out of control like that with Victor.

But it had happened with Travis.

Apprehension took hold of her. What now?

Timidly, she rose and shook out her blankets. "Travis, I feel peculiar."

"How so?" He rallied around the horses. She gave him her bedroll. He tied it to one of the pack horses while she clawed the night's tangles from her loose hair.

She nervously patted her saddle, checking its positioning but knowing full well Travis was an expert in saddling. "About things."

"What things?"

"Excuse me," she said, her frustration rising, "but did I dream last night happened or were you there with me?"

He squinted over the horse at her. "I was there."

"What did that all mean?"

He dodged to the other horse, checking equipment. "It doesn't have to have any meaning unless we give it some."

It seemed he was running away from discussing it and she was chasing after him, insisting they should. Baffled by his attitude, she walked to the fire pit, picked up the plate of food and bit into a biscuit.

"I guess Merriweather was right," hollered Travis. "He shouldn't have left us alone."

If he was attempting a joke, she wasn't amused. The comment intensified her guilt. It hadn't been a casual night for her. It had meant more. But now in the light of day, she wished she hadn't succumbed. She'd come off looking gluttonous, while Travis appeared squeaky with generosity.

She washed her face with canteen water, then brushed her teeth.

Travis kept talking. "I wonder how his hemorrhoids are doing."

Irritation increasing, she brushed her hair and stepped closer. "How could you ignore last night? Give it no meaning at all?"

His blue eyes glimmered like a cold, deep well. "Chalk it up to a good time."

"I am *not* a good-time girl!"

With a cool look of detachment, he sprang to another horse and checked its bridle. She stopped brushing. He was pulling his sentiments away from her, closing down as he always had.

"I feel—" she wheeled around the horse "—I feel beholden to you for the one-sided nature of our—our—"

"Alliance." He lifted Independence's foreleg. "Looks good this morning. No damage done."

"Alliance. That's the word!" She scratched her cheek. "No, that's not the word. The one-sided nature of last night's association—"

"Association? It sounds like a business agreement. How about connection? That's a good word. Yeah, I like that."

She chased him around Independence, trying not to display her humiliation. "If you think that I go around offering myself like that," she said, gesturing to the empty campsite, "offering myself to anyone—"

"Jessica. No need to feel beholden. At least I got to kiss your breasts." He winked.

That wasn't funny, either.

"I think we should take some care in…in how we behave," he said, suddenly serious, deflating her hope that last night might have held more significance for him. "I'm taking you to Riverpoint Junction today and Devil's Gorge from there. I think you should brace yourself, because you're going to be awfully disappointed at what we find."

She saw distrust reflected in his face.

He still didn't believe her.

Last night had been much more than physical on her part. She wasn't sure how she'd have described her feelings for Travis ten hours ago—perhaps concern for a friend, unexpected physical attraction, gratitude that he was taking her to the foster home. But mostly confusion. She'd wondered what it would be like to make love to a man as commanding, but also as tender, as Travis. She'd never witnessed a man so full of emotion, riding a wild mustang, and then later, getting angry on her behalf for the disappearance of her baby.

Now when he glared at her, shielded and withdrawn, she felt empty. She was alone again.

Feelings had definitely shifted between them, no matter how hard he tried to deny it. But they were raw, misplaced feelings that might interfere with finding and keeping her child.

With a sigh, she found her cowboy hat resting on her saddle horn, brushed it against her thigh, then swung herself onto her mount. No man would interfere with that again.

Chapter Twelve

Travis had wanted to get Jessica out of his system, had nearly attacked her with a pent-up desire that scared even him, and now he craved her more, not less. How in hell had that happened?

Dammit, he knew how. He'd wanted to make love to her and instead had gotten tangled up with her charms.

It was nearly noon and they'd been traveling in relative silence, save for the occasional stop to water the horses. He winced in the saddle. He'd never seen anything as enticing as Jessica by the firelight, her face and body outlined against the stark black of the woods. He recalled how less than a week ago, he'd described her looks as store-bought prettiness. Now that he'd gotten to know her some, the pride and commitment in her character shone through.

Did reaching out to her mean he was turning his back on Caroline? Logically, he didn't expect he'd never go near another woman again, but this surprised him. It felt rushed and unrestrained. Another woman had never factored into his future. Hell, he was selling everything he owned and had nothing to offer another woman, which proved how little he'd considered the possibility.

He never jumped headfirst into business or personal matters. It'd taken him a year to propose to Caroline. Indeed, he prided himself on how cool his head was—it formed a part of his character that had gotten him several good promotions. He was an officer of the law, and laws dictated he should remain impartial. He wouldn't be swayed by a woman he'd slept with.

It left him in a delicate situation. He had to endure two more days with the blond beauty. Two more days remembering what her hands had felt like on his body, how her mouth had trembled to meet his, how vulnerable she was to the outcome of this journey.

She was depending on him to lead her on the path to truth, as would his commander if he knew the situation. Seeing how emotional Jessica was when she awoke this morning, Travis knew he had to be the one to set the calming precedent.

No more touching.

No more feeling sorry for Jessica.

No more yelling.

His detachment lasted through the morning as the trail dipped and swelled through the mountainside. They had to leave the river behind to get to Riverpoint Junction in the fastest way possible, but would catch up with it again when they redirected to Devil's Gorge. The other option was to follow the Glacier River to Devil's Gorge, then head south thirty miles to where it intersected the Beaver River. But this was a shortcut.

They passed another rider headed in the other direction who said he had business in Calgary, then a newly married couple who were aiming to visit their folks in Strongness.

"What's going to happen to the McGraw brothers?"

Jessica called to him in the afternoon. "They won't know to follow us to Riverpoint Junction."

"They'll make a good decoy, leading those two other men directly to Devil's Gorge. I hired the McGraws to ride to Devil's Gorge, and that's what they'll do. Sometimes, when the wind blew right, I could smell their campfire so I knew they were heading there."

"Won't they see our tracks? Won't they know we've turned off?"

"They won't suspect it. Besides, the earth's dry. It's hard to follow tracks in dry dirt and grass unless you know what you're looking for."

"You'd know."

"Yeah, I would. But most wouldn't." He said it without arrogance, simply stating a fact. But he noticed the worry in Jessica's face. "I don't see any vultures circling the air behind us. There's the occasional one above us, but I haven't seen any behind us since yesterday when we were on the other trail. And no smell of campfires. Those men have gone. Don't worry."

She rode easier.

As the light began to fade in the late afternoon, Travis pulled the horses to a clearing and dismounted. Jessica followed suit.

"We'll be there soon. It's nestled in the side of that mountain. Listen." Travis stood and inhaled the cool air, rich with the scent of plants and minerals.

She looked worried again. "What do you hear?"

"Riverpoint Junction. The junction of the Beaver and Glacier rivers. I hear the sound of rushing water."

A smile came over her. "I hear it now."

It sounded like the soft gush of rain. Soothing.

"If you'd like to stretch your legs, we could walk the rest of the way. It'll take us twenty minutes."

Jessica paled. "Twenty minutes," she repeated. "I might know in twenty minutes."

Or you might not, he thought, but didn't say it. By the way she smoothed her pants and adjusted her belt, she was nervous enough as it was.

The trail widened. It allowed him and Jessica to step ahead leading their two mounts, allowing the three broodmares to follow behind.

"There's something I need to ask you." Jessica slipped one hand out of her glove. "The more I think about it, the more it puzzles me."

He picked up a fallen tree branch from their path. "This could hurt someone." He whipped the dry branch, most likely felled by the wind, into the trees beside them.

"What town was Pete Warrick arrested in?"

"Red Deer, north of Calgary."

"Does Dr. Finch travel there often?"

"He makes his rounds twice a year."

"You say he witnessed Mr. Warrick's theft?"

"That's right, he saw him in the alley right between the two stores."

"This is what I don't understand. It's already cold in November. There's lots of snow. Does Dr. Finch normally travel in the coldest months?"

"Not usually. He said he'd promised to look in on a patient just outside of town, someone who needed medicine badly. Mr. Cruckshank."

"Did you talk to Mr. Cruckshank?"

"He died before Dr. Finch could get to him. We have witnesses who attested to that. Mr. Cruckshank had a heart ailment, died with his wife and brother beside him."

She seemed defeated by that answer.

"But, Jessica, it didn't happen in November."

"But I thought you said Dr. Finch witnessed—"

"He came forward to identify Pete Warrick this past November, but the store robbery happened February before last."

"February," she said with a jolt. "Two Februarys ago. What day exactly?" She pressed a hand to his and they stopped. "What day in February?"

"The eighteenth."

Her voice became urgent. "I gave birth last February. February the third. Dr. Finch was in Montreal on February eighteenth."

"He could have made it across the country in the fifteen days after your delivery. Easily."

"Not two Februarys ago. There was an ice storm in Montreal. It downed trees and covered the roads. A winter freeze followed. It took the city two and a half weeks to clear the roads and rail lines in all directions."

"But you said your father visited you after your delivery. If he made it through, then so could—"

"The baby came a few weeks earlier than expected. My father didn't visit until three weeks later, as scheduled on the twenty-fourth. Besides, it took nearly that long to clear the railroad."

"Are you sure of your memory? You said you'd been heavily sedated that night and for days afterward."

"I gave birth during an ice storm. I heard the pellets jumping off the shingles. Around midnight, Dr. Finch barely escaped the house in his buggy, otherwise he would have been trapped with us for days. When I awoke, everything was covered with half an inch of ice. The trees, the buggies, the street. I'm sure about this!"

"If the baby came earlier, was he small?"

"I remember him being very tiny in my arms."

"Then there's a chance he might not have—"

"No."

He steeled himself for the brutal question he had to ask. "What did they say happened to the body?"

"Miss Waverly told me she had asked my permission for Dr. Finch to take the baby to the hospital grounds for burial. Those were the papers she said I signed. I don't remember, but I believe that's what she was told. She never saw my baby passing, she was too preoccupied with the other woman in labor."

"Did you go to the burial grounds to check?"

"I didn't...*I couldn't*...but the private investigator said he did. There was a wooden cross on a tiny plot of newly dug soil that Dr. Finch indicated was what they did with fallen children. I was to send the hospital money for a gravestone. My father gave me the money himself when he visited, but I...I...haven't yet. Don't you see? Dr. Finch couldn't have witnessed Mr. Warrick stealing anything. I have a private investigator who can prove he was in Montreal."

She pushed her hat backward so it fell to her spine, clasped by a leather thong at her throat. "Someone at the university told my investigator that Dr. King was apparently in Vancouver when I gave birth. Where was he, Travis? Vancouver, Montreal or Red Deer?"

At every angle, in every way he approached it, Travis's reasoning slammed into a wall. Had he put an innocent man in prison, based solely on the word of a crooked doctor? "What about the fact that Dr. Finch was paying a call to Mr. Cruckshank? There are witnesses."

"Witnesses that the man died before Dr. Finch arrived. Do you have witnesses of the doctor's arrival?"

Disturbed by the image of possible events, Travis shook his head. No one had actually seen Dr. Finch in Red Deer, he realized.

"So maybe he took the man's name from the newspaper obituary and fabricated the story."

"Why would he do that?" Travis asked. "He'd have to have something against Pete Warrick."

"Or Mr. Warrick has something against Dr. Finch, and Finch wanted to shut him up. Did Mr. Warrick resist in court?"

"Pete kept insisting he was innocent, but he never fought hard. He said he was alone in his cabin, drinking."

"Maybe that's the truth and he couldn't prove it."

Travis rubbed the back of his tight neck and swore. "It seems the doctor has a few unanswered questions. *I'd like to be the one to ask him.*"

They crested the hill. Jessica stopped and stared at the valley below. A cluster of log homes surrounded a short main street that housed several feed-and-supply stores.

"Riverpoint Junction," she said softly. "There it is."

Jessica stood there as Travis asked for directions, thinking of how far she'd come and who and what she'd find at the foster home.

"Excuse me, folks," said Travis to a young man and wife in a passing buckboard. "We're looking for a place called Murphy's. Murphy's Foster Home."

"We know William and Martha Murphy. Follow the main street, then turn right just before you get to the hardware store. It's the third cabin on the right, last one on the end. You'll likely see the children playing outside."

"Thank you." Travis turned to her. "Jessica, let's go."

"I don't know if I can."

"You came this far on your own. I'm here with you now." He tapped her elbow, took her reins and led their two saddled horses down the street. She walked behind with the broodmares.

Guarded, Jessica looked about the town with suspicion in her heart, but things appeared placid and normal. Newly painted storefronts, well-maintained and nailed together with precision, glinted attractively in the warm afternoon light. Friendly townsfolk passed by on the short boardwalk, the men tilting their hats in respect, the woman nodding, unafraid to peer directly at the couple leading five beautiful horses down their rutted street. A big green mountain framed the backdrop.

When they turned at the hardware store, she heard the sound of children laughing before she saw them. The tight nervousness in her chest threatened to suffocate her.

Travis pulled in the horses at the end of the street, along the grassy slope beside the third cabin on the right. As he tethered them to the hitching post, Jessica stared at the beautiful sight.

It was a large acreage and at least a dozen children were jumping, hopping or running across the fenced grass. Too many moving heads to count. Healthy, plump, rosy-cheeked children singing songs and playing finger games or tag, or racing around a teeter-totter and wooden slide. They ranged in age from about thirteen, she figured, staring at the oldest boy, to a one-year-old little blond girl who'd just learned to walk, judging by the jerky nature of her steps as she held a jangling rattle in her pudgy fist.

Physically, these children didn't seem to want for anything. Jessica gave thanks beneath her breath.

But there were so many of them. Were they all motherless and fatherless? All to be adopted?

The little girl dropped her rattle. She tried to bend down to pick it up, but fell down, as well.

Jessica laughed, pushed open the gate and picked up the rattle and the little girl. She fingered the eyelet apron on the girl's smock. "Hello, button."

"How-do," the little one replied. An attempt at *how do you do?*

Jessica jostled the girl in her arms. The youngster giggled. "Where's Mrs. Murphy?"

"Mu…fee." The cherub face peered around the yard. "Mu…fee."

"That would be my ma," said the oldest boy, moving closer to Jessica and Travis, who was now standing to her right. "I'm Sidney. My ma's out back." He gestured behind the house. "And my pa's in the barn, milkin' the cows. I'd be there, too, but I'm stuck lookin' after the children."

"It's a mighty important job." Jessica smiled and lowered the youngster to her feet.

Sidney smiled back. He had a slender face and slender hands, both heavily freckled.

"We'll speak to your mother first," said Travis. "While you tell your pa we're here. We're from Calgary. This here is Miss Jessica Haven and I'm Officer Reid."

"An officer?"

"With the Mounties."

Sidney raced off, saluting unnecessarily and stumbling over his gangly legs. "Yes, sir!"

They closed the back gate on the children but the little girl wailed through the bars.

A woman raced from behind the house when she heard the cries. A kerchief held back her dark brown hair, gold earrings sparkled on her lobes, and a freshly pressed apron covered her rotund figure. "Angie, is that you crying?"

The woman stopped and wiped her hands on her apron at the sight of Jessica and Travis. "Something I can help you with?" She spoke to them but reached over the gate and pulled the young girl into her arms. "Where's that boy of mine?"

Travis stepped forward. "We asked that he fetch his pa." Travis introduced himself, then Jessica.

"There's nothing wrong, is there, Officer?" Martha Murphy clutched the child closer to her chest.

"No, ma'am. We're on our way to Devil's Gorge and wanted to stop by and see your foster home. Miss Haven is a journalist. She's never seen a foster home and wanted to write about you."

"Write about us? Mercy! And by a lady writer, too." The woman laughed, squeezed the little girl, then walked to a clothesline half strung with wet clothing. She dropped the girl beside a basket full of children's clothing. "Hand me your wet dress, Angie. The one on top. That's the one. You'll have to excuse me," she said to Jessica. "I have to keep working or I'll never get these clothes done. Seems there's a never-ending supply of dirty laundry around this home. You can write that down for your article, miss. And a constant need for fresh milk. That's where my husband is, milking our three cows for suppertime."

Jessica's initial reaction was laughter. She liked this friendly woman.

Both she and Mrs. Murphy kept a watch on the other children as Sidney and his father came out of the barn to join them. Mr. Murphy, a bearded man dressed in overalls, balanced two pails of milk. He lowered them to the grass beside the clothesline, then shook hands and made introductions.

They learned that William and Martha Murphy had been living here for seven years. He supported his family with a small herd of cattle, supplementing his income with carpentry in town whenever there was a need.

"Are all these youngsters foster children?" Jessica asked the wife while Travis occupied the husband.

"Six of 'em are ours, the other six are up for adoption. Well, actually, only two now. Four, praise the heavens, are leaving for adoptive homes within the week."

"All at the same time?"

"We found good homes for them in the valley—the B.C. valley fifty miles west—but William isn't able to deliver them until next week. Folks couldn't come themselves because they're farmers. No time to leave their crops. William doesn't mind. He'll take Sidney with him and they're going to bring back a new plough."

"My pa's going to show me how to use it," said Sidney. "Says he thinks I'm strong enough to plough the fields myself this fall."

"That's a big job," said Travis. "But you look up to it."

Sidney kicked proudly at the grass. He lifted Angie off the ground, plucked her hand and headed toward the slide. "I'll take her, Ma. I'm gonna miss her when she leaves."

Martha sighed. "We all are. Thank you, Sidney. We'll be inside with our visitors. Send the six youngest in for their supper."

Angie wailed.

"Yes, you," said Mrs. Murphy. "Give her one time down the slide then she's to come in and wash up."

Jessica watched with a tremble to her heart. "Is she your youngest?"

"She's the youngest, but not mine. She's being adopted by my sister in the valley. My sister's got five boys but no girls and is tickled to be getting one so sweet. She helped find the homes for the twins and the other little boy, David. I don't know what I'd do without my sister."

Jessica watched Sidney lift Angie to the slide. "Where did Angie come from?"

"Devil's Gorge."

"How…how did her parents pass on?"

"Runaway stagecoach. They were inside when it tipped. Angie was, too, but she got trapped beneath the seat and the framework saved her from being crushed."

"Who brought her here?"

Martha beamed with sincerity, but Jessica was stricken cold by the explanation that followed. "A wonderful man named Dr. Finch. He's been our salvation."

"You know Dr. Finch?"

"Absolutely. He comes around every summer before he leaves for Vancouver. He was just here two weeks ago."

"When, exactly, is he leaving for Vancouver?"

"He's got his medical sales rally on Saturday morning in Devil's Gorge, he told us, then he'll be leaving right away."

Jessica felt nauseous. They had approximately thirty-six hours left to catch him.

Chapter Thirteen

"I've never seen twins before." With her journal on her lap, pencil in hand, Jessica sat on the Murphy's horse-hair sofa in the parlor. Martha had kindly insisted they stay for supper, they'd accepted and Jessica felt full. She watched the little boy and girl chase a red rubber ball along the braided rug. Looking across the room to where the men stood at the bookshelves, Jessica caught Travis watching the children.

In private, he'd told her to calm down, that if they left this evening they'd still have plenty of time to reach Devil's Gorge within thirty-six hours, that she could take two hours now to spend with the children.

"No one else in town has seen twins, either," said Martha with a proud glint in her eyes. "They're fascinating, aren't they?"

"Adorable. My great-grandmother was a twin." Jessica vaguely remembered the stories her father used to tell.

"My husband's got twins on his side, too. I reckon we all might, if you go back far enough in history."

They were active toddlers and seemed happy despite life's problems. Callie had thick brown hair done up in a single braid and ribbon, a round face and eager-to-please attitude. She caught the ball first as her brother, Bobby, with the identical little face, pert nose and rosy lips, tumbled after her. A yellow sheepdog in the corner rose and lunged for the pair. They stopped to pet his head and scratch behind his ears. The dog closed his eyes in contentment.

"Do they do that often?" asked Jessica. "They stopped at exactly the same time to pet the dog."

"They do seem to have an inner sense," replied Martha.

"Imagine being that in tune with a brother or sister. Where are they from?"

"The valley."

"And how did their folks…what happened to them?"

"Their mother died in childbirth. The father couldn't handle them alone and had no family to give them to. No one knows what happened to him. The twins have been passed down through a few homes already."

"Such a sad life for such little children. How old are they?"

"I'd say fourteen months. It's not documented."

They were three months younger than her son would be.

Jessica swung her gaze to the other children hiding behind various chairs and parts of the room. She settled on the other four who were up for adoption—Angie, an older brother and sister, and then the toddler, a young boy. "How old is David?"

"Seventeen months."

Jessica's pencil thudded from her fingers to the paper on her lap. She caught it, trying to contain her feelings of possibility. The blond boy joined in with the twins to pretend they were scrubbing the dog, Harper. Harper was good-natured and sat still in the midst of the commotion. Then David's plump fingers caught hold of the red ball and he tossed it across the room. Eight children tumbled after it. David had a catchy laugh and Jessica found herself laughing with the rest of them.

The older children were more reserved. After a while of watching them, she noticed that they were studying her and Travis. Jessica realized with a squeezing of her heart that the two who remained to be adopted—an eight-year-old girl and her nine-year-old brother—might be wondering if they were being assessed for adoption.

Jessica wanted to take them in her arms, rock them and promise that life would be good. That the world was a wonderful place full of delight and possibility. Instead, she stifled the lump at the back of her throat and realized how lovely and kind Martha and William were as foster parents.

"These two older ones, Rebecca and Roy," said Martha with a comforting hand on the eight- and nine-year-old, "I'm so happy no one has come for them yet. We don't know how we'd manage without them. They're my two best helpers." Turning away, Martha wiped her eye, but not so fast that Jessica didn't register the disappointment. Martha was making up a story that she was happy in order to salvage the children's feelings. "Could you two help me clear the table?"

With a giggle, they fled to the kitchen. There was a clatter of plates and cutlery, then a scramble of feet on the wooden floor. The twins crawled to Jessica's side. Bobby placed his sticky hand on her pant leg while Callie pointed to the pencil and cooed.

Jessica tugged on the little girl's ear. Her skin felt smooth and warm. "Write me something, sweetheart."

Jessica extended the pencil and allowed the girl to

pick a spot on the journal. She scribbled lines and circles in the top margin while her brother watched as if he could read. Angie joined them, staggering behind with David and the dog. The weight of the twins pressing against her knees gave Jessica an inexplicable calm. Surrounded by the children, she felt as if she'd come home.

When Travis came over and crouched beside them, directing Callie's tiny hand with his large one to make a *C,* Jessica stood back for a minute, amused to see the harsh edges around Travis's eyes soften.

Jessica's notes filled the other side of the journal—things Martha had told her. They'd started the foster home six months ago. The federal government had established the Children's Aid Society and had advertised they were in need of stable, temporary homes for displaced children. Martha had readily applied, received a small monthly fund for food and clothing and spread the word into the farming communities that she would accept any ward in need of help.

Dr. Finch had supplied needed medicine such as cough syrup and bicarbonate for upset tummies, and had promised to drop by once a year for physical examinations and treatment of the foster children. He charged only a small fee, much less than normal. Martha suspected his fees went up slightly when he'd discovered he could bill the government directly.

"God bless the man," Martha had rejoiced. "What would we do without proper medical care for these kids?"

Jessica grew jittery at the woman's words. If Dr. Finch were gone tomorrow because of Jessica's accusations, some folks would suffer, and that was difficult to accept.

Jessica lifted the blond seventeen-month-old to the sofa beside her. She enjoyed the feel of his moving limbs and wondered if her son looked and felt anything like him. David squirmed and wouldn't sit for long. With a smile, she set him to his feet where he immediately tore off after the dog.

Still helping Callie at Jessica's side, Travis watched the boy run away. "Where did David come from?"

"Strongness. The mercantile owner, Mr. Brown, found him. Someone left David at his counter one night. They left a note that only said, *please deliver to the foster home.*"

Sorrow hit Jessica. What if David were her son? He was the right age. And blond. Did she feel any pull toward him? As she gazed at the laughing boy, she realized she felt as much affection for him as she did for all these other children. Still, how could she find out?

"Do you still have the note?" asked Travis.

"Yes. We keep good records."

"May I see it later? Maybe in my line of duty, I'd recognize something you might have overlooked."

"Sure, but Mr. Brown said he had the Mounties from Devil's Gorge look at the note. They couldn't trace either parent."

Travis squeezed Jessica's knee in a gesture of kindness. It came unexpectedly and for some unfathomable reason, brought a sting to her eyes. He knew how desperate she was; how difficult it was to restrain her feelings and remain composed.

Callie had finished writing her scribbles and according to Bobby, it was his turn. With a chuckle, Travis guided his hand to make a big *B.* Several minutes later, Jessica closed her journal despite the twin's calls for more.

"We have to help in the kitchen," Jessica explained. She scooted into the warmth of the large room with the twins following her every move. With a giggle, she picked them up, one on either arm. "You're so heavy," she said with exaggeration. They fingered her gold necklace. Without thinking, she planted a kiss on each downy cheek.

Martha looked at her curiously and Jessica felt her color rise. The kisses had come unexpectedly. She hadn't meant to exclude any of the other children.

Sliding the twins to the ground, she helped tidy what clutter remained. When she turned around, Mr. Murphy was dragging an oblong wooden contraption into the parlor.

"Anyone up for churning butter?" he asked.

The children hollered in excitement while Travis and Jessica watched, baffled. "What's that?" asked Travis.

"It's a dog-powered treadmill. You can use a goat or sheep, but Harper here is good. Bought it from Dr. Finch two years back when money wasn't so tight." He hoisted it to the worn rug. "Dr. Finch uses it to power his medical gadgets, but we use it for household devices. You put a dog on the wooden treads, he walks for thirty to forty minutes, it turns a pulley on the front that churns the bucket of butter."

Jessica scoffed with laughter, *"No..."*

"Yes, ma'am," said Sidney, pulling the sheepdog on its leash. While his father got the bucket, his mother poured in fresh cream. She was the center of a storm of gleeful children.

The dog was leashed to the front bar and began walking, happily nipping at leftover supper scraps offered by the children as a lure. The clacking of wooden treads echoed in the house. Travis and Jessica stood captivated with laughter.

After ten minutes, knowing they were nearing the

end of their visit, she announced, "We've brought gifts for everyone."

Exclamations of wonder filled the room. Travis frowned.

"We'll have to get them from outside and we'll be right back." Jessica tore out the side door into the evening darkness with Travis at her heels.

"What on earth do you have in mind?"

"We can't leave without giving them something. They have so little. Anything small, it doesn't have to be grand."

Their packs were slung over the corral fence. She untied hers quickly but Travis took a moment to think. Then he raced through his.

The children were waiting in the parlor, all twelve of them seated quietly, but bursting with anticipation for the entertainment to begin.

"First, I've got two magic stones to give away." Jessica clenched her fists in the air and the children swooned. Martha and William sat on the sofa, taking pleasure in the laughter. The dog continued trotting and William patted his head.

"They're good-luck stones," Jessica continued. "For Rebecca and Roy." She stepped between the toddlers on the floor and presented her rocks.

"Oh," said Rebecca. "Mine's blue like the sky, and as shiny as a mirror."

"And mine's pure white, like a snowball," said Roy.

"I found them along the river. They were so pretty I had to keep them for someone special."

"Thank you," they said.

"Next, I've got a fancy rope to give away," said Travis, reaching into his pack. "Who'd like to learn how to lasso?"

When they all raised their hands, Travis turned to Jessica and winked. "I think it has to go to the oldest one here. And he'll teach the rest of you. Sidney." Travis passed the rope to the smiling young boy.

Next, Jessica gave away two pencils and two sheets of paper she'd ripped from the back of her journal. She gave them to the twins, who immediately set out to use them. They tried to get the dog to write something, too, but to everyone's laughter, he preferred to use his paws.

"*Two* pencils," Travis teased her. "I thought I told you back at the beginning you could only take one on this trip."

"I took three. I didn't listen to all of your advice."

"Somehow, I knew that."

In the next half hour, Jessica gave away a sewing needle and thread, a lace handkerchief and half a bar of berry soap. Travis was pleased to give away a shiny fishing lure, one of his smallest canteens, a spoon he claimed was an official Mountie spoon from the officers' barracks and a leather strap from one of his horse's saddles that he'd tied into a small bracelet.

"And my last gift of the evening, ladies and gentleman," said Travis, "is reserved for someone who likes to cook. Who here likes to help Mrs. Murphy?"

Again, they all raised their hands. When Travis pulled out a used but small cooking pot, Jessica found herself laughing again. It went to one of Mrs. Murphy's daughters.

Jessica took a deep breath and reached for the final item. She ran her fingers over the soft flannel nightgown and remembered when she'd bought it in Montreal. She'd just been told by the private investigator her allegations against Dr. King had proven false, and that her father had sent word he was ceasing employment. Distraught but unwilling to accept the news, she'd strolled for hours down the winding cobblestones of the French Quarter. When she'd come across a clothing store, she'd gone inside to buy this gift. Now she held it up to David. "I think this will fit you perfectly. Wear it in good health, sweetheart."

David insisted she tug it on over his shirt. She did, loving the warm feel of him.

"That's the gift I tore out of your hands," Travis whispered in apology. "Now I realize who it was for. Are you sure you want to give it away?"

Jessica watched David pat his new "shirt" proudly. And then her affectionate gaze rested on the twins.

It simply felt right to give away something she loved to the children here, who had lost everything and every-*one* they had once loved. "I'm sure."

"Can't you stay a little longer?" asked Martha, watching Travis and Jessica mount their horses. It was nearly seven-thirty as William held up a kerosene lantern to illuminate the corral where he, his wife and the children stood.

"Stay! Stay!" shouted the youngsters.

Travis turned to Jessica and noticed how divided she was in her sympathies. Watching her earlier with the children had riveted his attention. The care she'd taken to ensure that each child had a token gift had demonstrated her change from the woman he'd once regarded as selfish.

Jessica was more giving than he was.

"I'd like to stay longer, but we have to go," she said, pressing some bills into Martha's hands.

Martha shook her head. "I couldn't possibly accept—"

"I have enough money," said Jessica. "Please take it and use it for the household."

"That I'll do. Thank you kindly. Where are your companions staying? In the rooms above the mercantile? You're welcome to stay here for the night if you haven't got space there."

Travis moved in his saddle, unsure of how to answer. The Murphys thought he and Jessica were traveling with an entourage, or at the very least, a proper chaperon.

Jessica bit down on her lip and looked to him.

"They're meeting up with us on the trail," Travis answered to everyone's vocal disappointment. He was thinking of the McGraw brothers, but let the Murphys assume otherwise. "I'm afraid we have to go. We might be back some day, though, sooner than you think." As he pressed his legs against the horse and they trotted away, he wondered why he'd said they might return.

Tilting back his hat, he thought maybe because he'd felt just as relaxed and happy among the children as Jessica had been. There'd once been a time when he'd seen children in his future, too. How quickly things could change.

He heard Jessica say goodbye several times. She'd already hugged each child while William had passed him the note to read, left behind with David when he'd been abandoned. No clues there.

When Travis glanced back in the darkness, Jessica was turning in her saddle, unable to look away from the children. They were soon swallowed by darkness, though, and she turned to look straight ahead, solemn and deep in thought.

The mood was melancholy as they headed up the rocky trail. Travis knew they had to keep riding to find

Dr. Finch, but it was unsettling to go from all that laughter to a lonesome, starry night. The moon was three-quarters full to light their path, and they could follow the Glacier River again, which reflected some of the moon. If they rode till midnight, they'd make good time and maybe see Devil's Gorge in two days.

Travis would interrogate Dr. Finch and, if he needed to, enlist the aid of the three Mounties stationed at the outpost. Any delay of his return to Calgary could be explained to the commander as official duty, investigating an alleged crime. Because of the obstructing mountains, no telegraph or railway lines had been laid. Devil's Gorge was isolated. Any communication had to be done in person.

For the safe footing of the horses, Travis set the pace slower than he would in daylight. From travels with his father, he knew the trails well. This last leg to Devil's Gorge was the steepest and stoniest. The wagon trail followed the curves of the Glacier River, but would double back in spots, going around jagged rocks impenetrable by horse and man. Some foot trails existed in and out of the bush where over the years, miners had unsuccessfully tried their hand at finding silver, copper or gold.

They stopped twice to water the horses then reined in forty minutes to midnight. Travis slid his pocket watch back into his vest and called to Jessica, "We'll camp here for the night."

He saw exhaustion in her face and anxiety in her step as she hauled her saddle to a fallen log, where she hoisted it for the night.

"You weren't able to lift it that high five days ago."

She halted, gave a noncommittal smile, then slid her gloved hand into her jacket pocket. "I wish I could have stayed with the children."

"They're safe, and that's what we went to see."

She shrugged with the uncertainty his words seemed to evoke. "I don't know what I'm doing anymore, Travis. I don't know who I'm doing this for or why, or if I'm doing the right thing."

"Jessica, you're tired. Have a seat here while I finish up. You're not to lift another finger." He clamped his hands around her upper arms and led her back two steps until she sat on the dry log beside her saddle.

While he continued by the light of the moon, he found himself more and more concerned about her. A silent warning in his mind told him to guard closely…or maybe to stay his distance.

When he was finished with the horses, he began to build a fire. It was cold and they'd need to keep warm through the night. "It's too late to cook a full meal. If it's all right with you, we'll take something dry from our packs."

"I'm still full from supper. You go ahead."

The fire was blazing. They were heating their hands when she began again. "If my baby…if Dr. Finch isn't Dr. King and all I wind up doing is hurting everyone involved, I couldn't face myself if I disrupt the good that he's done for the Murphys. And the good that the Murphys are doing for those children."

He listened. He watched a slender branch catch fire and blaze. Unscrewing the cap from his canteen, he held it out to Jessica. "You need water. Drink."

She slid closer to him on the log, her thigh and shoulder brushing his, accepting the offer.

When she swallowed a few mouthfuls, he spoke. "What you're doing is one hundred percent right. We've got to find Dr. Finch."

"What if I'm wrong about him?"

She handed him the canteen and he drank from it. The water tasted cool and clear. "What if you're not?"

"For the first time in over a year, Travis, I'm having doubts… I don't know…" She shoved herself up from the log and stood near the fire, her face and front glowing orange from the flames.

He rose to follow, standing with her in her corner of the world. "I know," he said gently, affected by her strength, her stamina to get this far on her own when no one else bought into her story.

"Jessica." His voice was low and soft, like the wind. Lifting his fingers to her cheek, he stroked away a strand of silky hair. "I believe everything you told me about Dr. Finch. I believe he is Dr. King. I believe he did something shady to your son. I believe you."

Chapter Fourteen

A heartbeat passed while Jessica stood encircled in Travis's arms.

She hadn't realized how difficult her burden had been to carry alone. It felt as if a boulder had been strapped to her back for seventeen months while she'd been climbing an invisible hill. But now Travis was offering her his hand, if not to carry the weight then at least to make the climb with her. That alone spoke to every cell in her body, sparking gratitude and friendship.

"Oh, Travis." She pressed her forehead against his solid chest. It met with the satin feel of his cotton shirt. He smelled good, like fire and earth and a breeze caught in heaven. "Travis, what can I say?"

"Say you'll go on and see this to the end. There must be others who Dr. Finch has beguiled. No one else has spoken out, but I'll help you be heard."

"Angie—the toddler at the foster home—I'm worried about her background. Dr. Finch brought her and I wonder if her parents really died in a stagecoach."

"We'll check it out when we reach Devil's Gorge. I

won't stop until I've checked the background of every one of those children."

The emotions trapped inside of her for so long finally eased their way out. "Thank you…thank you."

He held her, her head buried in his shirt. She loved the way they rocked together. His body, wrapped around hers, felt like a massive mountain. He, too, had been weathered with age and unexpected storms. He'd been blasted by sunshine in his most favorable years and trapped in dust when his wife had died.

As they stood there, something altered between them. Something almost imperceptible. She knew Travis surprisingly well after these long five days. She'd studied the way his graceful body moved, the way his hands held his horses, the gentle sway of his hips when he donned his guns. She knew and felt and yes, even *hoped,* for the subtle change in his stance now.

Their bodies touched at a thousand points. Each point flared a spark of fire—her shoulder blade where one of his arms had sunk in, the back of her waist along her spine where his other hand slid up her jacket, the tips of her breasts which he pressed against, the muscles along her thighs where he braced his own. Her body wanted him before her mind knew enough to stop.

When she felt the brush of his warm lips against her throat, a quiver flared from her breasts to her thighs. She understood what he was doing, recognized the desires he was awakening in her body, peeling away her resistance in the promise of secret pleasure.

"I can't help myself, Jessica…" he whispered into her ear. The heat of his breath excited her more. "I'm trying to hold back…I've been trying for days…but I can't stop."

"Don't stop, Travis…" She tilted her head slightly

and he dived for her throat, touching, murmuring, fondling. An explosion of sensations gripped her. The warmth of his body pressed against hers. She looped her arms around his waist and let her hands roam at will down his sides. His muscles were ropy and warm beneath his shirt.

"I don't want to be alone," he whispered. "I want to be with you."

Their faces touched. His eyes glistened in the firelight. He looked down at her mouth, made a soft sound and then kissed her.

They moved their lips slowly at first, enjoying the sheer simplicity of a kiss. How could something be so simple yet stir so much feeling in her soul? His lips tugged hers in one direction and then another, and then he gently swirled his tongue along her bottom lip. She kissed his tongue and met it with her own, timid at first, which he seemed to savor. She felt his hand slide from her waist around her front and up until he found her breast.

"Mmm..." she murmured. His hand felt solid and good.

"You've got such beautiful breasts...and a lovely waist...and legs...hmm...gorgeous legs..."

She knew he was exaggerating, but she felt beautiful nonetheless. Beautiful and *wanted,* despite everything he knew about her. Or maybe because of everything he knew about her.

When he reached for her blouse buttons, she knew what his invitation was, and she knew what she was accepting when she let him peel the cloth from her shoulders.

At the time that she'd been intimate with Victor, she hadn't known how to prevent pregnancy. But since reading the medical journals, she'd learned plenty. Making love with Travis now wouldn't produce a child because she was aware of her monthly cycle and the timing was off. May the stars forgive her for she was still a single woman, but she ached for more children. She yearned for the presence of another beating heart inside her womb.

Travis kissed her shoulder. Her heart crackled inside her ribs. He flung the blouse to her blankets by the fire and with his eyes took a long, daring sweep of her body. She felt the wonder of her first time, filled with anticipation and knowledge of what was coming.

He untied the string from her braids and ground his fingers through her hair, clumping his fists around her ears. He brought the hair to his nostril and breathed it in.

"You smell like honey. You taste as sweet." To prove it, he bit her softly at the shoulder, as if he were tasting her skin.

She forgot everything except the harmony between them, the rise and fall of his chest, the pounding of her pulse at her wrist, elbow and throat as his mouth tickled her shoulder. She strained and swallowed quickly. He must have felt it on the palms of his hands, for he pulled away and stroked the ridge along her jaw.

He swung her into his arms, lifting her off her feet before she could resist. But he lowered her quickly to the ground again, five steps away in a cocoon of blankets. His were strewn with hers. He tried to straighten them behind her shoulders, giving them a tug.

He lay to one side of her. His long hard leg was splayed between hers and for the life of her she'd never forget the intimacy of the gesture.

"May I take this off?" he whispered, straining above her, trailing his fingers along the thin strap of her undershirt.

"It's old and ugly," she confessed.

"Not at all. The cotton has worn out comfortably and hugs you in the right places." He slid his forefinger over the mound of her right breast, circling closer to the apex, teasing her body and ripening her need.

"You know today when we arrived at the Murphy's, and I saw you looking at the first little girl we met...Angie...I wanted to pick you up and hold you like this. I wanted to tell you we'd find your son again...but I can't make that promise."

"Shh," she murmured. "Shh... Your trying is enough." She caught his fingers but he untangled them and kept exploring.

"It can't be enough."

Sighing, she closed her eyes and enjoyed the rubbing of his hand, flattened against her breast, then his fingertips drifting over the cloth to the other side.

His raspy voice broke the silence. "I've been afraid to touch you for days."

"Why?"

"I'm afraid I'll hurt you. That you'll be disappointed. That I'll be disappointed in myself."

"Because of Caroline?"

"Yeah."

"You're a youthful man with many vital years ahead. You can't expect yourself to be a saint."

"If this were meaningless—" he struggled to say the words "—my finger dipping up and down the hollows of your breasts, it would be easier. But being with you, I feel as nervous as if it were my first time. I don't know if I can walk away. But I don't know that I have anything to offer."

"Offer me your smile."

His cheek pulled unexpectedly into a grin. The

warmth in his eyes conveyed the difficulty and depth of his feelings.

She didn't want to think about anything except the joy they were sharing and the anticipation she felt for the hour ahead. But she was deeply moved by his words and his tenderness. She stopped his hand when it hovered above her breast and forced him to finally touch her nipple. He tugged at the cloth and the flesh beneath, sending ripples of sensation down her body.

"Can you kiss me like you did the other night?"

"Oh, Jesse…"

He kissed her first on the mouth, then the jaw, then her eyelid. His whispery touch possessed her. He tugged her to a sitting position, rolled up the bottom of her undershirt and chemise and drew them up over her head.

Before her head was fully out of the fabric, she felt his lips on her breast. His mouth was like molten lava, heating and engulfing her flesh. Adrift in pleasure, she murmured in response.

"You've still got your jacket on," she said when she opened her eyes, her voice humming with amusement.

"I can fix that." He rolled to the side of her, hastily slipping out of one sleeve, then the other, his sights remaining on her the whole time. His shirt came off next. "Mother Nature knew what she was doing when she made you."

She hitched her hands behind her knees, still encased in her worn ivory pants.

"I could say the same," she said beneath a roving stare of her own. She could watch the firelight dance across Travis's beautiful body for hours. The bare, broad muscles of his shoulders flexed as he removed his undershirt. A line of hair followed his musculature from chest to belly, dipping lower down his pants.

He came to her and overtook her on the blankets.

"You're disturbing my view. Now I can't see you." While she rumbled protests, he chuckled softly against her neck and bit lightly. His lips blazed a trail along her body. In return, she wanted to taste him and smell him and hold him, never letting go of this moment. She found it hard to believe that they were talking and laughing during such intimacy, but after years of restraint, the freedom to do as she pleased was exhilarating.

His lips reached her stomach. She giggled with the torture of light, fluttering kisses that made her muscles contract and release.

He tugged at her belt and pants. "Can I take these off?"

"What if I say no?"

He grumbled in reply.

She smiled. "Yes."

With swift dexterity, he unbuckled and tugged the fabric hard. His hands roved her thighs, calves and ankles before tugging at her bloomers and removing those, too.

She reveled in the instant feel of cool air brushing the hairs on her skin before she turned to the fire to let herself roast.

"Let me lie on the outside," he offered generously, "behind you where it's cooler."

"But then you'll be cold."

"I don't feel it. I'll roll a blanket behind me."

Turning to her side, she heard the rustle of denim. With him behind her, she felt his nakedness pressed along her spine, his erection against her bare bottom. Excitement raced through her.

He tightened his length against her, stroking her hair and nibbling on her earlobe. He didn't go near any private areas, which served to drive her mad with desire. Stroking her upper arm, he worked his way along to her wrist. When he ran his fingers along the bumps of her spine, he lingered at the top of her buttocks, then kneaded and pressed against the tense bundle of nerves there, sending such a warm feeling of relaxation through her legs she closed her lids and let herself drift in a sea of ecstasy.

Travis layered more kisses along her arm and waist. Gripping the outside round of her thigh, he kissed her throat. With an intake of heated breath, he plied his fingers over her belly, cupping the swell of flesh, then reaching farther for a breast.

He explored beneath the heavy sphere with long, tempting strokes. Travis had the ability to make her feel that sexual intimacy was deeply powerful and *normal* between two people who cared about each other. Unlike the sexual oppression she'd been taught all her life by her father and everyone else.

When he stroked her full breast, she was lost again. His large hand had no difficulty cupping both breasts at the same time. Lightly, he tapped and tugged the nipples. She felt the surge, the heated response between her legs.

"Do you like when I touch you here?" he asked.

"Um-hmm."

He murmured her name in a combination of laughter and undisguised passion as his hand moved to her upper buttock. Still lying on his side behind her, he slid a cool finger into her wet folds, sliding two outer ones along the creases.

"Ahh," she whispered, awash in a pleasure she'd never experienced.

He dipped his fingers farther, then out again, moving in a welcome, gentle rocking. Everything else seemed so far removed from the two of them sharing this time together, encompassed by darkness and forested mountain.

He surprised her by twisting her arm above her head, reaching for a dangling nipple with his mouth as he continued pleasing her from behind with his hand.

The sensations all at once trapped her there in bliss. She was his lover. Travis Reid was making love to *her.*

The rhythm gained urgency. He seemed to know exactly what she needed. She arched back on his hand so that it would reach deeper. Just before her first contraction came, he removed his hand and from the back, slid himself inside. With a breathless cry, she rode his shaft.

The rolling waves cascaded through her body, slowing her senses, making her believe she could feel and smell every sensation about him, every movement and scent in the woods around them. Spasms of heat pulsated deep into her stomach, downward, lower still.

Her climax faded softly. He didn't move, still as rock hard as when they'd begun.

He whispered in her ear, "I love the feel of your contractions squeezing around me. I can't bear to pull out."

But with a gentle nibble on her shoulder, he slid out and turned her. Giving her a kiss on the mouth, he swung his knees to the ground between her legs and lifted himself above her.

He kissed her breasts, leaving her nipples wet and aching for more, making her blood surge greedily again.

Sliding his rough, tanned hands beneath her legs, he lifted her bottom to position himself dead center. She craved for him to enter again, to feel him pressed against her, breast to breast.

With a wisp of sadness, she saw the scarring on his leg and wondered how much it had hurt.

He whispered that it was okay, half his face emblazed by the fire, the other half cloaked in shadowed mystery.

He gulped, his Adam's apple moving slowly as he thrust into her. She gloried in the wonder of mating, in the wonder of watching Travis savor the feel of her.

Reaching lower to cup her buttocks, he pressed their bodies closer. A rasping sigh wrenched from his throat as he released her thighs and lowered himself on top of her length. She enjoyed the feel of his satin hairs sliding against her silky nipples. He flanked her shoulders with his arms, one hand on each side of her head, whispering and murmuring words of passion as he plunged.

She urged him to roll over until she was sitting on top.

Her hair dangled against his matted chest. She lowered herself so her breasts swung against his skin, watching his pleasured face as he closed his eyes and abandoned himself to her touch. By instinct, she moved in a slow rhythm, as he'd done with her. Remarkably, she derived as much satisfaction in giving as receiving.

Then he reached his peak, lips parted in surrender, smothering her golden breasts with hands of awesome size.

She was smiling, she realized, bursting with joy because he made her feel so skilled and wanted, so unlike what she'd felt with Victor.

Collapsing beneath her in a heap of melted muscles, Travis reached for her face, drew it downward and pressed his sweaty forehead against hers. She kissed his looming shoulder and he laughed. "You're good... you're so good...."

"Jesse," Travis whispered in the cool darkness. "If you move just two inches, I can pull my arm out and stoke the fire." The tingles in his arm from having it beneath her neck while she slept began throbbing in a full cramp. Drowsy, she turned enough for him to withdraw it.

Sitting up at the foot of their bedroll, still naked beneath his wool blanket, he clenched and unclenched his fist. It relieved the spasm. A small stack of branches which they'd collected last night loomed to his right. From where he sat, he reached for three and slid them to the fire. He watched the flames curl around the new branches, enjoying the immediate flare of heat.

Jessica was covered up well with her blanket, he noticed. One long, smooth arm lay propped along her head, her wrist tilted against a mass of honey hair. Sleeping soundly, she was interesting to watch. Her eyes moved beneath her lids as if she was dreaming, long brown lashes sweeping upward, eyebrows gently arched, her slender nose with its freckles visible even in this dim lighting and full pink lips parted slightly.

He never would have imagined finding himself in this position with Jessica Haven. He would have readily told anyone who would've asked that not in a century would he ever go near the mayor's daughter. She was not for him.

Yet, look at him. Last night he couldn't keep his hands off her. Now when he looked at her soft figure sprawled in the covers he wanted to repeat their coming together.

He smiled and patted her calf above the covers. And that brought an unbelievable pounding to his heart. It was as if he'd been drugged into a stupor of sleeplessness combined with relentless pain for the past twelve months, and someone had given him an elixir—a dose of Jessica—and said try this, it'll take away your agony.

It wasn't possible, he would have told them.

But then he'd drunk her potion.

Jessica. He patted her calf.

He glanced up at the sky but it was pitch-black, still

the middle of the night. He tried to stop himself from wondering, but he thought about tomorrow. When they awoke, would she look at him with expectation? The forces of reality chipped away at his mind. How could he offer another woman comfort and security, when he hadn't had any himself in twelve months?

God, even while he slept with Jessica, he thought of Caroline and how she had looked and felt. He'd always imagined he'd honor her memory for years to come and not slip into bed with…

He knew material goods didn't seem to mean a whole lot to Jessica anymore, but they were out in the middle of nowhere and she had no need for money here. Would she be different once they returned to Calgary? Neither one of them had spoken about the future, but his mind wandered. If this continued…would he be able to satisfy the mayor's daughter?

But most importantly, what if he couldn't help her with her child? She'd stacked her hopes as high as the sun, and he was right there with her, unable and unwilling to dash them. If something terrible had happened to her son by Dr. Finch's hand or anyone else's, if they were unable to locate the missing boy, then it seemed that everything Travis and Jessica were feeling might come crashing down from as high as those hopes, too.

Nothing beneath their feet seemed to be of solid foundation.

The fire sparked. A flame shot toward him. It flickered on his arm but he brushed it off quickly. Jessica stirred. She was a deep sleeper. Smiling, he joined her in the blankets, glad she was able to sleep on the trip. The days of hard work had exhausted him, too.

When he rested his head on the makeshift pillow, her eyes flickered open. Her lips tipped up at him and she gave a groggy smile. When her hand slid over his bare waist, temptation flared through him.

"We should put our clothes on because it'll be more comfortable in the morning. Here." He thrust a bundle toward her. "Put these on. Jesse," he said, capturing her persistent hand. "You've got to get your sleep."

"I know," she moaned, but her hand explored his belly.

With a humorous tug, he fought with her fingers. He tried to think of what was best for her, despite what he yearned to do all night. "How are we ever going to rise in the morning? We've got to get some sleep."

One mischievous brown eye peered open. "We really should, I know." But her warm fingers slid lower down his belly, tangling with a soft plane of flesh and hair.

Fighting his urge as much as he could, he finally gave in to the drumming of his pulse and the red-hot feel of her skin. He pressed a hand to her stomach and reached up for the swell of her breast. He flicked his thumb over the soft nipple and smiled to himself at how quickly it rose beneath his hand. "We'd be crazy if we started again with so few hours of sleep ahead of us."

She nodded in exaggerated agreement. "I'd be mad to touch you here." Her hand explored the column of flesh that immediately hardened with her tender strokes. He closed his eyes and exhaled.

"We'd be insane to do this." He slid over her at an angle, pressing his lips to her awaiting breast.

With a repressed squeal of laughter, she buried her face in the crook of his neck as he mounted her soft, willing body. "Lunatics…we'd be lunatics…."

Chapter Fifteen

Travis awoke from his sleep, disturbed by a faint noise. When he opened his eyes, the sun was breaking through the tops of the pines. He glanced around and saw nothing but the horses and undisturbed trees.

"Ah," he muttered, sliding up on his elbow. They'd slept too long. He'd meant to get up before the sun. Jessica breathed heavily beside him, still in her night's trance.

It had been quite an evening, he thought, smiling. No wonder neither had stirred.

The horses whinnied. Something was wrong.

His muscles pumped at full alert. In a flash he jumped to his feet. With shirt buttons undone, shirttails flapping against his pants, he dove for his guns six feet away.

"Stop right there, mister."

"Christ," Travis muttered with a chill shivering up his spine. Turning around slowly, he already recognized the heartless, calculating voice of one of the men. Andrew Garwood. When Travis had completely spun around, there stood the other man beside his leader—the scrawny Jeb Lake. Both of them pointed their six-shooters straight at him.

Travis had never liked being on the wrong end of the gun. These men would pay.

"What the hell do you want?" A new terror gripped Travis, knowing Jessica was still asleep and in danger, remembering the bone-deep agony of his other loss a year ago.

"Wake her up."

Bridling his fury, Travis kicked her boot. She rolled over, her clothing rumpled, and smiled. "Lunatic."

Fear he'd never known before wedged in his throat. He nudged her boot harder.

"Again?" she muttered. "I can't keep up with you…let me sleep for a while longer."

"Jessica!"

She jumped to a seated position, bleary-eyed but looking up at him. "Travis?"

His stomach clenched. "Turn around slowly. We've got unwanted company."

She frowned, framed by a halo of messy hair, sitting in her wrinkled blouse. "Could it be Mr. Merriweather?" Concern dampened her expression as she studied his, then slowly turning at the waist, she gasped. "Who are you?"

"None of your business."

Vivid fright swept over her as she clutched the blanket, and she stared at the men.

"Jessica, get to your feet and come here," Travis said slowly.

She ran to his side and he slid in front of her, protecting her. "These are the men I told you about."

"But I thought no one was following us."

"We didn't come up from behind," bragged the scrawny one. "We came from ahead."

"Quiet, Jeb. No need to tell 'em more than they need to know."

"What happened to the McGraw brothers?" Travis asked.

"Can't say."

"Did you hurt them?"

"Can't say."

Damn them. Travis raced to think of a way out. His guns were three feet in front of him on the ground. He could dive for them, roll and likely wound them both, but dammit, that would leave Jessica open to the line of fire.

"Quit thinkin', mister, I can see it in your eyes." Garwood remained calm and steady. His long hair, tied at the back, glistened with dirt and body oil. "Quit thinkin' and keep still and no harm'll come to you. No siree, we're not gonna shoot an officer. We don't need to. We'll be a hundred miles away before you talk to anyone."

"Don't take them all," said Travis, gulping as he motioned to the horses. After all the wretched turmoil he'd been through doing everything in his power to rid himself of the damn horses...dammit after everything... "The Clydesdale's worth the most. Take that one."

"We're not here for the horses."

If they were here to take Jessica on some disgusting—

"Don't get us wrong." Garwood cocked his guns while the other one grinned. "We'll take the horses. Now that we've come this far, it's a bonus. 'Specially since we've crossed the Rockies. Nothing but flat valley beyond. But what we want is something of the lady's."

"What?" asked Jessica, massive confusion in her voice.

"Don't play dumb," Lake taunted. His loose shirt fluttered against his thin chest.

Perplexed, Travis pivoted toward Jessica. "She's got nothing of value. No precious stones, no jewelry, nothing."

Garwood scoured the campsite. He chuckled when he saw her bulging pack. "In there."

"No, please," she begged.

Travis felt her hands dig into his back and he tried to organize his scattering thoughts. "Would someone please tell me what's going on?"

Jessica inhaled rapidly, still ignoring Travis and speaking to Garwood. "How could you know? No one knew."

"We saw you at the bank the night before you left. We saw you go into the vault with the manager. You went in with a large satchel and came out with the same. But it's got to be a lot of money, otherwise you would have talked to a teller. And we know who your father is. He's got a lot of money."

"But I didn't notice anyone—"

"That's the problem with people like you. You never notice people like me."

Travis narrowed his gaze on the two ruffians and swore. He didn't know Jessica, after all. "How much money are we talking about?"

He heard her stammer in protest. He turned his head to see her face stain with guilt.

"Answer me!"

"Two thousand," came the soft reply. Her lashes dipped over the hollow swell beneath her eyes.

He blinked in the brilliant sunshine, unable to believe it. She'd brought a ton of money without warning him, without consulting him. She'd brought these thugs here as if she'd invited them herself.

"Holy thunder," said Garwood with a laugh.

"Please don't take it," she pleaded, her shoulders riveting beneath her uncombed blond hair. "I need it."

"So do we, ma'am. So do we. But you've got plenty more where that came from."

"I don't."

Travis swayed beside her. "Why?"

She raised hesitant fingers to her forehead. "For Dr. Finch. To bargain with him for the whereabouts—"

"Bribery money," he scoffed, shaking his head in the pounding silence.

"Ma'am." Garwood inched closer, looming over the dying fire. "I want you to lift the bag and carry it over here. Nice and slow and don't try anything funny. If you go for your guns," he said, motioning to Travis, "we'll shoot, officer or not."

"Let *me* bring you the bag," Travis tried to insist.

"No. Stay there. Don't move. Lady, you go."

With a shaky breath, she stepped out and around Travis to her saddlebag, ten yards away beneath a sprawling cottonwood. Travis looked on in utter disappointment. It mingled with the contempt he felt for the two bastards pointing guns. He took note of their size, weight and shape. He heard the thud of horses' hooves behind them, but couldn't glimpse more than two shapes of white and brown between the tree trunks. But before, when he'd first met them on the trail, he'd paid attention to the branding on their horses' rumps.

Realization dawned on Travis. "Jessica, when I met you and Merriweather Sunday morning at the fort, I heard the sound of two horses echoing in the town streets behind you." He flicked his chin at Garwood. "That was you."

Garwood shrugged but a small grin slid to his filthy mouth.

Jessica dropped the bag at Garwood's feet.

"Ma'am, if the opportunity were better, I'd haul you up on one of those horses and take you with us. Unfortunately, we've got to run."

As Travis and Jessica stood with their hands planted in the air, Lake untied all five horses. Garwood transferred wads of money from Jessica's pack to his. They didn't bother with the saddles lying across the logs before leaving with every last horse.

It was impossible to tell just by looking at Independence that she was in foal. Travis knew because he'd arranged for her breeding, then later had done the physical examination to confirm it.

These men were riding off with a mare that shouldn't be ridden hard. And could easily develop serious complications.

Travis choked with sadness.

Never in the past miserable year had he ever anticipated that he would be sorry to see that horse go. Never.

Behind him, Jessica groaned.

He wheeled around and, with deep accusation, glared at Jessica.

Distraught, Jessica paced the campfire ten minutes later. "Travis, please talk to me. I'm deeply sorry for what's happened, but I'm not the thief." Her hands trembled with hatred at what those men had done.

Without a word, Travis picked up two buckets and stalked to the river. She followed his long steps there and back, feeling as if she were a child, as she had the first day when she'd walked into the stables offering him a proposition.

Eager to make amends, she watched as he doused the flames. "That's a good idea. We've got to put out the fire if we're going to continue on."

He tossed the empty buckets to the dirt. They clattered on stones. She winced at the sound.

He stalked toward her and clamped his firm hands on her forearms. Then he shook her. "Carrying that amount of money without telling me was damn stupid." He pushed away, rubbed his mouth and peered down the wooded trail.

"I'd like nothing more than to point my finger down the road toward Riverpoint Junction and tell you you're on your own. Maybe you don't care about putting your life in danger, but you put mine there, too."

Shaken, she dipped to right the fallen buckets. "I had no reason to believe anyone knew about the money."

"Not only have I lost every saved penny I put into those horses, but Independence is in jeopardy. Dr. Finch is leaving for Vancouver in a little over twenty-four hours. And you and I are stranded in the middle of goddamn nowhere."

She knew he wouldn't leave her in the woods, alone. She opened her mouth weakly then thought it best not to reply. With his explosive temper, nothing was certain.

"What did you think you were going to get?" he demanded. "A congratulations for being able to keep your money a secret? It's not a bloody secret. They knew. You, adrift in your lah-dee-dah world, didn't even see them watching you!"

Twigs snapped beneath her boots as *she* flung the buckets this time. "They're wrong about people like me, and so are you. When I took a closer look at the leader, I realized I *did* notice him. When I came out of the bank, he and his scrawny friend were standing in the alleyway talking to Clive Monahan."

"The baker?" Travis flicked his Stetson upward.

"That's right. I passed and tried to nod hello to Clive, wanting to tell him how much I enjoyed the cake he baked for the social my sister gave on my return, but Clive ducked into the shadows so I kept walking."

"Why couldn't you tell me about the money? Why did you lie to me?"

"I didn't lie," she said, but knew he didn't see it that way. He flagged a hand at her, shook his head and backed away to begin hiding the saddles in the bushes. She realized that meant he planned on walking somewhere.

Remorseful, she picked up the buckets and stacked them beside the saddles. "What would you have done differently if I'd told you I was carrying cash?"

He kneeled and opened his pack, removing some gear. "I would have forbidden you to take it."

"Exactly." She rolled up a blanket.

"I thought you'd changed, Jessica. I believed you when you told me you were no longer that pampered woman. But money has never been a problem in your life, and just like every other time, you're trying to *buy* your way out of this one."

His words hurt. She sank to her knees, blanket in hand. "What choice did I have?"

"There are laws in this country." He hiked up from the ground. "You follow the laws. I'm supposed to help you abide by them."

She dragged her pack next to Travis's and fumbled with her ties. "Those laws didn't work for me. I told my father what Dr. Finch did and I told the private investigator. The only person I had left was myself."

"You had me. But you and your kind always run things by the almighty dollar."

She flinched at the awful words.

He dragged her pack closer to his feet and took over. So helpful with the packing, so cruel in his judgment. "I'll never take your word at face value again."

The statement felt like a blunt thrust to her chest. Opening her mouth to breathe, she answered quietly. "Do you know what I remember about that icy night in Montreal? Dr. Finch ordered my breasts to be bound tight with linen for seven days. To restrict the natural flow of milk so my supply would shrivel and I wouldn't get engorged. That's the merciful thing they do for women who lose their children. It's none of your business what I do with my money. It's not your child. You have no idea what I feel."

Half an hour later seated on a log, Jessica still hadn't calmed down. She felt her heart racing and wondered how circumstance could turn so drastically.

Keeping to himself, Travis finished hiding their gear and equipment, packing only the essentials they'd need to travel on foot. They kept their packs plus the extra items he'd tied to the bottom of his—one pot, a small ax, three canteens.

"Don't forget to pack your little gun," he said.

"Right."

He'd obviously concocted a plan but wasn't eager to share it with her. Where was the tender man who'd made love to her last night? The man who'd coaxed kisses from her lips and promises from her body?

Now when she looked into his eyes, she saw contempt and detachment. It chafed a part of her soul she hadn't realized Travis had touched.

She should have stuck to her original plan of not getting involved with any man—*not even considering it*—until she found her son. Rubbing her cheeks to freshen herself, she tried to focus. *Her son.*

Despite the robbery, she still aimed to get to Devil's Gorge, with or without Travis as escort.

Travis bent to her saddlebag. He tore it open and ripped out a page from the back of her journal.

Alarmed, she bolted to her feet. "What are you doing?"

He gripped her pencil. "Sketching the brands I witnessed on their horses. I'll use the information later."

"When do you plan on going after them?" Panic clamped her throat. They didn't need the diversion now. They needed to get to Dr. Finch first.

He didn't answer directly. "Do we both still agree we need to get to Devil's Gorge?"

She nodded vigorously and rubbed at the kink in her neck. He still believed her story about her son and was going to help. But his cool stare of disapproval let her know where she stood. He was an officer and as such would help her find the man who'd taken her child, but Travis no longer approved of her.

He hoisted his heavy pack to his broad shoulders.

She toyed with the straps on hers. "I know this is inadequate, but I'd like to compensate you for your horses. I'm sure my father will repay you when we get back." She wanted to reach out in some way to Travis, to remove the sole burden from his shoulders and take the responsibility of the theft upon her own.

He peered down at her. "You don't understand, do you? It's not about money."

Saddened by his response, Jessica flung her pack over her shoulders, adjusting the makeshift leather straps Travis had applied. She understood that no amount of money could replace his fine horses—could replace the wonder of Independence as she carried her unborn foal. Jessica understood his bond with those animals, but every time she mentioned it he tore her head off for that, too.

Travis pointed to the shrubs. "We'll leave the rest of our things here. I'll come back for them on my return or send a man. For now, we've got to put our energy into getting to Devil's Gorge and put our disagreements aside."

"I can do that." But seeing the disdain when he looked at her made her ache.

"Fine. Let's go, then."

Nodding, she adjusted her brown cowboy hat then tucked her derringer into her waistband. She stepped down the trail toward Riverpoint Junction, but Travis stepped in the opposite direction.

"Where do you think you're headed?" he asked.

She thumbed the air to her left. "Back to the Junction to borrow some horses. I thought we could borrow some from the Murphy's to get us to Devil's Gorge."

"That's an eight-hour walk in one direction. Finch is leaving for Vancouver in twenty-four hours. We'd never make it."

"What was your plan?"

He nodded at the forest. "We take a shortcut. Our only hope in reaching the gorge within twenty-four hours is by foot through the trails."

She peered into the shrubbery where he pointed but saw no paths. "What trails?"

"A number of them pass through these mountains. They were set up by old miners and fur trappers. They're impassable by horse. You could take a mule, maybe, but the paths are so overgrown and steep that you'd be taking your chances."

She hesitated. Climb mountains and river canyons? She rocked with self-doubt. Was she physically capable?

He studied the turmoil she felt racing across her face. "We could go back to Riverpoint Junction if you think you can't make it by shortcut. It would take us longer, but I could leave you behind when we reached Devil's Gorge, if I had to, to head to Vancouver and catch up with Finch."

The sound of ice pellets hitting roof shingles echoed

in her ears. A vision of a crying newborn peering out from a blanket popped into her mind. "I'm coming."

"You know," he added, "there's only one road for Garwood and Lake to take to Devil's Gorge before they can run in any direction to freedom." He pointed. "It's the same road we would have been taking."

"What does that mean to us now?"

"It means if we make it through the shortcut, we'll get there before they do."

"What?"

"Then all we have to do is notify the Mounties and wait for the horse thieves at the end of the trail."

As she staggered under the weight of that disclosure, Travis parted the branches and led the way. With a deep, uncertain breath Jessica followed, wondering how much harder this grueling expedition would become. How much more difficult it would be sharing the next twenty-four hours with a man who'd made love to her last night, but who couldn't stomach talking about it today.

Alarmed at the complexity of the wound, Abraham Finch removed his hanky from his suit lapel, wiped the strings of sweat from his bushy eyebrows and looked down at the bloody foot.

The lumberjack lay sprawled on the examination table, dosed with chloroform by Hopkins, who stood nearby waiting for further instruction. Yesterday while chopping a tree, the lumberjack had severed part of his foot. It dripped blood on Abraham's new leather cover, the sound ticking in time to the doctor's speeding pulse. He swore softly. The padding had cost him a fortune. Worse, this patient was one of a handful who might skewer Abraham's fine reputation for healing.

Abraham had insisted he couldn't help the man, but his fellow lumberjacks waiting outside the door had insisted he could.

Abraham squinted at the injury, wondering what to do next. Most of the toes were mangled and needed to be removed, but Abraham knew if he amputated the big toe, the man would have problems—perhaps unnecessary—ever again being able to maintain his balance while walking. Sweat continued to pour, weaving down the width of Abraham's broad jowls.

"Please hand me the biggest knife," he said to Hopkins.

The assistant did as he was told. Abraham felt sorry for the lumberjack—after this, he'd certainly lose his method of earning a living. But Abraham would be damned if he'd allow him to lose his gait. As a newly appointed surgeon, he would remove the minimal amount of damaged tissue, all the toes except the big one, and pray like hell for the man to recover.

When he was nearly through and bandaging the foot, a knock sounded on the door.

"Yes?" He looked up through the fading light slanting through the side window. It was getting dark.

A face he hadn't seen in quite a while peered around the thick plank of oak. "I know you're leavin' for Vancouver tomorrow, Doc, but you gotta help me," the man begged. " My son…please…you gotta ride out and see him."

Chapter Sixteen

After twelve strenuous hours of walking, every long muscle in Jessica's thighs ached. She heard Travis's rhythmic breathing three feet ahead of her in the dense brush—a loud exhale as he pushed low branches from her path, followed by a deep inhale as he looked back to ensure she was safe.

The sunset dimmed beyond the forested mountains and she prayed for a rest.

"We do know one thing more than we knew before," he said, coming into a clear spot, stopping on a grassy hillside.

She stood adrift in knee-high plumes of wild grass. The rich scent was intoxicating, inviting her to linger. Her legs pumped with blood. The soles of her feet ached. "What's that?"

"The baker." With a gloved hand, Travis tilted back his Stetson. "Clive Monahan. He's involved with the two who stole our horses. Thieves somehow tend to know about each other. They stay out of each other's path. Maybe Clive knows something about Pete Warrick and the trial."

She hadn't thought of it. "It's possible." Her lightheadedness caused her to roll back on her heels.

Travis inspected her, as he might an ill child, or one of his troops. "Sit down." He motioned to a looming boulder.

She stumbled backward, grateful to plant herself onto something immovable. It felt wonderful to remove the weight from her swollen feet. But if she removed her boots, she might never get her throbbing feet back into them.

He pulled out a canteen and offered it. "Drink."

His words were more like orders, but in some ridiculous way they were soothing, as if he was taking the time to notice her discomfort. *Leading* her through it, as a sergeant major.

"Are your feet sore?" he asked, sliding off his pack, then removing hers.

"Yes."

"Put on another pair of socks. They'll cushion your feet. I'll do the same."

"You mean we're not—we're not breaking for camp?" She tried to cloak her weariness, but it crept into her words.

Crouched low at her feet, he stared at her again but she couldn't see his face for the setting sun behind him. When he rose, he cast a shadow over her and the boulder, ten feet long. Peering above at the screeching birds, he slid out the compass from his pocket. He opened its cover, lay it flat in his palm and pivoted slowly, watching the needle.

"We've made good time. But Dr. Finch is leaving for Vancouver tomorrow."

His outrage at Dr. Finch was still driving him.

"We can't walk in the dark," she said.

"Why not? Animals do it."

"But they're nocturnal."

"We can be, too. We don't know if Finch is departing early in the morning or late afternoon. We don't know if he's taking the stage or the train. But what is certain is that we need to walk another ten to twelve hours to get there."

She rubbed her face, knowing that Travis was right. Devil's Gorge opened up to a fertile valley floor in British Columbia. Although no methods of transportation crossed the Rockies from there to Calgary, plenty hooked up to the western side, and Dr. Finch had several avenues of escape.

Jessica untied the laces of one boot and slid out her foot. The woolen stocking clung to pounding toes.

Before she could stop him, Travis fell to one knee, gently cupped her heel and propped her foot on his thigh.

"What are you do—" When his hands began to massage, she knew exactly what he was doing. "Ohh," she groaned in bliss. "Do you do this for all your troops?"

"Only if they're women."

She found that humorous and giggled. He remained composed.

"Ohh," she whimpered again when he exchanged one sore foot for her other.

He worked his way up her calf. Her lashes fluttered, unsure of where he would take his hands. Sadly, she recalled how deeply she'd wounded him by not telling him about the two thousand dollars. But he'd hurt her, as well, too stubborn to see it from her point of view.

She'd do anything to see her son again.

His fingers slowed. The massage finished.

"Let me exchange the favor," she mumbled, rising higher on her boulder. She reached for her pack for an extra pair of socks, pulled them on and then her boots. "Let me help you relieve the soreness in your feet."

He rose, cordial and blunt. "No, thanks. My feet are fine."

He closed his mouth firmly, reached for his pack and his extra pair of socks, and she realized there'd be no further discussion.

Travis always left her standing in the cold.

After five minutes of rest, she struggled to her aching feet. Her pack was trapped beneath his so she yanked. It barely budged. "Yours is so much heavier than mine."

"It's easier for me to carry more weight."

Her pack weighed about ten pounds, but his had to be close to thirty.

"Shall we go then?" Every bone, every organ, every hair on her skin throbbed with overexertion.

His gaze flickered over her body, registering a sentiment she hadn't seen in twelve hours—sympathy. "We'll rest here for two hours."

"Don't rest on my account."

"I need the rest," he murmured, but she was all too aware it was she who was dragging them down. "Unroll your blankets and try to snatch some sleep."

It was roughly four o'clock in the morning when Travis heard Jessica call. So she'd finally detected the limp in his walk which he'd been trying to hide.

"Travis, don't tell me you sprained your ankle."

He spun around, the weight of his pack feeling as if he'd strapped a two-thousand-pound cow to his shoulders. Even though she was walking only five feet behind him, he could barely make her out in the dark. "It's just my sore leg. But there's no sense worrying about something that can't be helped."

She joined him among the Douglas firs and dropped her pack. It hit the soft ferns and echoed through the trees. A faint waterfall tumbled in the distance. He could smell its coolness—runoff from the glacier's summer melt.

He motioned ahead. "Two to three more hours. We're almost there."

Peering down at his leg, she wouldn't be so easily swayed. "How much longer can you go? Let's rest."

"*I* don't need to rest," he insisted.

"I do," she said in much the same tone he'd used on her earlier when he'd pretended he needed sleep.

A squirrel scampered across their trail, scuttled up a fallen log and waited boldly for them to pass.

"Sit," she instructed. "Among the squirrels. And drink." She handed him the canteen.

It wouldn't hurt, he thought, and so relented. He sat on a fallen log. After several seconds of guzzling, he lowered the canteen to his waist. "There's something exciting about walking through a forest in total darkness."

"I know," she whispered. "I feel like I'm in church and we might disturb the congregation if we talk."

So far, they hadn't seen any large animals, for the animals could likely hear the couple approaching from a hundred yards away and therefore hid from view. But as they sat on the log, listening quietly, Travis pointed out a dozen elk passing fifty feet to their right. The animals created a moving black wall of shuffling beasts.

Travis tried to organize his thoughts. He was still angry with Jessica, but could appreciate her grit and endurance.

The taut pull on his muscled thighs screamed for rest. His eyelids felt so weary and dry that when he blinked, they seemed to scratch his eyes.

Jessica was a mother searching the earth for her lost child. He could appreciate that but somehow in the midst of it, she'd lost sight of Travis. He was here, too. By not divulging the money, she'd made him feel unimportant in her life. He wondered how much she'd actually felt in his arms, and whether she couldn't help knowing, however unintentional, that getting close to Travis would help her cause.

Well, he wouldn't have any more of it. After he deposited Jessica in Devil's Gorge, he'd go alone to the Mounties and get their help in tracking Dr. Abraham Finch. Jessica was too emotional to speak to Finch directly and Travis too affected to watch her. This interrogation needed a calm, deliberate head, away from a puzzling woman.

Despite his limp, he rose to his feet. He'd never had to walk on his sore leg this far and was unsure how he'd manage for another three hours.

But then, nothing had ever felt this important. "Let's go."

Dawn light glimmered over the rushing water as they broke through the forest to meet the river's edge, so close to Devil's Gorge it made Jessica tremble.

"We're here." Travis eased his pack off his shoulders and sat on a mossy boulder.

"Where?"

"Turn around," he said softly, pointing above her shoulder. "To your right."

In that second, a feeling of wonder rushed through her skin, of having fought so hard to get here and now the fear rushed in. Would her hands come up empty as they had so many times before? Or would they find Dr. Finch and would he admit…? She had no money to bargain with. All she had was her intelligence and the determination of the man—*the friend*—standing with her.

When she turned, she saw three mountains looming in the distance and nestled between them sat an ice field, rounded on top like the mountains, but translucent whitish blue. It extended for miles. In the foreground was a till of churned gravel and dirt that the glacier deposited as it retreated every summer.

"I didn't think it would look like that."

"What did you think?"

"It's like another mountain but it's made of ice."

"And that's only one finger of the glacier. It meets up with a massive block of ice farther into the mountains."

"How much does it melt in the summer heat?"

"Not as much as you might think. It retreats two to three yards a year. In the cooler months, it's covered with snow."

She sighed, enthralled by the beauty. A skinny lake rippled to the glacier's left, milky green in color and surrounded by a coniferous forest. The Glacier River that ran beside her boots weaved its path up to the glacier's right, leading to a steep gorge about a mile away. There, a village sprang out of the cliffs. *Devil's Gorge.*

She felt her pack lifting off her back.

"Take this off a minute," said Travis. "Give it to me."

Moved by the moment, Jessica stumbled backward and slid to the boulder beside him.

"We're here," he murmured. "The original proposition."

"I know you're not happy with me, Travis." She slid her hands along her pant legs and realized how filthy she'd become in twenty-four hours. Her nails, usually neatly trimmed ovals, were ragged and encrusted with dirt. Her pants were streaked with black loam. And beneath the looming brim of her cowboy hat, her hair, braided in two, felt heavy and flattened by sweat.

Leaning back against a tree, his body equally mired in dirt, Travis removed his hat.

"I know you're not happy with me," she continued, "but I'd like to say thank you for getting me this far. Whatever happens from here, thank you all the same."

He tightened his jaw and clenched one forearm across the other. If he was thinking about her thank-yous, he had no response other than a nod.

Thumbing his dark, matted hair, he still radiated masculinity despite his limp, which had worsened. She suspected he thought he was successful in masking it, but every time he'd turned a corner in the past hour, she'd winced along with him.

She peered through the golden haze of dawn, over the vision of lake and stream and glacier. "What time is it?"

He pulled out his pocket watch. "Six forty-five."

"When's the earliest time you think Garwood and Lake might be arriving with the horses?"

"They'll be nervous, so they'll be riding fast. Eight o'clock at the earliest, I figure. An hour and a quarter away."

A faint neighing disrupted them. They strained to find its source.

"The horses," he whispered, pointing past her to the green meadow. "It's the same herd of wild horses. This is their territory. They make this trek back and forth all summer long."

She noticed the pain expressed in his face as he watched the herd, the tight lines etched around his eyes, the muscles pulled around his lips, the flicker in his cheek. Was he sorry he was giving up his private life of horses and breeding? Was he agonizing about where Independence might be?

The sound of a bellowing locomotive echoed in the

valley, disturbing their placid moment. Squinting to find its source, Jessica saw the train chugging toward Devil's Gorge.

She jumped to her feet, knowing what it meant. "Everything I've been dreaming about for the past year is waiting for me there."

Travis cupped her shoulder. The peaceful touch of his hand rooted her, coming at a time when she thought she'd burst with panic and weakness. "Are you ready?"

Chapter Seventeen

From a distance, it appeared the town of Devil's Gorge and its people were still asleep, but when they neared, Travis noticed bustling energy in the early-morning air.

One man was herding a dozen bleating sheep through the center square toward the stockyards, another rolled through town with a wagon load of chopped timber heading for the sawmill, and several shopkeepers were rolling back their awnings and unlocking doors. The sound of the gorge waterfall rushed through the air, and when the wind blew right, a sprinkle of water refreshed their skin.

Since they were concerned about the train schedule, they stopped at the depot first. As they entered, Travis pointed to a flyer tacked to the door. "It's Dr. Finch's medical rally in the town square today. At eleven o'clock."

"It says he's selling medical supplies."

"When's the next train leaving?" Travis asked the man behind the ticket counter.

"Not till noon. Need a ticket?" The man looked over the two of them and seemed unaffected by their dirty appearance.

"Where's it headed?"

"The farming valley, then Vancouver."

"I don't need a ticket today but I was wondering if Dr. Finch has bought his yet."

"Can't say he has. I thought he was taking his own caravan this time."

"I've got a meeting with him before he leaves. Might you direct me to his office?"

"Just down the road," said the man. "Big yellow house on your left. Are you injured, mister?" He looked at Travis's leg as he limped away.

"I'll be fine."

Travis clutched at Jessica, his hand lingering on her pack. To an onlooker, the poor woman likely looked as if she'd been living in the mountains for weeks and was in desperate need of a good meal and a bath. To Travis, she looked like what she was—a resourceful, tenacious woman persevering against the odds and clutching to the hope that the doctor would be there when they knocked on his door.

"Travis!" A male voice called across the platform. "Reid, is that you?"

Travis peered around the log wall and waved to one of the men he and his father had sometimes sold their cattle to.

"Hey," the man shouted across an aisle of passengers disembarking from the train. "Ben at the livery stables tells me you're comin' in with three gorgeous broodmares. I'll drop by later to catch a glimpse!"

Travis withdrew. He nodded curtly over the heads of other passengers and felt Jessica's stare.

Leading her by the elbow, he gently weaved her through a mix of people—farmers, drovers, old men and young children, all seemingly interested in the soiled woman at his side.

Jessica ignored them but Travis was aware she was nervous.

When they reached the outer doors, he dropped his hand.

"Jessica, there's an inn by the livery stables." He peered in that direction and it was still there with its burnished wooden sign reading, Rooms to Let. "You could use a rest and a hot bath. Let me do this alone. The Mounties' outpost is just past the edge of town, overlooking the main trail to Vancouver. There should be three men inside. I'll enlist their aid and we'll—"

"Let me see Finch. I want to see his face when I ask if he remembers that night in Montreal, if he remembers which medications he administered that made me so groggy. When I ask what he did with a baby in the middle of an ice storm."

Although they were both plastered with dirt, Travis didn't look as rough as she did. Hell, all kinds of men came out of the mountains looking all kinds of ways, but a tirade from a crazy-looking woman like Jessica against a smooth-talking man like Dr. Finch wouldn't go down easy in this town.

"It's best if us men handle this, Jessica. Not because we're men but because it's our job and we're good at it."

"I'll be quiet. I won't interfere."

"You can't be quiet. You will interfere. The sight, the recognition of you might back him into a corner. He might not answer any of our questions."

"Nothing on God's green earth can make me stand outside his door while you're walking through it."

Travis heaved in a breath of morning air.

"I don't think he'll recognize me right off. We met briefly in Calgary years ago, and then in Montreal but only for a few hours that night. I don't look the same."

"Not today you don't."

"Why don't you knock on his door? If he's there, I'll keep him talking until you go and get the other Mounties."

"You'll keep him talking?" he asked in disbelief. "No. We'll knock on the door together. If he's there, *I'll* step in and talk and you get the other Mounties. You won't have any trouble finding the outpost. It's clearly marked at the end of this road."

They agreed and headed toward the big yellow house on the left side of the road. The waterfall rumbled beneath their feet.

The house stood on the opposite side of the street. When they reached it, they slowed to a stop.

The size of the mansion elicited a small gasp from Jessica. Workers were already out, tending to the spotless gardens. One man stood on a ladder adjusting the eaves, another collected wild roses planted in the flower beds. On the other side, a woman dipped her cloth into a steaming bucket of water then wiped one of the stained-glass windows. As if in a carnival, up from the side of the house bounded a man and three longhaired golden dogs. The trainer held biscuits above their noses and when he snapped his fingers, the dogs rolled over in unison.

Travis knew Dr. Finch had a home in this town, but he'd never had the need or curiosity to visit. He had no idea of the wealth the man had amassed. Finch could afford the finest lawyers and solicitors. Jessica had said she'd signed papers when she'd released her child. Although she couldn't quite recall what those papers were—a death certificate or not—Travis would bet his only compass that the papers protected Finch.

It wouldn't be as easy as simply walking in and asking questions.

Travis cleared his throat and led Jessica through the picket fence.

He went to rap on the door with his knuckles, but Jessica pointed out the shiny brass knocker. He used it instead.

A matronly woman dressed in a starched black-and-white uniform answered. "Good morning. May I help you?"

She glanced at Travis, then Jessica. Her eyes flickered over their soiled clothing. Then down to Travis's holsters and the tip of the derringer tucked into Jessica's waist. The woman didn't look pleased.

"We're here to see Dr. Finch," said Travis.

"Is he expecting you?"

"No. I'm a friend of his from Calgary. He told me if I'm ever in the area, to please drop by." Travis helped Jessica slide her pack to the porch, then removed his. He gave the woman his most charming smile. "Well, I'm in the area."

"He's busy. You'll have to try later." She tried to close the door.

Travis dived for the brass door handle and held it firmly. "I'm Sergeant Major Travis Reid with the Mount—"

"He has an injured leg that the doctor needs to see," Jessica blurted. "We need to see the doctor immediately."

Travis scowled. There was no need to talk about his leg, or to sound desperate. He slipped his leather billfold from the inside of his vest, opened it and showed her his police badge.

The tension in the woman's round face gave way to concern. "I see. Please come in. You look like you've been traveling for weeks. Have you been on duty, sir? Is that how you've injured your leg?"

"We've been traveling for seven days and had a mishap on the trail."

"I'm sorry to hear it. If you wait in the doctor's parlor, there's a basin of water and fresh towels you may use. I'll get someone to help you."

Someone? Travis didn't like the sound of that. They wanted to see the doctor himself. He turned around to tell her so, but the efficient woman had disappeared.

"My God, look at this," Jessica whispered behind his shoulder.

Suddenly aware of the opulence inside the home, Travis turned slowly, taking in the granite columns, the mirrored wall that reflected his grubby appearance, the tin ceiling above his Stetson and the highly polished pine floor beneath his spurs, inlaid with a border tile of granite to match the columns.

He hissed in disgust. Then he saw the waiting room. With windows reaching to the floor, the sunny room was at least sixty feet long and thirty deep. Bigger than the entire cabin Travis had been born in. Plush upholstered chairs lined the walls, mingling with low tables. Packed in every corner and on every tabletop were newsprints, advertisements, samples of medical products and modern gadgets that you, too, could own for a very small sum.

"Son of a bitch," said Travis. "He's got a hunger for money."

"And limited medical know-how that he lords over his patients." She picked up a pamphlet, read to herself, then commented. "What person wouldn't want to extend their lives, to live pain free and supply their loved ones with good health?"

Travis walked among the gadgets. He didn't know what half of them were, but they were shiny and polished and promised relief. He picked up a hairbrush attached by wires to a square battery. The newsprint beside it claimed the electric hairbrush would cure headaches. It also stated that in no case should more than one person use the same brush, or it would lose its full curative powers. Travis shook his head. That ensured that each member of the family would get their own.

If Travis's mother were suffering from horrible headaches—as some women did—and Dr. Finch came along and said, *Here, try this,* wouldn't Travis spend the fourteen dollars to buy her one?

Dammit, he would. And that's why the despicable bastard needed to be stopped.

Travis picked up a brown jar and shook it. The tablets inside rattled. He read the label. "A Remedy for Gaining Healthy Weight." He sighed.

Picking up what looked to be a corset rigged with wires, Jessica snorted. "This is what my sister wants to order. An electric corset sure to cure anything bothering a woman."

Travis shook another bottle, this time filled with liquid. "This one says it's a cure for gonorrhea."

"There's no cure for gonorrhea, only ease of symptoms."

Travis unscrewed the cap and sniffed. "It smells like pure alcohol."

"It probably is, mixed with colored water."

"How do you know all this, Jessica?"

"From my research for the journal."

"If you know so much, then so do the circles you worked in, and so how can men like this get away with lying?"

"There are good people trying to put an end to it. These days, doctors are required to get a medical degree from a proper college. Licensing of physicians and surgeons is a vital component, too. But North America is large and some of it yet untamed. It will take some time." Her face tightened. "But we're here, aren't we?"

He looked above her shoulder to the wall. "A medical degree."

Jessica set down the corset and stepped over to read the certificate. "Glasgow."

"It looks authentic."

"It doesn't make sense. Did he graduate? Is he doing this simply for the money and because he has a blackened heart? Couldn't any of his professors see him for what he is?"

Beside the degree were several other frames mounted to the wall—two plates containing labeled spiders and another one harboring a metallic gray rock which was labeled as a meteorite fallen from the sky.

Looking farther to the corner of the room, Travis spotted a sideboard holding a basin of water and folded towels. There was a closed door beside the corner and as he walked closer, he heard muffled voices. Maybe one of them was Dr. Finch's.

His stomach tightened with anxiety. "Let's wash up. There's a mirror."

Jessica's hands shook as she splashed her face with water. The freckles on her nose paled in color as she gazed to and from the closed door.

Travis was just drying his hands on the towel when the door opened.

Jessica sprang to his side.

It wasn't Dr. Finch who stepped out. A man, a bearded farmer it seemed, sauntered out in overalls. His skin had a sickly gray tone. Clutching a piece of paper, he spoke to a thinner man dressed in a satin vest, cravat and ironed white shirt. "Thanks. I'll get this filled at the apothecary and I'll—I'll send my wife around with a pie as payment."

"Don't worry about payment, Grady. And getting it filled at the apothecary—" he lowered his voice "—is a little cheaper than having me fill it here. I know you've got another kid on the way. You should be feelin' more yourself by the end of the week. Take care."

As Grady left, the thin man looked to Travis and Jessica. "Come on in, folks." Clean shaven, he smiled at Jessica. "What seems to be the problem, here, with your husband?"

A hand shimmied up her throat. "No, no, we're not married."

"My leg isn't bothering me that much," Travis offered, sidestepping Jessica to peer through the open door. "How did you know we were waiting? I didn't see the housekeeper go through this door to tell you."

The man gave a jovial laugh. "We've got another private door inside. She told me you're a Mountie. How can I help you, Officer?"

The inside room smelled clean, of disinfectant and floor soap. A new leather examination table sparkled in sunlight. Bottles glistened. A row of instruments lined a cupboard counter. However, the room was empty of people.

"We're here to see Dr. Finch."

Jessica stepped boldly into the inner office. Travis didn't want to upset the man, but he readily followed Jessica.

"Dr. Finch isn't here. But I'm his assistant, Taylor Hopkins. I'd be pleased to be of service. I've been workin' here many years and often pick up the slack when he travels. No need to be timid. I imagine there's no illness you can confide that I haven't heard before."

Disappointment washed through them. Travis noted

Jessica's lips parting nervously. "Has Dr. Finch left for Vancouver?"

"Not yet, ma'am. He's out on a call at the Baker ranch."

Travis scratched his chin, noticing the sparkle return to Jessica's face. "How far is that?"

"Three miles west."

Mr. Hopkins continued smiling and Travis realized he might know this man. "Are you related to Fitz Hopkins?"

"I'm his son. One of two. My brother is the tax collector. You know him?"

"Well, son of a gun," said Travis, hopeful that this was a good man. "My father and I sold some cattle a couple of years back to your old man."

"Ah, the Reids from Calgary."

Travis heard Jessica grow impatient. She rubbed her hand along her waist and cleared her throat. But Travis knew there was a fine line between being friendly with folks and getting them to talk. Some officers barreled right through their inquisitions, but he felt the fine hand of camaraderie went well with polite questioning. Besides, he knew this man's family and Travis's immediate reaction looking into the fella's clear eyes was that he wasn't aware of what his boss was doing.

They chatted for a moment about the town and the weather. Jessica inched toward the cupboards.

"What are these?" she asked, stricken with a look of horror.

Travis glanced down at the wooden trays filled with implements—tiny steel saws, scalpels and sutures.

"Surgeon's supplies, ma'am. No need to fret. They're necessary tools—"

"Dr. Finch performs *surgery?*" she said, aghast. Travis felt his heart kick.

"Yes, if you think you might need help with a problem, I'd be happy to have a look—"

"Since when?" she demanded. "Since when does he perform surgery?"

"A couple of months. He's had an interest in it for years. Ask him—he'll tell you all about the surgical courses he's been taking in Montreal."

"Do you travel with him?" Travis asked.

"No, sir, I never go. I hold down the fort here."

"What sort…what sort of training do you have?"

Mr. Hopkins rocked back on his heels, perfectly relaxed and at ease. "Nothing formal. Dr. Finch trained me for the past six years. I've read every volume of his medical texts—the ones that line this room." He pointed to the shelves. "I can't get enough of learning about medicine. Of course, he's taught me the practical things."

Travis twitched. Performing surgery cast a whole new light on the despicable Dr. Finch. "When do you expect Dr. Finch to return?"

"Well, he was up all night with one of the Baker boys. Appendicitis, he figures, but not acute enough for surgery."

"Thank God," Jessica muttered.

"Beg your pardon, ma'am?"

"I'm glad Dr. Finch won't be operating."

"That what Mrs. Baker said, too, when I visited this morning." He glanced at the wall clock. "Dr. Finch told me he'd be back in two hours. Roughly ten o'clock. We'll start the medical rally on time, pack Dr. Finch's remaining bags and he'll be leaving by two this afternoon."

"Two o'clock," Travis repeated.

"That's right."

"We'll be back to see him sometime before then. We

don't have a medical problem, just wanted to drop by and say hello."

"Mighty kind of you. He appreciates the company. Take care, now."

Mr. Hopkins walked them to the front door. As they left, he hollered, "By the way, where are you stayin' in town?"

Travis exchanged a worried look with Jessica. The man seemed trustworthy, but he didn't need to know they'd be staying at the inn. "At the outpost with the Mounties."

There wasn't a spare room at the outpost, certainly not one for a woman, but Travis was betting Hopkins wouldn't know that.

A hollow feeling wove through Travis as soon as they left the house. Looking at Jessica's despondent face, he knew she felt it, too. It was as if they'd been building their expectations for days to see a magical wizard. They'd been inside his house and seen inside his craft, but the wizard wasn't home. And all their emotions leading up to this—anxiety, fear and tension—were reaching a breaking point.

"What do you think of Mr. Hopkins?" Jessica asked Travis ten minutes later as they hurried along the boardwalk. She peered down the road to the large log building with a wooden tower and lookout. The Mounties' outpost. The sound of the gorge waterfall echoed off the buildings behind them, anchoring her orientation to the town.

"I wanted to find some reason to dislike him but I couldn't. Even when we overheard him tell that other man—Grady—to get his prescription filled somewhere cheaper, it indicated an honest man trying to do an honest day's work. What do you think of him?"

Her eyes flashed. "Sorry, but I don't trust anyone."

Travis carried both packs, one slung on each shoulder. Jessica marveled at his stamina. She was so tired she could barely put one foot in front of the other.

"That nervous knot in my stomach only seems to be getting bigger. This has to end soon, Travis."

"For the moment, I think it's going to get worse." Travis looked at his pocket watch to make his point. "Seven-thirty."

She sucked in a breath, making a soft whistling noise. They could expect the men who stole their horses to be passing through within half an hour. She peered over her shoulder and Travis did the same. Nothing had changed from previously—folks were going about their business on an early Saturday morning. There were no signs of Travis's broodmares.

Relief bombarded her weary frame when they walked through the doors of the outpost and were met with three friendly faces. One of them was a sergeant. He commanded two constables.

"Travis Reid, you old dog. Have a seat."

Travis introduced Jessica. He seemed to know the sergeant, but the constables were new to him from when he'd last visited. Travis outranked them all.

"Sergeant," said Travis. "Can we go inside your office? There's pressing business to discuss."

"Certainly. Would you like a cup of coffee, miss?" He pulled the pot off the cast-iron stove. "Just cooked it."

"I'd love one."

They stepped into the private office and sipped those coffees as if they'd never tasted anything finer.

Travis explained the situation to the sergeant—the theft of their horses, and then the allegations of Dr. Finch being a charlatan. Travis held back on Jessica's accusation that Dr. Finch had taken her child and sometimes went by the name of Dr. King. She would have held back the information, too, at least until she knew she had the utmost security in trusting the sergeant.

"May I speak frankly, sir?" asked the sergeant.

"Of course," said Travis.

"We'll help you in the matter of your horses. If the men are caught red-handed with the broodmares, the crime is easy to prove. But sir…Dr. Finch…he delivered my sister's child last year and has taken good care of my own when tuberculosis befell us last year."

"I want him for questioning. That's all. There's more to this story but this is all you need to know for now. Don't allow him to leave for Vancouver until I've questioned him. That's a direct order."

"Yes, sir. Shall we go to the Baker ranch and get him?"

"There's no reason to disturb the Bakers. We can wait." Travis rose and slid his empty coffee cup to the desk. "I'd like to take one of your men to the inn with us to guard Miss Haven. We need to wash up and perhaps Miss Haven would like to rest her eyes."

"No, Travis. I'd be afraid to put my head on the pillow in case I slept right through to two o'clock."

They hurried out of the room. The sergeant briefly summarized to the constables what Travis had told him, then swore them both to silence.

Travis described his stolen horses and the two thieves.

"Constable Kenyon," said the sergeant. "Go with them. Keep your eye on the main street. From the trail, they have to pass through town and by the inn. Blow your whistle if you spot the broodmares. We'll set up another watch on the far end of town. One shrill blast on a whistle means trouble. When Dr. Finch returns from the Baker ranch, I'll be waiting for him at his home. The sergeant major will join us at any point he sees fit."

Travis and Jessica left the building with Constable Kenyon, leading three horses between them—one belonging to Kenyon, two borrowed for Jessica and Travis.

The three of them walked to the inn with the constable insisting he carry both packs. Jessica was so grateful to get the cement brick off her back she could have kissed him. And equally grateful to get it off Travis's, so that he might find relief for his limp.

The rush of the waterfall filled the street. It lulled her with its melodic sound. It was half a block from their inn. Travis took a diversion so she could witness the falls in person. They approached the gorge from its top. Trees lined the river on both sides, thicker on the other ledge where no buildings stood.

Ropes cordoned the area for five hundred feet, likely to keep animals and children from falling over the gorge. Rooted on a rocky ledge next to Travis, she looked down over the falls, its clear greenish depth mesmerizing her, the speed of the water making her heart rush. "It's the most dangerous thing I've ever seen."

"Magnificent," said Travis.

They reached the inn and took two adjoining rooms on the second floor, facing the street. They ordered a meal to be sent to their rooms, then headed straight up the stairs. Constable Kenyon would watch from outside the front door, beneath their balcony.

The balcony flanked the building and after Jessica washed up and changed into clean skirt and blouse, she stepped out to feel the breeze on her sticky skin. Travis was already there in his fresh black clothes, leaning against the rail. He looked formidable dressed in black, muscles tightening like a black jaguar ready to pounce, a daring look in his eye.

She leaned in beside him, her blue blouse tucked inside her clean brown skirt. Their sleeves brushed and she felt the hair on her arm bristle in arousal. "When I'm with you, Travis, I feel safe."

It was a strange reaction in the middle of such a dangerous situation, but she wanted to acknowledge how she felt.

He angled his head in her direction. The movement emphasized the tense muscles in his face, the power in his jaw. "Don't drop your guard yet, Jessica. You never know what's coming."

Someone knocked on the door. Travis pressed his finger to his lips to silence her, withdrew his gun and moved her behind the wall. "Who's there?"

"The innkeeper with your food."

Travis let him in and, after the man departed, they ate their delicious barbecued beef and rolls on the balcony.

Jessica rested her head against the chair back for just a moment, it seemed, when Travis was nudging her shoulder. "Wake up, Jessica."

Alarmed by his tone, she reeled forward on the chair and slammed both feet to the ground. She'd fallen asleep. "What is it?"

Travis whispered, staring out at the street. "Andrew Garwood and Jeb Lake just rode in."

Chapter Eighteen

Travis watched as a fearful hush fell over Jessica. Peering over the balcony, they watched the two men lead the five horses straight through town, headed west toward the coast. Travis came alive with fury. These men had held them at gunpoint and had stolen every last dollar of investment Travis had in the world.

But with relief he noticed Independence—and the other horses—seemed to be unharmed.

Garwood and Lake tilted their hats low to shield their identities and stuck to the outside perimeter of the road, as if to lose themselves in the crowd. No one paid them notice.

Travis remained still but glanced down at the landing. Constable Kenyon was there, whistle perched in his lips, staring nervously from the thieves up to Travis. Travis shook his head to signal the man to refrain from whistling. The thieves would hear it and run.

"You've got to go after them," whispered Jessica.

Hell, he wanted to. He clenched his fists, primed for a fight. "It's almost ten o'clock. Finch is due back any minute. I can't leave you alone to face—"

"You've got to go after them. You've got to get Independence. She doesn't belong with them."

Travis looked again to the constable, who still held the whistle in his lips and motioned with his hands. *What do you want me to do?* he seemed to be asking.

You're too close. Don't blow the whistle yet, thought Travis.

But the constable blew the whistle.

Garwood's horse jerked in response. Garwood turned his head to the inn to identify the noise. The Mountie ran out of sight, likely to get his horse. Garwood's gaze shot straight up the balcony to Travis. Garwood's eyes blazed with disbelief. Alarmed, he clamped down on his hat, sunk his spurs into his horse and tore off. Independence spooked, and tied to the other horses, bolted behind Garwood.

Folks in the street screamed. They scuttled their children out of the path of oncoming horses.

"Wait here for me!" Travis yelled to Jessica. He vaulted over the balcony as she let out a cry. It would have been a vertical drop except for the roof slope of the first floor. Travis slid down the rough cedar shakes, barely noticing the splinters and scrapes along his legs, keeping a firm grip on his guns.

He raced for his horse, untied it and galloped west. He hollered for people to get out of the way. One astonished man, turning the corner with his dog, dived for the boardwalk.

Travis saw the constable a hundred feet ahead. Out of the side street came another mounted constable who followed his partner. Travis suspected the sergeant was likely taking care of business, waiting at Dr. Finch's house. A cloud of dust rose from the street, but at least all the people had cleared out.

Travis felt the wind at his ears, whizzing around the leather ties of his Stetson, whipping at his skin and racing over the blood pounding in his veins.

Slow down, he called silently to the thieves ahead, slow down so no harm comes to the horses. Garwood and Lake were free in their saddles, but Travis's five horses were roped together and didn't stand a chance if Independence remained spooked. Galloping in a frenzy, they'd tumble mane over hooves and snap their necks. If one went down, they all did. And this stress on Independence could cause her to abort.

A cry tore from Travis's throat.

Goddammit, everything he ever wanted—to be rid of Independence for good—wasn't what he wanted at all.

They left the town behind. The cloud of dust following Garwood and Lake and the stolen horses loomed a mile ahead of Travis. Hell, they weren't slowing down but speeding up.

This could only end in disaster. If Travis gave up now, maybe the men would slow down. Maybe Independence and the other horses might be saved. But the Mounties in between them made it impossible for Travis to make that choice. Even if he stopped, they wouldn't. With heads pressed low to their mounts, they were racing with guns drawn. One fired in the air.

Travis's heart careened.

The riders dipped into a green meadow and he followed. From the corner of his eye, he spotted the herd of wild horses. Their ears pricked up. More trouble. They spooked easily and if they ran, if they caused a stampede…

It happened quicker than he thought possible. The horses began to gallop parallel to them. Fifty beautiful animals, neighing, some with heads tilted in the direction of the riders, a moving mass of lean muscle and power.

Garwood and Lake couldn't seem to hold on to the rope of stolen horses.

Travis's team of five, led by Independence, began to drift closer to the wild ones. Independence began to slow and was soon enveloped by the herd.

Travis no longer cared about Garwood and Lake—he galloped closer to his animals. Lost in the herd, he rode with them for half a mile before he felt a slackening in the pace. The gallop soon became a trot, which subsided to a complete standstill.

Every muscle fluttered in his body.

Travis sat on top of his horse in a sea of animals, trying to get his heart to slow down. Twenty feet away, still tied to the others, Independence was silhouetted by a looming, glistening wall of ice.

He slid to the ground. His legs buckled with exertion and emotion. He reached out and stroked Independence's muzzle. She moved beneath his hand and he let out a long, wonderful sigh.

"You scared me," he said softly, patting her sleek soft hide. "You scared me."

She nuzzled his hand.

Travis heard trotting hooves in the distance behind him. Turning around, he watched as the Mounties swung closer. They stopped two hundred yards away so as not to disturb the herd. They held their guns pointed at Garwood and Lake who were still mounted, but disarmed and holding their hands in the air, both seething.

Travis snarled at the thieves. "I'll give you one guess. Where do you think you're going?"

* * *

Abraham Finch fussed over his cravat as he peered into the gilded mirror in his front-hall entry. Blazes, for a self-appointed surgeon, he'd better learn to make his fingers work better over knotted cloth. They were a bit stiff.

Hopkins opened the door, sales equipment in hand, baggage spewing with tonics and medical devices. "Shall we go, Doctor? It's eleven o'clock and I believe the crowd is waiting."

Abraham stepped off his front porch into the lovely morning. "What's all this ruckus, then? I heard galloping horses and people screaming."

"I'm told the Mounties are after horse thieves. That's what the sergeant told me as he raced by."

"Thieves?" He clicked his tongue. "Good grief, some people are lazy. Refuse to lift a finger to make an honest day's wage. They don't work as hard as you and I, do they, Hopkins?"

His assistant nodded. The man was reliable, thought Abraham, proudly. This morning when Abraham had returned from the Baker ranch, where the boy's fever had subsided, Hopkins had quickly finished the packing for Vancouver. He'd told Abraham that an acquaintance had dropped by to visit, Travis Reid. Apparently, his limp was bothering him, but so far, Reid hadn't returned. Abraham's bags lined the hallway and the porter was already loading the private stage that would take Abraham and two hired hands to the coast. If Reid reappeared, Abraham would be happy to treat him. But if not, it would have to wait for another time. Abraham was bound for Vancouver to visit with his only sibling, his brother, an honest businessman who advised Abraham with his investments while he enjoyed the warm weather of the coast.

Things had turned out well this morning. Abraham had given the Baker boy an elixir that had chased the eight-year-old to the privy. It seemed that was all the boy had needed.

With hands free, Abraham tipped his silver walking cane to and fro as they marched to the town square. "Were the horse thieves caught?"

Hopkins puffed beneath the weight of the baggage. "Yes."

"Good. Ah, here we are." Abraham beamed at the waiting faces. A splendid crowd, indeed. A splendid crowd for a splendid surgeon. Lord, he did love the way that sounded.

Approximately forty people crowded around the temporary platform as he took the three steps. It was nothing more than a corner of the boardwalk, but Hopkins had already been here. Medical bulletins had been tacked to the posts, proclaiming the wonders of galvanized spectacles, powders for lice and foot fungi, tobacco and pipes for gastric disorders, and personal hygienic tools.

"Last chance, folks," Abraham shouted from the platform. "I won't be back for eight months, so it's your last chance to buy directly from a *surgeon* for any ailment you may have!"

Hopkins stood beside him but two steps back. That was the man's only flaw, Abraham realized. Hopkins didn't seem to take to the blatant advertisement in Abraham's summer rallies.

"How does that thing work, Doc?" shouted a youthful man, pointing to a metal box balancing on the rail.

"Well, now, let me show you, Mr. Johnson." Lifting the lid, Abraham saw a movement in his peripheral vision. It came from the intersecting street. The town's

Mountie sergeant raced around the corner and stopped when he reached the crowd. He puffed out of breath, scanning the heads. The man always seemed to be rushed, so Abraham didn't pay him heed. When the sergeant glanced up at him, the doctor nodded in acknowledgment.

The sergeant placed his hands on his hips and didn't seem as friendly as he usually was, but then he was trying to catch his breath.

Abraham turned back to his work. "You've got a frail grandfather, don't you, Johnson, that could use muscle development?"

The young man shouted, "How's that supposed to help?"

Abraham removed two steel dumbbells from the case. They were wired to a battery. "Electric weights. The small jolt—nothing that hurts or might harm your granddad—stimulates the muscles and makes them bigger."

"Well, I reckon if Grandpa ever tries out as a circus weight lifter, I might get him a pair!"

To Abraham's disgust, the crowd snickered.

A woman in the back raised her hand. "Why are your prices so high?" Her voice shook.

Abraham scowled. Troublemakers sometimes created a stir at his rallies. He had a quick tongue and could usually put them in their place, but he'd never been harassed by a woman. A cowboy hat shielded her face, but two blond braids dipped around her shoulders. A blue blouse, tucked inside the pleats of a brown skirt, clung to her figure.

"My prices aren't high if your husband's working, ma'am."

The crowd murmured in embarrassment for her.

"If he's not," Abraham cooed in the sincerest of tones, "I will gladly work out an arrangement, if you'd be so kind as to hold your questions for me privately."

"Why does the apothecary sell some prescriptions at half your cost? I compared prices thirty minutes ago. The apothecary is standing there, ask him yourselves!"

A thunder of voices rumbled through the crowd. This woman grated on his nerves. He turned to Hopkins for help, but the assistant's mouth dropped open in dismay. His eyes widened as if he recognized the woman.

"My tablets and powders are better made, madam!" shouted Abraham. "They're purer and more effective!" Desperate, he looked to the sergeant and gestured—*commanded*—that the man shut her up. With a sigh of relief, he saw the sergeant headed her way.

But then the son of a bitch just stood there beside her with his arms crossed as she continued ranting.

"Most of your lotions don't work! Does anybody here…*anybody*…feel that Dr. Finch has ever over-charged them?"

No one spoke. The rumblings died down to utter silence so deep that Abraham heard the horse tethered at the hitching post twenty feet down lapping water from the trough.

Johnson spoke up. "You charged me a fortune for my grandpa's crutches, Doc! When I visited Calgary two months ago, I saw them at half the cost!"

"That's—that's the price of doing business, lad! You can't expect me to transport crutches all the way from Calgary and charge you what it cost me."

"That's right!" shouted someone on the doctor's side. "Last year when my tooth needed pullin', there was no one else in town who'd go near it. You all know what a toothache feels like! And Abigail Withers, don't you recall how he set your broken arm? And Grady, how he fixed your heart?"

"I don't know about my heart," said Grady, placing

his hand on his chest. He looked awfully pale, thought Abraham. Almost gray.

"Come see me after the rally, Grady!" shouted the doctor, his vigor returning. "I'll hold off on my private journey just to have a look at you!"

A horse and rider turned the corner at the mercantile, capturing Abraham's attention for a second. A large man dressed completely in black stared at him with unwavering cool eyes. He was too far away for Abraham to recognize.

"Haven't you done enough for Mr. Grady?" the blond woman persisted. "Where were you on the night of February 3, 1890?"

Abraham lost his temper. In a flash his rage surfaced, something he never displayed in his rallies. "Who the hell are you to speak to me like that?"

At that moment, the rider slid off his horse and strode to the woman's side. Abraham tilted his head in faint recognition, but the stranger's face was also masked by a hat and several days' growth of whiskers. He put a hand around the woman's shoulder and Abraham realized their connection. Likely a penniless man and wife who wanted medical care but could ill afford it. "Mister, get a handle on your woman! Sergeant, take her away! She's a troublemaker!"

People gasped. Voices boomed. Heads turned.

"I recognize you," some man mumbled at her.

"That's right," said Johnson. "I grew up in Calgary. I remember you from your father's campaigns when he used to put you on his shoulders. You're the mayor's daughter."

The crowd murmured. "The mayor's daughter!"

Abraham Finch tasted bile at the back of his throat. Perspiration drenched his forehead. February 3, 1890.

He had been in Montreal. First as Dr. Finch, and then as always for his lecture series, Dr. King.

Frantic, he packed his wares, stuffing them into sacks.

A commotion rippled through the crowd.

"Grady!" someone shouted.

Abraham continued packing, cold sweat gripping him, terror squeezing his heart.

"Grady's collapsed! Dr. Finch, please help!"

"Mr. Grady!" Struck with fear, Jessica fell to her knees. People swarmed around them, shouting at the gentleman to rise.

But he couldn't. Mr. Grady's skin had mottled, his hand was cool and sweaty. His lids closed. When Jessica placed a finger at his wrist, she noted his pulse flickered in and out.

"What can I do?" Travis, dressed in black, kneeled beside her. He removed his jacket and placed it beneath the fragile head.

"Unbutton his shirt. Give him air. Everyone, please stand back!" Desperation clung to her words. She jumped up and scanned the boardwalk to see the old man running. "Dr. Finch!"

The doctor stopped and pivoted. He looked to his assistant, Hopkins, who stood frozen on the platform, not knowing which way to turn. A storm of fury lit Finch's eyes as he glared at Jessica. "I tried to help you in Montreal."

"What medicine did you give Mr. Grady? *He* needs your help. Please prove me wrong and show us that you're a healing man."

Fear took hold in Dr. Finch as he looked from her to Travis to the sergeant. "Officer Reid," he said, barely audible. "The Mounties." With a burst of fresh anger, he slapped his leather bag and scurried down the boardwalk. "Hopkins! Come along!"

Jessica dived to give Mr. Grady emergency aid—things she'd learned in Montreal lectures—anything to help the now unconscious man.

"Sir, Mr. Grady needs our help!" Mr. Hopkins yelled over the crowd as she unbuttoned the poor gent's collar to get him to breathe.

"Hop-p-p-kins!" Dr. Finch shouted, his voice lost behind a building. "Come alo-o-o-ng!"

"Go to hell!" Hopkins raced to the fallen man and dumped the doctor's bag to the ground.

"It's not the right medicine," Hopkins whispered to Mr. Grady. "I tried to tell him you have angina, but he laughed at my appraisal and insisted on the newest heart tablets from Montreal. They're triple the price. I tried to tell him."

Gently, he slapped the man's face but there was no response. He rifled through his medical bag and found ammonia. He waved it beneath the man's nose but still no response.

In a panic, Jessica realized he'd stopped breathing. Her mind racing, she remembered reading about the Paris Academy. They recommended assisted breathing for drowning victims and she wondered if it could work here. She puffed into his mouth twice. It didn't seem to help.

The crowd gasped. "What are you doing?"

She ignored them and, checking his pulse again, turned to Mr. Hopkins. "He's lost his pulse."

Without hesitation, Mr. Hopkins took his fist and thwacked him on the sternum.

Mr. Grady responded with a grumble but the crowd began to push Mr. Hopkins. "He's beating the man! Stop him!"

"No!" shouted Jessica. "He's responding. There's a European doctor who claims that compression squeezes the heart so it begins to beat again."

If that *one* whack didn't work, though, there was nothing more she could do to help.

Mr. Grady tossed his head and muttered incoherently. The crowd murmured. "He's comin' back!"

Swamped with relief, Jessica sat back on her legs and watched the man regain his healthy color. His breathing recovered and pulse rebounded.

Mr. Hopkins was overcome with emotion. He rubbed his mouth with the back of his sleeve and sobbed, "Grady, you've got another little one coming into the world. You've got to stick around."

"Looks like he's going to be all right."

She felt an arm around her shoulder. When she glanced up, Travis was peering down at her. "Mr. Grady is in good hands with Hopkins and the sergeant. Let's go find Dr. Finch."

Terror struck her again. Finch had disappeared and there was no telling, now that he'd recognized her, if he'd tell her the truth about her son. She'd spent precious moments with Mr. Grady while Dr. Finch had time to think. All he had to do was stall them. Keep his mouth shut and there would be very little they could prove. *If* they found him.

"He went this way," said Travis, leading her down the street toward Finch's home.

Compared to previously, the grounds were eerily deserted. Travis didn't bother knocking. With his guns drawn, he threw open the front door, hurried past the frightened housekeeper, and called out, "Finch! We know you're in here! We just want to ask you a few simple questions!"

As members of staff came slowly through closed doors, Jessica and Travis didn't know who to trust. So Travis pointed his guns at everyone as he waved his badge. "Mounted police. Police business, folks, nothing to panic about. The town sergeant knows I'm here. We just want to speak to Dr. Finch."

"He's in the back," whispered a butler. "He's packed his carriage and he's left."

Jessica ran for the back door and stumbled into the yard. A closed coach sped out of the carriage house. "Stop!"

"Stop in the name of the law!" Travis hollered beside her.

Jessica took her pistol from her waistband and began running.

"Don't shoot him," warned Travis, running beside her.

"Like hell I won't." The carriage careened around a corner. She held up her left hand, propped the gun she held in her right across it and took careful aim. Her shot missed but when Travis fired, the front wheel popped off.

Crippled, the carriage crashed to the ground. It skidded. The two drivers slid off their seats. The horses neighed and reared.

Jessica trained her gun on the carriage. She drew closer and kicked open the door while Travis flashed his badge at the coachmen and ordered them to sit at the side of the road beneath his guns.

"What is the meaning of this?" Dr. Finch bellowed from inside the broken coach. He flung the curtains back and glared through the window.

"Come on out of there, you yellow coward," said Jessica.

"No one talks to me like that."

"Get out, I said, before I blast a bullet hole between those ugly eyes."

Dr. Finch gasped. "You won't get away with this. Officer Reid, may I say that after the last time we met, when I gave you evidence against that criminal Peter Warrick, may I say I'm shocked that you would stand there with your hands in your pockets. You tell this crazed woman to step off."

Travis raised his hands in the air, indicating helplessness. "She's pretty hard to convince. I've tried. It's best you go along with her requests."

The old man glared at Jessica and, since she wasn't under the influence of medication this time, saw him clearly. He was withered and scared. Trembling, in fact. Yet here was the man who everyone feared to go against.

"I'll tell your father about your rude behavior," he warned. "He'll be ashamed that his daughter could point a gun at a surgeon of my caliber."

Her hand tensed on the trigger.

"Easy," drawled Travis.

"Get out." She kicked at the door again. Pride was this man's flaw, and she would goad him till he exploded. She believed he *wanted* to explain how smart he was. He *wanted* to tell her what he'd done with her child.

The man stumbled over the first step and fell to the ground. "Please, the mayor would be happy if…if I opened one of my shops in your town. Think of the business it would bring to Calgary."

"You're nothing but a frail, tired man. My father wants nothing to do with you," she said, prodding. "He told me…in fact he told me to tell you never to set foot in Calgary again after what you did."

Finch didn't like the sound of it. His eyes bulged. "Your father doesn't know what's good for him. I was the one who took care of business for him, wasn't I? I was the one who got rid of the bloody problem before he had to carry it back to Calgary, unwed daughter and all!"

Finch began to disintegrate. He rocked to a sitting position and tried to heave up, stretching out his arms for help, but no one offered. With a wail of self-pity, he pushed himself to his feet and dusted off his fine suit. The coachmen stayed their distance, shocked to see their employer held by the law.

"My father says you're on your own." Jessica shook as she continued to push. She believed whatever plan Finch had concocted, he'd done so without her father's knowledge. She'd seen the look of sorrow in her father's eyes after he'd been told his first grandchild had died. He'd even hired a private investigator to help her. "My father says he won't stand behind you. Not since he discovered the truth from Pete Warrick."

She gambled by mentioning the trial and didn't look at Travis to see what he thought of her trick.

"That son of a bitch Warrick!" Finch shouted. A small crowd had begun to form. "You're going to believe him over me?" He pointed to several curious faces in the crowd. "I graduated with honors, I tell you! I don't care what he says, my degree is not a forgery!"

Jackpot, thought Jessica, gasping in delight. She glanced at Travis whose eyebrows shot up in surprise.

"And," said Travis, walking up beside her with his intimidating stride. "We'll go easier on your sentencing if you tell us what happened to Jessica's baby."

Jessica agonized at the words. She lowered her weapon and silently pleaded for her baby's life.

Travis showed the man some kindness. He sat him down on the steps of the coach. "Abraham, I know you've never been behind bars. Prison looks nothing like the homes you live in. Shorten your sentence. Tell us what happened that night."

A sob broke from the old man's throat. "No one was harmed. The judge will see that. I'll tell my lawyers…I wanted to help the mayor with his shameful situation. When he confided in me, I recommended Miss Waverly's Home for Unwed Mothers. I was going to save the baby for adoption…for my brother and sister-in-law who…who had problems conceiving. I'd heard the mayor once say that his family was descended from English royalty…I thought the baby would be special, and safe with my brother in Vancouver."

Jessica swallowed hard, lifted her chin and forbade herself to fall to pieces.

The broken man continued. "But when I returned from Montreal heading for the coast, I got word that my sister-in-law had delivered. I didn't know what to do… I—I…meant them no harm…I made up a story and gave the babies away. They're in a foster home."

"Babies?" Jessica whimpered. Blood drained from her limbs.

"Twins," said the doctor, full of shame. "You gave birth to twins. Callie and Bobby."

Jessica sank to the curb, too stunned to react. "I don't believe it," she whispered. "Two?"

Abraham could barely meet her gaze with his remorseful one. Travis, wordless, peered at her with tender amazement.

"How is this possible? I was recently told they were fourteen months old. They're not the right age."

"They are. They were born small. Twins often are but they'll catch up with their growth."

"But how could I not know I was carrying twins?" Jessica asked.

Finch sighed, broken and shaking uncontrollably. "Sometimes in the womb the positioning of one baby is directly behind the other. When I examined you, I never heard a second heartbeat because one twin must have been lying behind its mate."

Could she dare allow herself to believe? Her heart thumped madly. "That's why I remember holding a boy in my arms, but the records say it was a girl. It was both."

Dr. Finch closed his weary eyes. "I'm…so…sorry…. Please tell the judge I'm so sorry."

Tears sprang to her stinging eyes. Travis was a blur. Could it finally be over? "My great-grandmother was a twin," she said. "I heard stories of how they had to keep the girls warm by the fire all winter because of their size."

The sergeant came barreling around the corner toward the coach. Chaotic activity whirled around them. Twenty minutes later, Dr. Finch was led away in handcuffs.

While Jessica was still trying to come to terms with the news, Travis eased in beside her. He planted one soothing, warm hand at the back of her neck. They stood in the street. He rubbed her neck gently as she contemplated the astounding news.

Travis rocked her. "They're alive."

"And I've already kissed their soft cheeks." A cry of relief burst from her lips. She closed her eyes and buried her face in Travis's waiting arms.

Chapter Nineteen

In the livery stable six hours later when things had settled, Travis had shaved and they'd slept—as much as they could—Travis watched Jessica. She sat in a pile of hay fingering the children's imprints in her journal. Within an hour, they planned to leave for Riverpoint Junction on their quest to meet the twins.

She looked up as he approached. "Is he here yet?"

"Any minute." The buyer of his broodmares, Duke Shepherd, was due to arrive and Travis hoped his new proposal would be accepted with the same thought and consideration he'd given it. Negotiations over horses were never easy, and Duke had high expectations.

Travis eased himself to the hay beside her. After his six-hour sleep, his limp had nearly disappeared. He put a large hand over the scrawling on the page.

"B for Bobby and C for Callie."

Running her fingers over the page, she smiled but the smile was shaky. Then tears welled in her eyes and spilled over. She rubbed her cuff over wet cheeks.

Through this whole ordeal, he'd never seen her cry like this. "Hey, hey. You *found* them," he repeated.

She inhaled a laughing sob. "These are happy tears."

"And tired ones. You've been through a lot."

"And scared ones. The twins are supposed to be adopted."

"Not when their mother is alive." He grinned. "No, sir."

He watched her grope for words.

"Travis, I...when no one else believed me, you came along...and I...and I wanted to say how much I appreciate you."

He dipped his finger along the swell of her cheek, marveling at the soft hairs. Her nose was runny and her eyes swollen from the emotion of the last six hours, but he'd never seen a finer-looking woman.

"Your children are lucky."

"Oh, Travis, it's been so *un*lucky for them—"

"Lucky," he insisted. "They've got a mother. And she doesn't take no from anyone."

She no longer had to worry about Abraham Finch. Although his solicitor had turned up to protect him almost as soon as the sergeant had taken him to the jailhouse, his confession had been witnessed by four people. Finch's solicitor had refused to allow Finch to answer questions about Pete Warrick's trial, so Travis would need to speak to Warrick himself when they returned to Calgary. Finch was using some sort of blackmail on the man, but Travis would get to the bottom of it. Warrick had to be guilty of something because he went to prison without disclosing his hand.

The horse thieves were sitting in the other jail cell. Travis had learned no physical harm had come to the McGraw brothers. The horse thieves had confessed they'd untied the McGraws' horses while they were sleeping. So it was anyone's guess what direction the brothers had headed when they awoke. Any shots they might have fired to catch Travis's attention would have been too far away to be heard.

Jessica's money had been retrieved. The thieves had no time or place to spend any of it.

And Grady had recovered in his home. Hopkins was tending to him and together with the apothecary, they'd figured out a new plan for his medications. Blood dilators, Hopkins had insisted, and Grady's color had returned immediately.

"Travis Reid!" A lanky red-haired man entered the stables.

Travis took a last, lingering look at Jessica before he rose to join Duke.

"Thank you," she mouthed silently, and he filled with a deeper pride than he'd ever felt for anything else he'd ever accomplished in his life.

He hadn't anticipated or prepared for the toll her journey would take on him. He felt elated that Jessica had found her children, that they were healthy and happy and just as taken by the beauty of life as she was. And when he sat beside her, his pulse raced and his mind flew, trying to untangle the web of difficult emotions he felt.

Twenty minutes later, Travis had finished shooting the breeze with Duke and was down to the business of negotiation. The three of them, standing in the stall, huddled around Independence. The mare had seemed spooked at first, but had recovered nicely after the six-hour rest. Jessica stood quietly on the other side with a brush in her hand, grooming the mare.

"You can have the Clydesdale and the other quarter horse," said Travis, "but I insist on keeping the mare that's in foal."

"And I insist you sell her to me. She's a beauty and the one I was looking forward to the most."

"Let me keep her, Duke."

Duke waved his papers. "We've got a contract. We shook on it."

Discomfort settled on Travis. He rubbed his neck. "I'll abide by the contract. My word's my word. But I was hoping you'd allow me to buy her back."

Duke stared at him for ten seconds, narrowed his eyes and then sank back against the stall boards. "Hell, Travis. You don't make this easy."

"Let me buy back her contract."

"You're placin' me in a difficult position."

"I didn't mean to do that."

Duke picked a length of fresh straw from the pile beside him and stuck it in his mouth. He chewed. "You take the horse, then, but give me the foal. Leave the mare with me until she delivers and then come back next spring for her."

Travis patted the smooth red flanks. "I've got plans for the foal, too."

"Aw, hell. I hate it when I lose out on a good horse."

Travis grinned. "We've got a deal then." He held out his hand.

Duke grumbled and slipped his palm against Travis's. They shook. "Yeah, we got a deal." The huge man tore up the paper that pertained to Independence. "I don't reckon you owe me extra for breaking the contract, since I never spent a penny to get her here."

Travis shook his head, amazed at the man's generosity.

"But listen," said Duke. "Next spring, I get first choice at any other horses you might own."

Travis rubbed his clean-shaven cheek.

"You are continuing, aren't you? Don't give me any

bullshit about you quittin' the business. You are gonna buy more horses and breed 'em, aren't you?"

Travis glanced at Jessica's pinched face as she nervously awaited his answer.

"Yeah," said Travis, tilting back on his boot heels, filling with a deep calm. "I've got something else in mind for Independence, but when I get home, I'm buying a new ranch."

"Are you sure this is the right thing? That you want to do this?" Jessica's soft words rolled through the green pasture as they rode their horses along the crest of the mountain slope that overlooked the glacier.

Travis inhaled the early-evening air, enjoying the solitude invading his body. "Couldn't be more sure."

The setting sun hit a mountaintop and streaks of red emblazed the valley and the massive block of ice. Travis nodded to Constable Kenyon, who was accompanying them to Riverpoint Junction, and the man fell behind. He carried official, written instructions for the Murphys about Jessica's children, and would help investigate the whereabouts of the McGraw brothers along the trail.

On their mounts, Jessica and Travis weaved a path to the top of the grassy ridge. Travis led Independence by a rope.

Down below, the herd of wild horses galloped in the wind, their manes flowing like ribbons, their muscles flexing in the ripe rays of the sun. Fillies and colts galloped along the outer edge while they watched, and Travis knew he was bringing Independence home.

Wearing his worn leather gloves, Travis swung off his horse. His spurs jangled when he hit the grass. Stepping to Independence, Travis gave the horse a final pat.

Then with an ache which burned at the back of his

throat, he removed his gloves and allowed himself the joy of stroking her glossy hide one last time. She felt smooth, warm and calm. She turned her head and nuzzled the air in his direction.

A saddle creaked, then Jessica was standing beside him. "She's been a good horse," Jessica said.

"Yeah, she has."

Travis removed the rope around the broodmare's neck. Her saddle and lines had already been stripped and given to Duke Shepherd, her front shoes removed by the farrier at the livery stable and hooves trimmed. Mother Nature would take care of the rest, as she had for the mustangs.

"Have a good life," Travis whispered to the horse. He gave her a pat on the rump and she was gone.

Shoulder to shoulder, he and Jessica stood staring as the horse plowed down the grassy slopes, headed straight for her new herd. Sunlight caught her dark forelock, outlined the proud lines of her head, the majestic curves of her neck and mane, and the regal proportions of her legs.

Her dark tail rolled gently in the wind as she bore down the meadow. The other animals stood and watched and when Independence slowed to approach, their ears pricked up and they hesitated.

Then Independence whinnied. Other horses responded, and soon she was lost in a wave of undulating colors as the horses sped through the valley—an ocean of chestnut, roan and black as they galloped past the milky-blue glacier.

Jessica touched his sleeve, entranced by the vision below. "Tell me again. Will she be all right? Will her foal be all right?"

"She'll be fine. The horses will take care of each other."

"Do you think you'll ever see her again?"

Travis rubbed his hand along his arm and thought about the question. But he knew he no longer mattered to Independence, and that was the way it should be. "I don't imagine. Especially not if they're headed in that new direction."

"Where are they going?"

"I don't know," he said, watching them turn into a bottleneck between the mountains. "I haven't been around for a couple of years. I guess they learned a new path. Headed west where there are fewer settlers, away from here."

He and Jessica pivoted into the sun, her head reaching to his chin. She placed a hand to her forehead and squinted, and he did the same, using his hat to shield his eyes.

It seemed, as he watched the magnificent horses weave their path through the lush mountain valley, that he'd been on this never-ending journey for more than a year. But the cruel tide had slowed and his pain had dimmed, and just like Independence, there was a glimmer of new hope on his horizon.

He pressed his hat over his heart and whispered as the last horse galloped out of sight, "Goodbye, Caroline."

Chapter Twenty

If they took their time riding the trail, it would take the three of them two days to reach Riverpoint Junction. They rode, silent and single file, along the narrow, difficult terrain. The intimacy that had once bonded Travis and Jessica had now turned stilted in the presence of the other Mountie.

However, the emotional distance gave Travis time to think.

Time to think about making love with Jessica and what it had meant. *How* much it had meant to him, and how much he wanted it to continue.

As he sat in the saddle leading the other two, dipping his head beneath branches, stopping to water and feed their horses, listening to a hawk's cry and then later, snaring a rabbit for a late-evening dinner, Travis couldn't pretend there was nothing between them. He and Jessica had shared everything that mattered in this world.

Jessica grew quieter as the hours passed. At first, Travis noticed, she was talkative with the other Mountie, then she grew pensive, huddled around the campfire with her slender arms wrapped around her knees, a sheen of reflection in her gaze.

She was no doubt contemplating her children.

He realized how desperate she must have felt to stash two thousand dollars into a bag and head out with a stranger—*with him*—to chase after and then bargain with a devil.

What right had Travis had to belittle her for bargaining with her money, the only means she had left at her disposal? Travis had fought her every mile of the way and was ashamed at how many of her obstacles he'd created. Abraham Finch was behind bars and Jessica had been right.

And now she sat at arm's length from Travis whenever he slid to her side, or offered to walk her to the river to haul a bucket of water.

"I can do it," she said, wiping her furrowed forehead.

"I'd like to apologize, Jessica," he said gently. "For all the doubts I had against you."

"That's behind us." She straightened her sleeve, picked up the bucket and stepped over crackling branches on her way down the slope. "I…I need time to think, Travis. What I'm going to say to the children and…and dear God, what if they don't want to come home with me?"

"They will," he said simply. "I've seen them and how they reacted to you. They will."

Her body was cloaked by the trees. "What if their adoptive parents don't agree…and what if I do bring them home and…? I mean, of course I'll bring them home, I'm their mother…but I don't know anything about *being* a mother."

"You'll learn."

"You'd think, with two thousand dollars in my saddlebag, I'd find comfort that I'll be able to provide for them for a little while. But I'm terrified I'll have to use that money. When I tell my father and stepmother what's happened, I may be living on my own with the twins. And yet I can't wait." Her eyes glistened. "I can't wait to see them again and hold them."

She fled through the trees, engulfed by darkness. Travis stood staring, numbed by the gravity of her doubts, and his inability to soothe her when he yearned to help her. But an idea was formulating in his mind.

The day had come.

Hoping to make a good impression with the twins, Jessica insisted on changing from traveling pants into her fresh, brown skirt and blue blouse four hours before they entered Riverpoint Junction. Travis and the constable took the time to check on the saddlebags and other gear he and Jessica had hidden behind the shrubs after their horses had been stolen. Kenyon promised he'd come back with a narrow cart then get the property delivered to Travis in Calgary.

Standing behind the tree, Jessica buttoned her collar, ran a brush through her hair and adjusted her gold necklace to lie on top of her blouse. She pressed a newly washed palm against her clenched stomach and took a deep breath.

Bobby and Callie's lives were about to change forever. Her mind fluttered with a thousand misgivings. She had no father to present them with, but was determined to let them understand that she would try to compensate with every ounce of her love.

It was noon when they rode into the village, turned right just before the hardware store, then followed the road to the end house. The children were racing around the grounds. She lifted herself off the saddle to look for her two beloved faces, but saw neither.

Jessica's fears multiplied when she spotted Mr. Murphy packing up his team of horses and one covered wagon.

"Whoa," he said, taking the reins of Jessica's mare when she reached the grounds. "What do we have here? Back so soon, are you, miss?"

"Howdy," she said tensely, trying to smile as she dismounted. "The twins haven't been taken already, have they?"

"No, no. They're out in the back with the missus, helping with the laundry. I'm packin' us up now and as soon as my brother arrives, we'll be headed to the valley." He nodded in the opposite direction from where she'd come.

"Ah," said Travis, coming up beside her and anchoring a firm arm of support around her shoulders. "You'll be taking the wide trail to the town of Beuford, I see. It's a safe route."

Mr. Murphy peered at Jessica. "Did you get your interview with Dr. Finch?"

"Yes, Mr. Murphy, I did. But there are some things you need to know."

He stopped knotting his rope. "What kind of things?"

She couldn't speak. It was agonizing standing there, waiting, hoping, peering around the house and seeing no sign of them.

Travis pressed his fingers into her flesh and a warmth of unspoken understanding rushed between them. "Sir, we'd like to speak with you and Mrs. Murphy in private, if we might."

Angie screeched in jubilation when she spotted Jessica and Travis.

Jessica responded with instinctual laughter. Walking

over to the fence, she reached over and picked up the little girl. She heard Travis introduce the constable to Mr. Murphy. Then the constable waited behind while Travis opened the gate and the rest of them walked through it.

Cooing in her arms, Angie fingered Jessica's golden necklace. "Shiny," she mumbled.

"It is, sweetheart." Jessica kissed the soft face. "It's your big day. You're on your way to meet your new mama and papa."

"Mama," the girl repeated.

"Miss Jessica!" Roy and Rebecca were running around the corner playing tag when they spotted her. Out of breath, they bade her good day. "Your magic stones worked!" They eagerly rushed to tell her. "They worked!"

Angie squirmed in Jessica's arms so she set the toddler on the grass.

"We're getting a family of our own," explained Rebecca.

"Oh," gasped Jessica. "That's wonderful. Who?"

The eight- and nine-year-old gazed up at Mr. Murphy, then went over to stand at his side. With a big grin, he flopped his hat on one disheveled head of hair, then the other.

"Us," said Mrs. Murphy behind the group.

Jessica spun around, wide-eyed. "You're taking them permanently?"

"Couldn't bear to part with them."

Six other children came racing behind Mrs. Murphy, all talking at once.

"What's for lunch, Ma?"

"Shall I set the table?"

"Thanks for the lasso, Officer Reid. Can I show you how good I am?"

Roy hollered to Jessica, "They're signing papers and everything."

Then his sister tapped his shoulder and hollered, "You're it!" Off they ran toward the laundry.

Clapping her hands in delight, Jessica followed them a few steps behind the house but they tore away and there standing by the basket of wet clothes were her own two.

Bobby was leaning over the hamper with a wet cloth in his hands, directing Callie, who was plopped on the ground and playing with wooden clothespins.

The sound of ice pellets hitting the roof tingled through Jessica's thoughts. A tiny red face swathed in blankets… She wondered if she'd ever held Callie, or had it just been Bobby in her arms.

The others were still distracted behind her, but Travis was here. He was always here.

Clasping his fingers through hers, Travis led her to the twins. When he slid to the ground to his knees, she followed.

"Can we help you with these?" asked Travis.

Bobby puckered his lips. "Help."

Callie offered Travis a clothespin.

"Thank you kindly." Travis grinned. He turned to look at Jessica, his blue eyes twinkling with good humor.

Jessica sat rooted. Staring at the perky faces, she noticed a unique fold in Callie's ear, then Bobby's, much like the fold in her own. They *were* her children.

Callie thrust a clothespin in her direction.

Jessica gulped, reached out and clamped her hand on top of the child's. The plump skin was warm and fragrant. Jessica took the offered gift, tugged the girl by the arm and pulled her to her lap.

With Callie seated facing out, mumbling at her brother, Jessica leaned into her brown hair, inhaled the scent of powder and cocoa, closed her eyes and rocked her baby.

After a spell, Jessica felt Travis's firm hand on her thigh, caressing her skin beneath the fabric of her skirt. She felt lulled by his presence, as if the world had stopped spinning wildly on its axis to finally turn and start again, slowly, in the right direction this time.

With a few questioning groans, Bobby came to gather the rest of the pins from his sister's hands since the pins weren't coming to him. Jessica opened her eyes wide, and with a laugh, tumbled against her son. She whisked him to the other side of her lap and rocked them both.

"I'm your mother," she said, gazing with joy from one face to another, aware that Travis was watching her. "I'm your mama and I'm never going to let you go again."

"Ma...ma," said Bobby, trying to catch her collar with his clothespin. His fingers felt gentle at her throat.

"Mama," whispered Travis, beaming with wonder and pleasure. "The nicest word I've heard in a long time."

"I just cannot believe Dr. Finch would do such a thing." Martha Murphy cradled her forehead in her hand, with elbow resting on the kitchen table. They'd already eaten, the Murphys insisting that Jessica and Travis stay for soup and dumplings. The children had been shooed outside within easy view of the kitchen window.

Travis heard Jessica sigh softly beside him as she gazed at Bobby and Callie climbing down the slide, supervised by the Murphy's oldest boy, Sidney.

Travis found himself drawn more to the children than he'd expected. Now that he looked closer, the little girl had her mother's beautiful brown eyes, and the boy's chin jutted with the same determination as Jessica's when he was trying to convince his sister to do things his way. Callie wasn't afraid to lunge in her own direction, despite what her brother wanted her to do.

Travis turned to William who was leaning alongside his wife, comforting her.

"There, there. Sometimes good people aren't as good as they seem. And the doctor sometimes seemed…too good to be true."

"You're sure it's him?" Martha dabbed her eyes with her apron. "You're sure, Jessica?"

"I'm sure, ma'am."

William rubbed his beard and eased back into his chair, studying the police documents spread on the pine table. "These certainly look official. Charged with kidnapping, fraud and theft." His mouth twisted. "Just what kind of man was he?"

"Misguided," Travis offered. "As far as we can tell, he did attend the university in some capacity. But we won't know what exactly that was until we get back to Calgary and write to the authorities. But he confessed the twins are Jessica's."

"Oh, dear," said Martha, dabbing her eyes again. "That is blessed news. Their mother didn't die in childbirth after all."

"No," said Jessica. "But I was told *they* had."

"How awful."

William shook his head. "And what happened to the father of these children? Where was he? Where *is* he?"

Travis watched Jessica grapple for an easy explanation. He wanted to jump in and take over and shield her from further pain, but he gave her the option of answering.

"He drowned on his way to England, before the children were born."

The clock on the wall above them ticked in the silence.

"You were alone, then." Martha covered Jessica's hand with her own.

Jessica nodded.

"But I imagine your father will see to it that the children are safe and well-fed."

Travis answered. "They will be, ma'am."

"You've told the twins already." Martha motioned to the window brimming with a view of a dozen playing children. "They called you their mama as they ran outside." Martha smiled for the first time in thirty minutes.

Jessica smiled back. "Thank you for being here for them. I will never forget what you did."

"Take good care of them." Martha nodded as the men rose and reached for their hats on the pegs by the door. "And thank you kindly for the five hundred dollars. It'll last us a long time."

Jessica had told Travis privately she intended on sending a trickle more once she got established on her feet, and he was proud of her. She murmured and hugged the older woman. "What will you say to the adoptive parents when you get to the valley?"

"The truth. They'll be happy for the children."

Sunshine hit Travis square in the eye when they exited the cabin to inform the rest of the children about the twins. A burden lifted from his body. Jessica seemed to come into her own awakening, walking arm in arm with Martha, whispering something about what nursery rhymes she did and didn't know and then getting caught in a soft burst of giggles.

"They like the one about the cow jumping over the moon."

"I'll remember." Jessica coaxed all the children off their swings and teeter-totters, happiness glowing in her eyes.

With the twins clinging to her legs, she explained to the remaining children who she was and that she and Travis would be taking the twins home.

The older children had many questions and she answered them with patience and respect.

Travis asked the Murphys to delay their trip until morning so he could verify the validity of all the other soon-to-be-adopted children, to which they agreed. The Murphys in turn insisted the travelers spend the night. Due to limited space indoors, Travis and the constable slept in the barn while Jessica stayed in the parlor. When the children went to bed, the two police officers took the opportunity to thoroughly sift through the Murphys' paperwork. With verbal accounts from the couple, who had known several of the deceased parents—or knew a neighbor who had—Travis was satisfied that the other adoptions were legitimate.

In the morning after breakfast when it was time to bundle up Callie and Bobby, Travis laid a hand along Jessica's back. "Time to go."

But he had so much more to say to her.

Chapter Twenty-One

Hours later with the warmth of her daughter's body pressing against her in the saddle, Jessica savored the moment. They rode behind Travis, who was balancing Bobby against his chest. The constable stayed behind, as planned, to scout the area for the McGraws. Travis and Jessica were once again alone, at least as the only adults.

All the agonizing months of waiting and wondering what this moment with her child might be like drifted away until Jessica was left with a peaceful spirit. She'd been blessed with not one, but two. The mare moved beneath them, her straining muscles jostling the child to and fro, but mostly mesmerizing the little girl into murmuring a soft chant.

Every once in a while, Travis grabbed hold of his Stetson and turned around. "You girls okay?" He smiled as he asked.

"Yes," Jessica would holler cheerfully, her delight permeating her posture.

Every time one of them spotted a crow, a rabbit, an owl or a weasel, they shared it with the others and it became a game.

Jessica tried not to think of the problems that awaited her in Calgary. It would take them six or seven days to reach the town, considering they traveled slower with two toddlers. Surely her father would welcome her and his grandchildren at least for the first night. From there she would look for a small place to rent until she decided what to do. Now, however, she would make up for lost time with the twins rather than let her mind drift to the uncertain future.

Travis loomed heavily in her thoughts. When she laughed into the wind at one of Bobby's expressions, Travis squatted beside them, grazing her leg with his, making her pulse dance. When Callie wandered too close to the hitched horses at mealtime, Travis ran after the girl in dismay, always ready to be their guard.

Yet ever present at the perimeter of her thoughts was the memory of his demanding kisses and their private nights of lovemaking. She tried to brush them away. She had responsibilities now, youngsters to tend to, and the frivolous hopes that Travis would touch her like that again seemed selfish in comparison.

With the children, mealtime preparations were the most difficult for Jessica and Travis. They struggled to heat the goat's milk they carried, to keep the children's drinking cups spotless, to crush the wheat biscuits and coordinate the meal's timing. They gave up trying to eat at the same time as the children, doting on them first and then relaxing later as adults, sipping coffee and sharing in the pride of having provided for Callie and Bobby.

Changing diaper cloths was another struggle. Travis did his best to rinse as Jessica changed the bottoms and passed him the soiled ones, but there was no time to dry them in one place until evening hit. By that time, poor Travis had a bulging accumulation of rinsed, wet cloths in his saddlebag instead of guns, ammunition, shaving gear and anything else manly he usually kept in his back right bag.

When they stopped for their first evening campfire, they watched Travis chop four thick branches to make a traveling flatbed for the twins. Travis strapped the branches together with leather ties then unrolled a woolen blanket in the center. Two long handles would attach to the saddle of his horse, dragging the flatbed along the trail behind him where the children could rest or nap.

The first day had exhausted them all and they quickly fell asleep, with Travis and Jessica each bundling a child against them in their bedroll in case animals decided to prowl.

The second day passed much the same as the first. But on the second evening as darkness found them, Travis and Jessica put the children to bed first, hoping for a quiet moment to unwind and catch up on adult chores.

Situated on a flat grassy hill, the campsite overlooked a steep bank of the river. Jessica promised herself she'd wash thoroughly tonight and so grabbed her cake of soap along with a fresh towel and slid down to the water's edge.

Sitting cross-legged on a large flat boulder, she removed her boots and wiggled her toes in her socks, enjoying the freedom. She began to unbraid her hair when Travis slid quietly to her side. She startled in the gentle, warm breeze. Then she finished gliding the blue ribbon from her hair, ever so conscious of his nearness.

Travis watched Jessica weave her fingers through her golden hair, dropping the blue ribbon.

Inhaling the scent of riverbank moss, he detected her scent woven among the sod and the water. "I'd like to do that for you."

Her fingers stilled. The crush of water raced by in the blackened river. A partial moon clung to the sky. Clouds, like a sliding lid, rolled over the moon, clamping a cover over the steamy night below.

"There are many things I'd like you to do, too, but they can't happen."

"Why not?"

"Within a few days we'll be gone from here. Our journey will be over and we'll be back to where we always were in Calgary. Me as the mayor's daughter...and you as the Mountie ordered to be my escort."

"Is that how you see me?"

"I've got two children who depend on me. There's no room in my life for nights of...uncommitted pleasure."

Travis seemed disappointed. He looked over her shoulder at the campsite and she did the same. Fifty feet away, past earshot, the fire blazed and the children slept safely beneath their covers.

"They're finally asleep."

Her lips turned upward in a warm smile. "I never knew how exhausting it would be, but I love every minute with them. I'm grateful that you took me with you on your journey. Despite your commander's orders, you went above and beyond what I expected."

She reached for her hairbrush and stroked it through her tangles.

"Your children are incredible."

"Oh, Travis, aren't they? Those two little lumps are smart." She twisted to look again at the shapes by the fire. "Callie can count to five and Bobby can stack a pile of sticks a foot high—"

"Jessica," Travis interrupted. His voice rasped. "Look at me."

He reached around her slender, pulsing throat to tug her cheek to his direction.

"I'm going to go crazy," he whispered, "if you don't come near me."

He watched her throat tighten. The muscles along his stomach clenched.

"What you're suggesting, Travis, is so difficult for me to refuse. The most difficult thing I've ever had to do. But I can't. I'm sorry, I can't."

Rising swiftly to her feet, she reached for the soap and towel and then tore off into darkness along the river.

He leaped up and pounded the shoreline behind her. "You're not going to leave me here, are you?"

She turned slowly to face him. Shadows from the trees swirled about her figure. "I can't continue to do…you know what. There are consequences to our behavior."

He stood with feet planted wide. "Nice ones, all of them."

Clutching at the towel, she crushed her hands together, jamming five fingers into the grooves of the others. "Don't think you can simply make me laugh and then I'll fall into your bed and peel off my clothes." She tucked her arms to her sides, the movement causing him to notice the small intake of her waist. God, she was so much smaller than he was. "This isn't a joke, Travis."

There seemed to be a shortage of air as he breathed. "I'm not laughing."

"My answer is no."

"But I didn't even ask—"

"I know what you were going to ask."

"What?"

Her eyes fired, but rather than make him withdraw, her

stance caused his blood to light on fire. Then amusement found him. She couldn't know what he wanted to ask.

She clicked her tongue. "For heaven's sake, you're not going to make me say it."

He moved closer, towering above her with the river crashing on one side and his heart on the other. "I think I will. Tell me what you suspect I want to ask you."

"You want to…to sleep with me, Travis Reid, and my answer is *no.*"

This time he did laugh.

She scowled and tore off again.

Frustration rumbled from his throat as he caught up to her. "Where the heck are you running to?"

"As far away from you as possible."

"Why?"

"Oh, for God's sake, you are daft!" She stomped away to stand in a circle of sand, flinging her hands to rest on wide, beautiful hips. "Because I can't handle standing an inch away from you. I can't take wondering when you last shaved and when you're going to shave again and could I please watch. I hate that I wonder if you're hungry and what's that song you're humming and—and where did you learn to kiss!"

He felt drugged by her clean scent.

"Do you think it's easy for me?" came the husky reply. "Tonight when I watched you singing Bobby to sleep, and then comforting Callie about the darkness, do you think it's easy for me to stand by and not wonder what you're thinking as you care for them? And then when I see the soap in your hands and you unbutton the top clasp of your collar, just enough to let me see the hollow of your throat—do you think it's easy to keep my hands from tearing off the rest of your buttons? And now when I see the moonlight skimming over the freckles of your nose, do you think it's easy for me to stand here with my hands at my sides?"

"I'll not give in to urges of the flesh."

"Then give in to me. You're the most incredible woman I've ever met."

A quick line of pain etched her face. "It's sweet talk again. Stop it." She tore away and raced up the riverbank, still clutching towel and soap.

He climbed behind, clawing at the stones to gain the speed to overtake her.

She ran ahead, dodging between the trees. "Leave me alone!"

"Jessica Haven!" he hollered into the wind, stopping to press a hand to his throbbing side. "I want to marry you!"

She froze against the trees. Towel and soap dangled from her hand. The wind tousled her loose hair. Her blouse clung to the curve of her spine. One leg bumped against a rock. When she turned around, she was so far away that darkness masked her face.

He began walking, running toward her. "The question I've come to ask is not will you sleep with me, Jessica, but will you be my wife?"

"Travis..." Her oval face tilted upward, her eyes misted and her rosy lips trembled.

He laughed gently, grabbed hold of her slender body and reeled her into his arms.

"Do you know what I love about you?" He kissed her throat as her free arm came to rest on his forearm. "I love that you speak your mind to whoever comes up against you, but when I come near, you're at a loss for words."

"...marriage..." she whispered, hesitating. "To be your wife?"

He looked into her soft brown eyes, pressing his forehead against hers, cradling her body against his. "While you're thinking about that, do we have to have all these clothes between us?" He tugged at her buttons.

She clasped his roving fingers and peered over the hill toward the campfire that was still visible, the children still sleeping. "I've got two young children. You don't know what you're getting into."

He tugged at her towel. "Can you drop these darn things and put your arms around my neck?"

The towel and soap thudded to the soft grass.

"Now do as I say. Put this arm here." He planted one pliable hand up his shoulder. "And the other here." He tugged it around his waist. "That's better."

"Did you hear what I said, Travis? These children aren't yours. I had them with another man and how will your family accept that?"

His jaw pulsed. "Nothing you've said so far has made me angry, but if you talk like that, I may need to—" He halted. Gazing into her probing eyes, upturned eyebrows and straight, awaiting mouth, Travis knew what she feared. "I don't give a damn what anyone says. I love you, Jessica."

Her lips parted. He felt the resistance in her body soften.

"And I'll learn to love your children. *Our* children."

Her eyes glistened.

He thought she'd give in, succumb to his embrace and he waited for her to do so, but she took her time thinking. She wiped her nose with her sleeve and as difficult as it was to wait for her answer, he allowed her time to grasp what she wanted to say. It surprised him. "I misjudged you when we first began this journey."

"You misjudged me? I thought *I'd* made the mistake of assuming you were a rich, spoiled woman."

She shook her head as he cradled her. Her hair fluttered against his shirt. "I thought you hated me and would never give me a chance to prove who I was. I thought you were an overbearing, self-righteous critic."

He didn't take offense. He clenched her waist, loving the sensation of her soft body pressed against his firm one. "I'd once dismissed you as frivolous. But without you, I never could have made this trip and returned home sane. It was arrogant of me to assume that I had matured since my adolescence, but that you hadn't. We all change, Jessica, and you forced me to see that."

He felt her body tremor, but he continued. "I was an idiot for coming down on you about the money. Seeing those two children tucked in their blankets… I now understand what you felt. They're worth more than any amount of money."

"But you were right," she said. "I put you in danger. I shouldn't have kept it from you, especially after we made love. It only put a wall between us and negated what we felt."

"The wall is gone." A flare of desire tightened his throat. Her touch on the hollow of his spine felt good. "The most difficult part for me," he said with a quiver he couldn't control, "dealing with Independence…you never once flinched at anything you witnessed pouring out of me…all that hatred and sorrow."

"I didn't flinch because I understood it." Bringing her fingers to his collar, she fondled the fabric and uttered, "I'm in love with you, Travis."

He hadn't realized how wonderful it would feel to hear those words. She electrified him. The current raced to his heart. "Will you marry me, Jessica?"

Her breath came in a long surrender. Passion flushed her skin. "I will."

He was almost too filled with emotion to speak. Swinging her above the ground, he settled her on top of a rocky ledge so she was standing at the same height. He outlined the tips of her mouth with his fingers. "Touch me."

"May I?" she asked with wonder, lifting her hand to cup his bristly cheek. He felt her heavy breasts skim across his chest, scorching his skin with heat.

Her fingers fluttered over his back, leaving a trail of arousal. Their lips met, melting together, soft and silken and promising more. Many years more. She tasted of fresh air, smelled of grass and soap and felt like satin beneath his fingers.

Their tongues met, the whispering sensations throbbing through his mouth down his throat, giving pledge to what would happen soon between their bodies.

She bent her head to rest on his solid shoulder, running her fingers over the smooth expanse of fabric along his chest.

"I want more," he demanded.

"How much more?"

"All of you."

"I'm yours."

They kissed and she raced to keep up with his hands, which tugged her blouse from her belt and then skimmed up the soft cotton nightshirt that clung to her breasts. He fumbled with the cloth and finally, unable to find a front opening, raced his hands beneath the waistline until he found bare, warm flesh.

"This is what I need."

She laughed gently into his mouth as she tugged at his shirt, pulling it out of his pants with such vigor it made *him* laugh. "Who's seducing who, Mrs. Reid?"

"I have every right to please my soon-to-be husband."

He burned with desire so urgent he thought he might explode. Her murmurs were swallowed by his kiss. He felt her hands skimming his bare waist.

"To the ground," he commanded hoarsely. "I want to make love to you."

"Sergeant Major, that sounds like an order."

As he slid her down, they turned their heads and saw that the campfire was burning softly, the children safe and still.

He slid the towel to the grass and she tumbled to the soft mound in a sitting position. He dropped to his knees before her, ripped the nightshirt and camisole off her body, tearing it above her head, watching her breasts bob and shudder with her movements.

He could barely breathe looking at her generous curves. Capturing a golden sphere with his large, tanned hand, he flicked his fingers over the crest. She circled his waist with her warm, suggestive hands and watched the expressions flick across his face.

"I love you, Jesse."

Her lids closed. "I feel it. I know it. Let me show you how much I love you."

He kneaded her shoulders, caressed the smooth crown of her head, planted his hands at either side of her throat as she unbuttoned his pants.

She uttered sounds of approval as she placed her hand over the fabric covering his hardened flesh. He closed his eyes with the rush of sensation as her fingers pressed against his erection. She moved her hand lower to cup him gently and he gasped with pleasure.

He lowered her to the ground, determined to take his time no matter the torture. He tried to slide off her pants, but they clung to her womanly hips. He tried the other side then moaned in defeat. "Wiggle out of your pants before I take my pocketknife and slash them off."

"Then I wouldn't have anything sensible to wear on the ride," she teased.

He growled. "Sensible. The last thing that comes to me around you is anything sensible."

While she removed her pants, he quickly slid off his own, then his socks, till he felt the rush of warm air stirring his naked skin. Sighing, he propped his head on an elbow and stared at her half-clothed body.

"You're done in half the time I am," she whispered. "Where did you learn your quick maneuvers?"

He watched the circles of her breasts move up and down, the swell beneath her arms rising and falling as she tugged at her pants. "One look at you and any man would learn to race."

Desire flared in her eyes as she scrutinized his body. "And one look at your nakedness and any woman would weaken."

"Why didn't you let me know that in the beginning? Maybe I would have walked around naked." He found her mouth as he removed her pantaloons. Grasping her waistband with two fingers, he slid his thumb along her belly button, then her satin hairs, then down the midline of her crotch. He felt her quiver beneath his touch.

"Because it would have made you swagger even more."

His hand stopped at her crotch. He let her pantaloons linger above her knees. She opened her eyes in dismay as he continued to kiss her. Then she understood when he pressed his thumb into the slick awaiting center. Moaning, she lifted her knees off the towel to allow him to press deeper while her hands explored his shoulders and her kiss gained momentum.

He wanted to please her, to look at her face as he made

her climax. She'd been through so much...was so strong...yet he loved how she withered beneath his hand.

She'd agreed to marry him. Bobby and Callie were safe and protected, and nothing else existed.

Travis let another finger explore her moist, hot warmth, and then another. At the same time, he bent lower and kissed her stomach, marveling at the way her muscles bunched at his feathery touch. He swallowed what seemed like a mouthful of saliva, an indication of his arousal as he played his way up the centerline of her body. His tongue licked around her belly button, up her rib cage, beneath the breast closest to him, then over the curve till he reached her nipple.

She opened her eyes, lifted her breast up to feed his hungry mouth. Her body undulated beneath him and he knew she was near.

He slowly withdrew his fingers—to her amusing groans of displeasure, then slid her pantaloons down her thighs and off her ankles. Rolling on top of her so his knees were on the towel, he placed a hand on the grass above each of her shoulders, stared at the enchanting depth of her dark eyes, then lowered himself to the center of her splayed legs.

He was as rigid as a rod, but took the time to stroke himself along her moistened folds before slowing, dipping, testing, teasing the inner warmth.

"Now, Travis."

With a steely grip on her buttocks, he raised her bottom slightly, lifted her legs then raised her ankles up tight against his shoulders on either side of his face, and obliged.

They intersected.

She surrendered.

He thrust.

A wave of intense heat rolled through him. He plunged into her depths with a primal rhythm, urging her body to reach its peak before his own restraint gave way.

Holding her ankles in the air against him, he lost himself in the ecstasy and wonder of Jessica, melting with the tide and buckling against her as deep as he could go.

Then smoothly he spread her legs, slid her ankles gently to her sides, lowered his chest to hers and kissed her mouth while still inside of her. He slid his fingers between her legs, as well, above his penetrating shaft, back and forth in unison. He reveled in her wetness.

She came then, as their lips rolled together and tongues pressed. He could no longer restrain himself. A current of glorious release surged through him, gripping his muscles, coiling his spine, making his legs shudder with its massive power.

She thrust against him as good as he gave, her own muscles shuddering in forceful response, once, twice, then again, then easing slightly as they panted for breath. He shimmied his hands beneath her back as she went lax and her arms fell back against the grass.

He found his voice. "I don't want to let you go. I don't want us to part."

Her mouth drew open and she smiled in that ruffled, erotic way. "Roughrider," she said softly.

"What?"

"Nothing. I just wanted to say it. Like this. It's what I imagined the first day when I was watching you from the bleachers at the fort as you rode that bronco."

He kissed her throat. Pulling out of her, he rolled to the grass, buttocks on the raw ground, gazing up at the moon.

"The ground's hard," he said.

"So are you."

From the corner of his eye, he witnessed her studying his body. "That's what you do to me. I'll be ready for you in another minute, Mrs. Reid."

"I reckon you will." She raised herself on an elbow and peered through the trees at their campsite. "They're still sleeping."

"Amazing what a crackling, warm fire will do for youngsters."

She pushed against his hip with her bare toes. "And what the sight of a naked breast will do for you."

He laughed. "We'll have to remember the trick about the fire. We've got five more nights ahead of us, and then a lifetime of nights." Rolling on his side, he watched her extend her arms over her head, enjoying the way she stretched her legs at the same time she pointed her toes.

"I'm glad I was given the chance to repair the mistakes I'd made with you when I was younger. You were the only person who never commented on the fact that I was an unwed mother."

He thumbed the fallen hair away from her cheek. "You did the best you could and moved on. You and your children are wonderful. You never were the mayor's privileged daughter. That's something someone else put into my head and I never took the time to weigh on my own."

"You make me feel proud of myself, Travis, and not ashamed. Not anymore. I love you for that."

He kissed her on the tip of her pink nose. "And you and the twins give me something I haven't had in a long, long time. Something to hope for."

She smiled. "I'm planning to write a letter to the children's grandparents in England. Victor's folks. Callie and Bobby were taken from me and I don't want to do that to them. I want to tell them they have grandchildren. Would you object?"

"No, silly. It's a good idea."

She tucked her elbow up against her waist, and he reached out and stroked the weight of one breast as it tipped toward him. He could see the concern building in her face as she lay lost in thought. "Don't worry about what the town will say about your children, or how your family will react when we tell them. I've got my speech planned."

She rolled to her back and faced the twinkling sky. "I'm more worried about what your family will say. You know how they feel about me."

Chapter Twenty-Two

Six days and incredible nights later, Travis and Jessica rode into Calgary. The midmorning light shone across the flatbed where the twins sat perched in observation. It seemed strange to Travis, having been cloistered for more than two weeks in the forest trails, to be in the wide-open prairie again where dust rolled through the streets, and pine buildings instead of trees buffered the warm wind.

He turned to Jessica, whose spine seemed to stiffen even as they rode. Her skirt blew against her knees, clinging to the fine shape of her calf, hinting at the treasure they'd shared for the past week and which he knew he'd never get enough of.

The youngsters in the back mumbled to each other, fingers pointed at a passing pup and excited to be reaching *home.* The week on the trail had given them a chance to grow accustomed to each other as a family and Travis had never felt so renewed and invigorated.

But at this moment, as he nodded his head and tipped his Stetson in greeting to passersby on the boardwalk and on horseback, Travis felt the grip of anticipation as he headed for the mayor's mansion.

"Are you as nervous as I am?" Jessica leaned toward him, ruffling her lips.

"Not nervous. Excited."

Her hands rested on the saddle horn and he gave them a gentle pat to reassure her, but her cheeks washed of color and the line of her lips remained flat.

When they reached the broad, spotless house, Travis slid off his saddle, tore the blanket off the twins so they could hop out, then circled to Jessica's side. She hadn't budged from atop her horse.

He held out a hand. "Come now, Jesse, don't think too hard of all the things that might go wrong. I promise to protect you."

She smiled softly as she took the help he offered. Encircling her waist with broad hands, he lifted her gently to her feet, facing him. The twins stumbled off to collect leaves from one of the courtyard gardens.

Travis planted a gentle kiss on her nose. "Those chocolate-brown eyes are killers. I knew it the minute they set their sights on me."

They were interrupted before she could reply.

"Miss Jessica!" Merriweather, dressed in starched white shirt and black pants, bolted from the front porch. "Officer Reid! I'm so relieved to see you both. How did you fare?"

"Wonderfully," said Jessica, beaming at her friend. She gave the gent a big hug.

Merriweather moved briskly to shake Travis's hand.

"You're moving better," said Travis. "Glad to see it."

"Quite right, quite right. I can sit in a chair again." He beamed at Jessica, unaware of the twins behind him. Merriweather lowered his deep voice but Travis overheard him nonetheless while securing their horses to the hitching tree. "Did you behave yourself, young lady?"

"Mr. Merriweather," said Jessica in a stilted tone. "Please don't ask."

"I don't like the sound of that."

Travis wheeled around. "I take full responsibility."

"Uh-oh. I really don't like the sound of that." Merriweather caught a flash of movement behind Jessica's shoulder and said matter-of-factly, "There are two children running in our garden."

"Quite right," said Travis, gently mimicking the butler. "Good-looking kids, aren't they?"

"Who on earth do they belong to?" Merriweather peered down one side of the street and then the other, but none of the pedestrians looked the least interested.

"Jessica!" Franklin Haven barreled down the stairs.

Jessica pressed her hand against her stomach, darted a hasty glance at Travis and stepped out to greet her father.

"I've missed you, daughter." He planted a kiss on her cheek as Jessica embraced him.

"And you, Officer," boomed Franklin, turning to Travis. "My butler tells me you went on without a chaperon."

"Yes, sir." Travis extended his hand.

The man glanced at it briefly, hesitated, then extended his own. They shook.

And then in a flash, everything happened at once. Callie raced to Jessica's side with Bobby chasing. They pulled at her skirts with soiled fingers, calling, "Mama."

Merriweather and the mayor stared from child to child, then at each other, exchanging a stunned look of disbelief. If Travis hadn't known the situation weighed seriously on Jessica's thoughts, he would have found the scene comical.

"Jessica?" Franklin peered at her from over the rim of his spectacles.

She scooped down to pick Callie off the ground, and Travis hurled Bobby into the air.

The boy laughed. The mayor didn't.

Travis weaved his arm proudly around Jessica. "They're Jessica's children, sir. Our children, I might add. I've come to ask for her hand in marriage."

Merriweather slapped his forehead. "I knew I shouldn't have left you two alone. I knew it!"

"Your children?" wheezed the mayor. "I didn't even know you knew each other that well!"

"No, no, you don't understand," said Jessica, bobbing her face around Callie's pudgy fingers as the girl played with Jessica's dangling silver earrings.

The mansion door flew open again and two women dashed out to join them. Travis recognized them as Madeline and Eloise.

It took another moment of more hugging of Jessica and handshaking with Travis before the group stilled and waited for an explanation.

Travis tried to explain to save Jessica further anguish, but she leaned into the side of his rib cage and interrupted. "It's all right, Travis." She turned to her family. "He's trying to help me through this, but I think it's my duty to tell this story."

They walked through the gardens from the front yard, down the side path to the quieter back, watching the twins explore the grounds. Jessica began from the beginning, and though her father knew that part of the story, it was news to Merriweather, Mrs. Haven and Eloise. Shock registered in their faces when Jessica told the rest of her story. Twenty minutes later, she concluded. "And then the Mounties took Abraham Finch away in handcuffs."

Franklin heaved his large body onto a bench and

pulled out his hankie. He mopped his forehead, his gaze focusing on Bobby and Callie by the carriage house.

"Oh, daughter."

Jessica slipped to the other side of the bench. "It's a lot to grasp at once, I know."

"Sir, if I might say, Finch was a difficult man to confront, but your daughter never gave in to doubt. Even though at times I did." Travis stepped up from behind and gripped her shoulder.

She brought a hand to lie on his, acknowledging his gesture.

Franklin sighed heavily. "As did I." He glanced up. "And so, these are my grandchildren."

Jessica sat hushed, gripping Travis's hand, glancing from her stepmother standing beside her father's side, to Eloise, who was playing catch ball with the twins.

Madeline fell to her husband's feet in the grass. Her glossy dress billowed around her legs. She placed a hand on her husband's knee and looked kindly to Jessica. "You showed more bravery than I ever could have. How delightful that we'll have small children in the house."

Travis heard the tug at Jessica's throat. He knew that most of the household decisions hinged on Madeline, and she was giving her blessings.

Franklin mopped his forehead again, and then rubbed the hankie over his eyes. He blubbered, "I'm so sorry, Jessica, that I didn't believe you about Finch. You managed this all without the help of your father. I should have been there."

"Travis was here for me. We owe him a lot."

And that's when the real hugging and crying began. Travis watched the happy scene unfold. He never thought he'd be grateful to see women's tears, but he was. He led the twins by the hands into the arms of their new grandfather.

"Sir, I'd like your permission to marry Jessica."

The mayor smiled and reached out to embrace Jessica along with Bobby and Callie. Squeezing the three together, he planted a loud kiss on Jessica's cheek, which caused her to smile. "I reckon you better marry after the trip you just made."

"Quite right, quite right," said Merriweather with his usual charm.

"Are you sure you wouldn't like to rest a spell before we do this?" With Bobby firmly planted on his shoulders, Travis tapped his Stetson. He walked alongside Jessica as they headed to Quigley's Pub.

Gripped by another pang of nervousness, Jessica squinted in the noon sun, gently squeezing Callie's hand. She slowed her pace so that Callie could keep up beside them, and prayed that it would go well.

They'd spent two hours at Jessica's home, telling stories and giving a tour to the twins. Her father had immediately offered them his home. Jessica felt wonderfully refreshed in her change of clothes—a dress she'd taken from her bedroom wardrobe and not her saddlebag—and peered proudly at the twins with their newly brushed hair and scrubbed faces.

"We'd better do this now," she said. "Word spreads quick in this town. Mr. Merriweather has already been to the neighbors and they've certainly asked him questions. I'd rather we told your sister and the rest of your family personally before they hear through gossip."

"You're smart. My family appreciates directness." He winked. "Let me do the talking this time."

When Travis gave her that boyish grin, the nervous flutter in her stomach ceased. Almost.

"You did well with your folks," said Travis, placing a hand at the small of her back and leading her up the pathway to the side of Quigley's Pub where Quigley and Shawna lived. He stole a kiss at the back of her neck before lifting the door knocker.

The door creaked open and Shawna peered through. "Travis!" She flung the door wide, her three-month-old infant snuggled on one shoulder. She rubbed the baby's back and he burped softly. "Goodness, you're home. Who's the little one on your shoulders?" She laughed. "You look wonderfully rested!"

Stepping to the landing to give her brother a hug, she spotted Jessica, then looked down to Callie, whose little hand rested in her mothers.

"Miss Haven." Shawna's expression immediately tensed. Travis slid away from her to stand by Jessica's side, and Jessica surely needed the encouragement judging by the severe look on Shawna's face.

Travis began his speech. "Shawna, you've always been my baby sister and I know I've pushed you around a lot, but this time I need you to listen before we argue. You know that Jessica and I went to Devil's Gorge."

Shawna nodded. Her baby wiggled and she shifted him to the other shoulder.

"Baby," said Callie.

Jessica squeezed her daughter's hand and smiled at the beauty of the new mother and babe. "That's right, it's a baby boy."

Travis continued to explain to his sister. "What you don't know is that Jessica is a mother. These are her children. Their father passed away before they were born, and she's been chasing the man who took them from her for seventeen months."

Shawna staggered at the news.

Travis looked as if he didn't want to say more in earshot of the twins—he and Jessica had agreed earlier that the children weren't to know the sordid details.

Shawna looked up at Bobby, her face still solemn as she weighed the information.

Bobby reached for the brim of the Stetson, but Travis's large hands swooped to pin the boy's before Bobby had the opportunity to knock the hat to the ground.

"I've asked Jessica to be my wife, Shawna, and she's agreed."

The dark eyes flickered across her brother's face.

"I'm going to marry her because I love her. I love everything about her. She's decent and patient and encouraged me to stay with horse breeding."

Shawna's mouth parted slightly. While Jessica basked in the glow of Travis's beautiful words, his sister gaped at him in amazement. "You're not leaving the horse business?"

"No. And it's because of Jessica."

Shawna's eyes glistened as she looked from Jessica back to Travis. "But you have to know that not everyone in town will rally to your side."

Jessica knew she meant the Reid family. It was an honest statement of fact and Jessica bore no grudge.

"They will," vowed Travis, "once they get to know Jessica."

In that moment of shared honesty between brother and sister, as Jessica watched the expressions change from doubt to concern to tender hope, Jessica knew the man she'd chosen to be at her side would remain there forever.

Gently rubbing her baby's back, Shawna timidly turned to Jessica. "You were separated from your children for all this time?"

Jessica nodded, clinging to the hope that the woman would show her some kindness.

With a sigh of deep understanding, Shawna smiled and gently opened the door. She offered the simple, warm word that would bind the two as sisters well into their old age.

"Welcome."

Epilogue

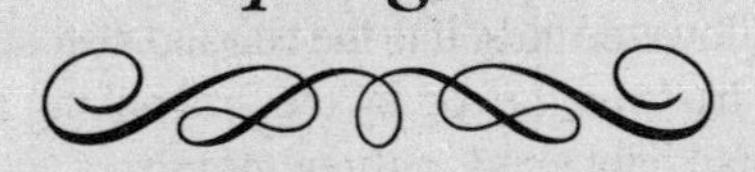

Three months later

"It's here!"

A letter arrived from England. The stage hand, doubling as the postman, delivered it one evening to Jessica while she ran along the hilltop chasing after Callie and Bobby. The tawny kitten that Shamus, the stable boy from the fort, had saved for them scuttled behind the twins. Jessica was shooing them indoors for bedtime but they were begging for one more turn on the swings that Travis had put up two months earlier when they'd first bought their small ranch.

Travis was working in the stables when Jessica rushed in to tell him, cheeks reddened by the cool October wind, twins in flight bundled in winter frocks, hats and mittens.

"It's here! They answered!" Jessica shouted across the stalls.

Travis peered around his new broodmare, pitchfork in hand. A kerosene lantern lit the night air. "Who has?"

"The Sterlings from England." Jessica slid the bonnet off her head and steered the twins to Travis's side.

"Well then, let's go indoors." Travis, built as solid as

ever and dressed in denim from head to toe, adjusted his gloves. He set the pitchfork inside an empty stall then pulled Bobby and Callie into his arms and they raced into the house.

It would be a full hour before Jessica got the children asleep in the loft above their main alcove. Travis had the fireplace kicking heat by that time.

Jessica lowered herself to the bed and watched as Travis sat on his heels on the rug by the fire, poking at the logs.

A lot had happened in three months.

She and Travis and the children had grown inseparable.

Abraham Finch—not a doctor at all but a failed student of medicine, the Mounties had discovered—had gotten a speedy trial and was starting his twenty years in the district penitentiary.

The judge had reopened Peter Warrick's case. It was discovered he was innocent of the accused robbery but he was wanted for counterfeiting money. Angry at the shoddy medical care he'd once received from Finch when Finch had treated his gastric ulcers with expensive placebos, Mr. Warrick had discovered that some of the doctor's labels were "handmade" yet claiming to be from Switzerland. Upon closer inspection of Finch's medical degree, Mr. Warrick had recognized the slick forgery. Finch had fabricated a story to put the man behind bars. The counterfeiting charges, however, put Mr. Warrick in jail for eight years of hard labor instead of seven.

Clive Monahan turned out to be the leader in the string of robberies Warrick had originally been accused of, with Andrew Garwood and Jeb Lake as accomplices.

The McGraw brothers who'd had their horses untied while they were sleeping had walked safely all the way back to Strongness.

David, the seventeen-month-old boy who'd been

abandoned at the mercantile, was adopted by a loving young couple in B.C. Travis had discovered that David's natural mother was a sixteen-year-old girl passing through on her way West with her folks, who was relieved to know her boy had been adopted.

The gravesite in Montreal that supposedly held Jessica's baby came up empty, the Mounties discovered. Finch had turned the ground only to justify his story.

In Devil's Gorge, the town was taking up a collection to send Taylor Hopkins to the University of Toronto for a proper education in medicine, and he in turn promised to return to the town to set up his practice. The Murphys had been ecstatic to hear that news.

Jessica and Travis's families had been slow to come around, but each had accepted the invitation to share their first Christmas together later this year, seated around Jessica and Travis's kitchen table.

Now rocking on the bed, staring at her husband's wide back and dark handsome profile, Jessica filled with joy at the man she'd married.

"Read me the letter." Travis turned around and slid to the mattress beside her.

She pressed her thigh against his and carefully opened the envelope.

"Dear Mrs. Reid,

Jessica if we might call you that. Thank you kindly for your letter dated July 16. My wife and I were surprised to hear from you. We remember your first letter came shortly after Victor's passing. We had no idea you were involved with our son.

It was difficult news to hear about your relationship with Victor, but thank you for your honesty. Please forgive us for not being able to write sooner. We're old and not used to such unsettling news. Now that we've had the opportunity to digest it, and the accompanying letter Officer Reid posted as confirmation of the news, we have come to some decisions.

We realize with sadness that Victor must have hurt you enormously. We loved our son. He was our only child. Bearing this in mind, we would like to accept your kindest offer of visiting Calgary to meet you and your new husband, and our only grandchildren.

If the spring would be convenient, it is our wish to travel then. Please write to advise and let us know which hotel is most conveniently located next to the new ranch you mentioned you were buying.

Affectionately, Mr. and Mrs. Albert Sterling."

Jessica gripped the letter for a long time. Travis bent over the edge of the bed, removed her shoes and urged her to lie down beside him. She snuggled into the crux of his arm.

"That's a nice letter," he said.

"More than I expected." She basked in the warmth of their new home and the man she'd grown to love.

She laughed when he rolled over and lowered himself on top of her. She nuzzled his neck.

"I know what you want," he whispered. He traced the outline of her cheek. The fire blazed in the corner, spreading its heat.

"You do?"

It was hot in the room. Her face flushed, but more from Travis's smooth fingertips sliding to unbutton her blouse than the fire itself.

"The fire's set," he said. "The kids are sleeping. It's just you and me." He parted her blouse, gulped at the swelling of her breasts perched above her corset and kissed her flesh.

Then he rose and headed to the desk that she used to write her articles for the *Pacific Medical Journal.* Now that he'd read a few, he understood her talent and her drive for work. Lifting the oak lid, he reached inside and pulled out a tablet of writing paper. He brought the quill to the nightstand and laid it by her side. "Go ahead. Write to your heart's content."

"You know me so well."

He patted her backside. "It's the only way I'll get your undivided attention later."

"Have I ever told you how much I love you?" Jessica slid the quill from its resting place and leaned over the paper.

From behind, Travis kneeled over her and massaged her back while she began writing.

October 22, 1892
Dear Mr. and Mrs. Sterling,
Spring would be lovely. The children will be more than two years old and eager to spend a full day of activity with us. I've told them you live in England and they dearly wish to meet you.

You must, of course, stay with us. It's a small cabin, but the weather is beautiful in the spring and we can spend many hours outside. Travis is expecting the arrival of several more horses during the month of April, at spring melt....

While Jessica continued writing, Travis ran his hands over her slender shoulders and thumbed the curve of her spine. He listened to the gentle hum of her breathing and the gliding of the quill over paper. Above him in the loft, rafters crackled as the twins turned in their sleep, and Travis marveled at the unspoiled woman he held in his hands, who'd had the courage to face him in the stables one morning to offer her proposition.

* * * * *

Be sure to watch for The Bachelor, coming only to Harlequin Historicals in March 2005.

Author's Note

While researching this story, I spent many entertaining hours in the medical library archives of McMaster University in Hamilton, Ontario. You may be surprised to learn that, although the characters of this novel are fictional, all of the products and medical gadgets used or sold by the charlatan existed in the late-nineteenth century. This includes electric corsets, eye massagers, dog-powered treadmills, weight additives, electric hairbrushes, electric dumbbells, shock boxes, hearing horns, nose straighteners, Queen's Herb, medical museums and forged medical degrees. Abraham Finch was a figment of my imagination, but he was drawn from a compilation of fascinating charlatans who really existed.